DARKFALL

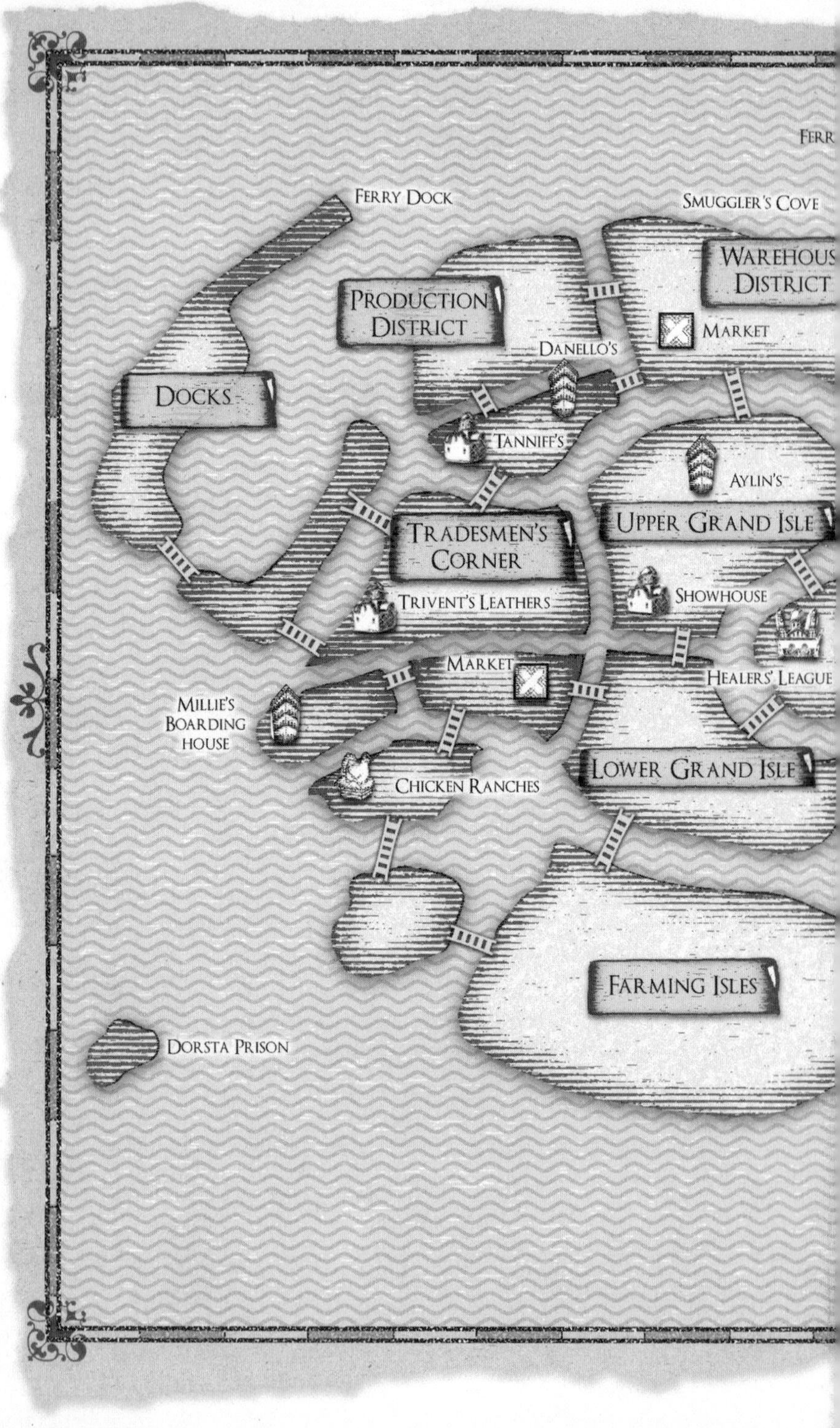

FERR
FERRY DOCK
SMUGGLER'S COVE
WAREHOUS
DISTRICT
PRODUCTION
DISTRICT
MARKET
DANELLO'S
DOCKS
TANNIFF'S
AYLIN'S
TRADESMEN'S
CORNER
UPPER GRAND ISLE
TRIVENT'S LEATHERS
SHOWHOUSE
MARKET
HEALERS' LEAGUE
MILLIE'S
BOARDING
HOUSE
LOWER GRAND ISLE
CHICKEN RANCHES
FARMING ISLES
DORSTA PRISON

THE THREE TERRITORIES

BASEER

SORILLE

GEVEG

VERLATTA

GEVEG ISLES

COFFEE ISLE

SANCTUARY

TOWNHOUSE

NORTH ISLE

PAIN MERCHANT'S

SOUTH ISLE

HALF MOON BAY

ARISTOCRATS' ISLES

ARISTOCRAT DOCK

GARDENS

THE TERRACES

GOVERNOR-GENERAL'S ISLE

Also by Janice Hardy:

THE HEALING WARS: BOOK I
The Shifter

THE HEALING WARS: BOOK II
Blue Fire

THE HEALING WARS: BOOK III

DARKFALL

JANICE HARDY

Balzer + Bray
An Imprint of HarperCollins*Publishers*

Balzer + Bray is an imprint of HarperCollins Publishers.

The Healing Wars: Book III: Darkfall
Copyright © 2011 by Janice Hardy
All rights reserved. Printed in the United States of America.
No part of this book may be used or reproduced in any manner whatsoever
without written permission except in the case of brief quotations embodied
in critical articles and reviews. For information address HarperCollins
Children's Books, a division of HarperCollins Publishers,
10 East 53rd Street, New York, NY 10022.
www.harpercollinschildrens.com

Library of Congress Cataloging-in-Publication Data
Hardy, Janice.
    Darkfall / Janice Hardy. — 1st ed.
        p.   cm. — (The healing wars ; bk. 3)
    Summary: With the rebellion in full swing, fifteen year-old Nya's loyalties
are put to the ultimate test, and she is forced to choose between leading an army
against the Duke or abandoning her people to save her sister.
    ISBN 978-0-06-174750-2 (trade bdg.)
    [1. Fantasy. 2. Healers—Fiction. 3. Fugitives from justice—Fiction.
4. Sisters—Fiction. 5. Orphans—Fiction.] I. Title.
PZ7.H22142Dar   2011   2011001946
[Fic]—dc22   CIP
                                                                    AC

Typography by Carla Weise
11 12 13 14 15   CG/RRDB   10 9 8 7 6 5 4 3 2 1
❖
First Edition

For my family.
Those I was born to, and those I chose.

DARKFALL

ONE

The missing are harder to accept than the lost. My parents had been dead five years, but my sister? She'd been missing only three months. I'd grieved those who'd died, but I didn't know how to feel about Tali. Guilt, fear, anger, hope—they came and left as fast as water birds taking flight.

She was out there, somewhere. A prisoner of the Duke's, stolen from me just as he'd stolen the city of Geveg, the pynvium from our mines, the food from our tables. His greed had turned to war, and he'd crushed all of us under his boot, racing to get even more power. No one was safe, certainly not Tali.

Late at night, safe at Jeatar's farm, I wondered if it was time to stop looking for her. I hated myself for thinking it, but it wasn't just my life I was risking by trying to find her. My friends put themselves in danger every time we left the farm, and some had even gotten hurt because of me.

But then my guilt would haunt me. How could I stop looking? I'd made so many promises. Others had sacrificed so much to help me. It wasn't just about one lost sister anymore, but thousands of families ruined by the Duke of Baseer and his desire to control everyone in the Three Territories.

If I gave up on Tali, was I also giving up on them? On any chance we had to be free of him? To just be *free*?

Someone knocked on the door to the room I shared with Aylin. I didn't want to answer. I'd tossed and turned all night, worrying and planning, and was really hoping to grab a few hours of sleep this morning now that Aylin wasn't hogging the bed.

"Nya?" Danello said through the door. "Are you awake?"

Yes, but I didn't want to be. We'd argued again last night. One of those dumb fights that started over nothing and ended with both of us storming off. If I opened the door he'd smile at me, and then I'd want to forgive him, and I wasn't *ready* to forgive him.

Trouble was, I couldn't remember exactly *why*

we'd argued. But it had been his fault. I was almost sure of that.

"Nya, come on." Danello knocked again. "You can't still be mad at me."

It had been over scouting reports, hadn't it? Troop movements outside Baseer. I'd said that gave us an opening to sneak into the city, but Danello said it could be the army moving around again to make way for more soldiers. I said I wanted to leave by the end of the week—he thought we should wait until we had more information. I said something stupid and he said something stupid back.

"I have food," he sang.

My mutinous stomach grumbled and I sighed. That was cheating, plain and simple.

"I have *good* food." His sweet voice was light and playful. Hard to stay mad at him when he sounded like that. I pictured him out there, leaning on the door, his hair a mess from the breeze coming off the fields.

Okay, maybe it wasn't *completely* his fault. Aylin said I'd been grumpy lately—probably from lack of sleep. It wasn't like he was telling me I couldn't go, just that I should be extra careful, think things through first. Without knowing why the Duke was moving those troops around, caution wasn't a bad idea.

And Danello *had* brought food.

I slipped out of bed, walked across carpet thick as my thumb, and opened the door. Danello carried no plate in his hands, but he did have a picnic basket.

I sensed a trap.

"I packed this full." He held up the basket. Handmade from the looks of it, blue-reed weaves, too. Those didn't come cheap. "All you have to do is come with me to get it."

I hesitated. He wasn't out of the weeds yet, but if he had sweetcakes in that basket, I could manage a *little* forgiveness.

"Where?"

"Just to the gardens. Sunshine, fresh air." He grinned, wide and silly. "It'll be fun, and we could use a little fun."

Aylin had been telling me the same thing. I grinned back. It had been a dumb fight anyway. "Let me get dressed."

I shut the door and threw on some clothes, then ran a comb through my still-black curls. The dye Aylin had used to color our hair and disguise us was starting to grow out, but unless I cut it as short as Danello's, it would be months before I looked normal again.

Have you ever been normal?

I pushed the thought away as I opened the door. Danello beamed, his short blond hair ruffled just like I pictured, his smile just as sweet. He offered me his arm and I took it.

"Did you pack sweetcakes?" I asked.

"You'll have to come with me to find out."

I followed, actually looking forward to something for a change.

Voices drifted up the stairs, folks laughing, talking, even arguing. So different from the first week we were at the farm, when half the people had huddled in corners and the other half run around setting up defenses. We were safe for now, but how long would that last? Faces turned when we walked past the reception room, and the laughing ceased.

Those in the back leaned their heads together, awed gazes darting to me. Some I recognized— those who'd been in the underground resistance Jeatar had been secretly running in Baseer, soldiers on the farm, friends and friends of friends who'd escaped before the Duke sealed the city and began recalling his troops. The others I didn't know, but new folks arrived every day.

"Any news yet, Nya?" someone called.

"Not yet." Seemed like everyone knew about Tali. I guess that was a good thing, since the more people who knew I was looking for her, the better the chance that someone would hear something that could help me find her. Still, it bothered me that everyone knew my problems. And knew that she was my sister. As much danger as she had to be in right now, she'd be in a lot more if the Duke knew who she was. He'd sure as spit use her to get to me.

"When's the next trip out?"

Danello's hand tensed in mine, but he stayed quiet.

"Hopefully the end of the week," I said. No commitment there.

"You'll find her, don't worry."

"Thanks."

Danello hurried me out the side door and we headed across the sun-baked courtyard. I drank in the humid air, the heat chasing the tenseness from my limbs. Fields spread out past the farmhouse grounds: tall, bright-green cornstalks with yellow tops waving in the wind, smaller, darker-green sweet potato vines in bushy rows. One pasture held grazing cattle with long, twisting horns.

Not at all like the islands and canals of Geveg. Even though we were miles from the river, and a two-day sail from Baseer, I still felt exposed with so much open space around me. There were no corners to hide behind, no side streets, no bridges. Just miles of fields. Geveg's mountains were hazy in the distance, looking more like storm clouds on the horizon than rock.

To the north of the farmhouse was a grid of dirt roads and buildings, the houses of those who worked Jeatar's farm. He had thousands of acres and hundreds of farmhands, and some merchants and traders had established shops there like a small village. I didn't know if it had a name, but Aylin called it Jeatown.

The fields closest to Jeatown were dotted with dozens of tents, makeshift homes for those who'd also fled Baseer. Horses grazed in roped-off corrals, with wagons nearby. I even spotted a few carriages mixed in, proof that wealth didn't protect you from the Duke's soldiers.

"It's getting crowded out there," I said. "We might have to start making food runs twice a day." We'd been helping Jeatar's people hand out food and supplies to the refugees, and the bags were going faster every day.

"I heard the guards say there are even folks from Verlatta now."

"Verlatta? What are *they* running from?" Verlatta had been under siege by the Duke's army the last six months, but when I'd shattered his palace and started a city-wide riot, he'd recalled the army to subdue his people. Verlattians should have been rejoicing.

Danello shrugged. "I don't know, but rumors say there's fighting in all the cities."

Even Geveg?

I tried not to picture my city in flames, people I knew fighting in the streets, their bodies in the canals, but I'd seen far too much for those memories to stay silent. War was coming.

Saints, war was *here*, and I'd probably started it.

I still had nightmares about being trapped in the Duke's weapon, locked to the misshapen pynvium by cuffs of silvery metal that made you do what you didn't want to do. The pain cycling through me and the other five Takers chained to it with me. Being forced to trigger it, to flash its pain and kill.

Of losing control of it and turning it into something that drained life.

I prayed the weapon had been destroyed when the Duke's palace was, shattered by its own pain when the walls came down around it, but I knew better. It was still there, and the Duke was still trying to make it work.

If he figured it out, none of us would ever be safe again.

A soldier by the perimeter fence waved at Danello and called hello. He elbowed another soldier and pointed at me, but they were done gossiping by the time we reached them.

It was the same everywhere we walked. Knots of people watching me, whispering about me. You'd think they'd be bored with me by now, but there was always someone new on the guard who hadn't heard what I'd done. Their words reached me, some from people who didn't even *try* to stay quiet.

"That's the girl who destroyed the palace and almost killed the Duke."

"It's the Shifter, the one who rescued all those Healers in Geveg."

"There's Nya. She saved our lives in Baseer. Took on the Undying to do it, too."

My skin twitched with so many eyes on me. I'd spent my whole life hiding who I was— *what* I was— but my secret was gossip now. And gossip traveled faster than a four-footed hen.

Maybe even fast enough to reach the Duke's ears.

"Here we are." Danello pushed open a gate to a low-walled garden. Cool green shade greeted us, smelling of honeysuckle and white ginger. It was beautiful, but my uneasiness was rising like the tide.

"Maybe this wasn't such a good idea," I said.

With all the new folks on the farm, one or two could be spies—or worse, trackers—for the Duke. He finally had control of Baseer again, and that was making everyone nervous. We should be preparing to fight back, defend ourselves if needed, not enjoying the sunshine.

"Nya, it's okay. It's quiet here, no one will bother us." Danello squeezed my hand and rubbed his thumb across my knuckles. I took a deep breath and nodded. He was right. Until we knew what the Duke was doing, there wasn't anything to prepare for.

We followed a stone path that curved among bright yellow flowers and trees with white bark and circled around a small pond. Danello stopped and pulled a blanket out of the basket. He shook it open and spread it out by the water.

"Breakfast is served," he said with a flourish.

I sat, scanning the bushes while he rummaged through the basket. Leaves rustled in the wind like footsteps crunching through dry grass, but I didn't see anyone around.

"Do you want fish cakes or stuffed peppers?" He held both up and wiggled them as if that made them more appealing. Didn't help the food, but it did make *him* look adorable. His warm brown eyes. The cute little scar above his lip.

I was a fool. A romantic picnic with Danello and all I could think about was what the Duke was up to? Danello deserved better.

"What's the pepper stuffed with?" I asked, scooting closer.

"Um . . ." He poked a finger into the breading. "Looks like fish."

"The same fish?"

"Maybe, if it was a *big* fish." He grinned.

I chuckled, the first laugh I'd had in, Saints, I couldn't remember. It felt good. This *was* good. Me, him, together all alone for once, with no one trying to kill either of us. I needed more of this—*lots* more. "I meant the same *kind* of fish."

"I know, but it made you smile." He set the pepper on a plate and grabbed a knife from the basket. "We'll split both. That way you won't have to choose."

Like I chose to leave Tali behind? My grin faltered. I hadn't meant to think it, hadn't *wanted* to think it. Shouldn't have thought it, not with the sun and flowers and a cute boy bringing me food.

A sweet scent drifted past on the breeze. White ginger. Tali's scent. No wonder I'd thought of her.

Danello looked at me, uncertain. "You okay?"

I nodded and he resumed cutting.

It hadn't been my choice to leave her. Danello and Aylin had kidnapped me, carried me screaming out of Baseer, thrown me on Jeatar's boat, and locked me in a cabin until we were far enough away that I couldn't swim back.

That's not the choice you regret.

No, it was the one I'd made my first night in Baseer, when I could have saved Tali from the tracker Vyand and kept her out of the Duke's clutches. But Danello and Aylin had been captured, too, imprisoned in a Baseeri jail and facing execution. Their certain deaths had weighed against Tali's life.

And I'd chosen them.

Tali had been in trouble for sure, but Danello and Aylin would have been killed in just a few hours. I'd thought I'd have time to go back for her. Thought I could save them all, but I'd been wrong. I'd left her in a city tearing itself apart with a man who wanted to turn her into a weapon and force her to kill.

"Here you go." Danello handed me a plate, a smile on his face but worry in his eyes. "One half of a mystery-fish-stuffed pepper and one full fish cake."

I took my food. The first bite tasted like rock, but I kept eating. He'd gone to so much trouble, and all for me.

Footsteps thumped over stone and I tensed. Another couple appeared but kept walking around the pond. They didn't even look at us. Maybe we were far enough outside the farmhouse grounds that people didn't recognize me. My name was a lot more famous than my face.

"It's okay, Nya, you're safe here," Danello said softly. "I won't let anything happen to you."

He wouldn't, either. He'd face any soldiers the Duke sent after me. Watch my back no matter what I tried to do. Even when he disagreed with it.

"Thank you," I said. I should have said more, but the words wouldn't come. I looked at him, hoping he'd know how I felt anyway. *Eyes say more than lips ever could.* Danello had nice lips. I smiled.

He smiled back nervously and leaned toward me, just a little, as if waiting to see what I'd do. I leaned in as well, my heart pounding. Hoping he'd come closer, so I could go closer and—

"Excuse me?" a woman called, stepping out from under the trees.

Danello blew out a sigh and turned around. I frowned at her. She looked too nicely dressed for a refugee. A Baseeri merchant perhaps. A man stepped out next, his face scarred, three scratches on one side, forehead to chin, like a giant bird had clawed him. He looked more like a soldier.

"Yes?" Danello asked.

The woman smiled at us. "Have you heard about the Great Flash?"

"Great Flash?"

She nodded. "It happened in Baseer. A flash bright as the sun, caused by a girl who channeled the Saints' power to crush the Duke's palace."

I shivered. She had it all wrong.

"Um, that's not what happened," I said. "It was a pynvium weapon that overloaded and flashed."

Danello grabbed my hand. "Don't say anything else," he whispered.

"The Saints sing of this girl," the woman continued. She glanced at the scarred man. "They gave her the power of Their light so she could save us from the darkness."

I couldn't even save my sister. How did they expect me to save *them*?

"She sounds, uh, great, but we need to go." Danello inched away, tugging me with him. He kept one hand near the rapier at his hip.

"Were you there?" the man asked. His desperate gaze bored into mine. He reminded me of some soldiers I'd seen at the end of the first war—the ones who gave up fighting and sat inside the Sanctuary all day, praying for salvation and begging everyone around them to pray, too. Ones who were lost, angry, wanting help and blame in equal measures.

"Will you tell us what you saw?" he asked. "Share your story with us and others who believe as we do?"

My story was being shared quite enough already. "Sorry, I didn't see anything."

The woman and the scarred man frowned but nodded. "Truth is a hard stone to swallow," he said. "If you want to share, you can find us in the east camp. Look for a red carriage with gold stars."

Carriage? Maybe they weren't merchants if they could afford a carriage. But they didn't look like aristocrats.

"Thanks, we'll keep that in mind," said Danello. We backed away, ready to run if they so much as stepped toward us, but they left and headed deeper into the garden. I heard the woman speak again, probably to the other couple we'd seen earlier.

"What in Saea's name was *that* all about?" I kept my voice low until we passed through the gate and into the safety of the open courtyard. If we needed them, three guards were within shouting distance.

"I'm not sure it was in Saea's name at all. They sounded like those sainters who hassle people in the park by the Sanctuary."

"The ones who think the stars are going to go out?" I'd seen them too, shouting to all who'd listen that the stars would go black and the dark would fall, but one light would shine bright enough to, oh, I don't know, chase away the shadows or something. I never listened for long. Their rants always brought soldiers, and soldiers brought trouble.

"Yeah. Maybe Baseer has its own sainters," Danello said.

"Who are ranting about *me*." It was worse than the gossip and the whispers. What I'd done wasn't a sign from the Saints. It had been an accident. I'd only been trying to stop the Duke's weapon and keep it from killing half of Baseer.

"It's not you personally. They're just trying to fit their crazy beliefs onto what happened. They did the same thing with that lightning storm last summer, remember? The one that set all those villas on fire?"

"True. Fingers of the Saints or something." No one had listened to them, and some had even laughed. It *was* a pretty silly name.

We reached the farmhouse and pushed open the kitchen door. Ouea, Jeatar's housemistress, sat at the table, peeling mangoes. Two girls sat on either side of her, smaller baskets of gold peppers in front of them. They twisted off the stems one by one.

Ouea looked up. "Nya, what happened? You're white as salt."

"A bunch of refugees think I'm the eighth saint."

"They think what?"

Danello smiled. "Nya's exaggerating, but there are some sainters out there talking about the flash in Baseer like it's a sign from the Saints."

Ouea tucked a graying strand of hair behind an ear. "People turn to faith when they're frightened. I'm sure it's nothing to worry about."

"Probably not." Especially when there was enough in my worry bowl already. "Maybe Jeatar knows where they came from."

"Could be." Ouea nodded.

"Can you ask him tomorrow?" Danello said. "I was hoping we could spend the day together. Fun, remember? You've been working so hard lately."

With nothing to show for it. Three times we'd sneaked out to Baseer—or as close as we could get— to search for Tali. But the rumors had been false, and the leads had led nowhere.

Ouea cleared her throat. "Danello? Where's my picnic basket?"

"Um." He winced. "In the garden."

"You weren't going to leave it there, were you?"

"No, ma'am."

"Then go get it."

Danello looked at me, then at the door. Ouea kept staring at him over the basket of mangoes. Her two young helpers kept their eyes on the peppers, but both girls were trying hard not to giggle.

"Wait for me in the kitchen garden?" he asked. "We still have a picnic to finish."

I smiled. "Definitely."

Danello dashed out, and Ouea went back to peeling mangoes. "He's a good boy, that one is. Even if he is a bit forgetful at times."

"Yeah, he's great." I glanced toward the door to the rest of the farmhouse. It would take Danello a while to run all the way out to the pond and back. Surely I had time to see if there *was* any news about Tali or those sainters. I'd be in the kitchen garden before him. "Jeatar in the library?"

"Last I checked."

Hope and dread tugged at my heart. Maybe today I'd find out where Tali was. Or maybe I'd learn there was no reason to look for her anymore.

And Saints help me, I wasn't sure which would be worse.

TWO

The library door was open but I knocked anyway. Onderaan and Jeatar looked up in unison. One smiled, one didn't.

I frowned. "What happened?"

"Forget about going to Baseer," Jeatar said, stone-faced as always.

"Why not?" *Please don't say Tali's dead. Please don't.*

"There's massive troop movement along the river, and transport ships are being moved into the harbor. Looks like the Duke is mobilizing his army."

"Do you know where?"

"Not yet, but from the number of ships, it looks like an invasion."

My chest tightened. "Geveg?"

"Or Verlatta, the mining towns, any of the river provinces."

"If not all of them." Onderaan shook his head and sighed deeply, for a moment looking so much like Papa I had to look away. It was still hard to believe he was my uncle. That I even *had* an uncle, let alone a Baseeri one. "This could be the start of a major campaign."

I'd seen one of those before, five years ago when the Duke invaded Geveg and killed my parents. My Grannyma. When he burned the city of Sorille to the ground to kill his brothers—rivals for the throne.

"Any news from Geveg?" Last we'd heard, there were still riots, though it hadn't turned into a full uprising yet. Information was sparse, since Jeatar had sent most of his spies and scouts to Baseer, but he had a few Gevegian contacts left.

Jeatar hesitated, glancing at Onderaan. Not a good sign. "Unconfirmed rumors say the Governor-General is dead."

"Seriously?" A surprise, but it didn't bother me none if he was. He'd been appointed by the Duke and treated Gevegians like we were trash. "Who's in charge now? Another Baseeri or a Gevegian?"

"I'm waiting to hear from my contacts there, but so far, nothing."

"If Geveg's in full rebellion," Onderaan said, "then the Duke would certainly want to end it before it inspired anyone else to fight back."

I nodded. "Like the mining towns." The Duke invaded us the first time for our pynvium, and he had to need more of it. I'd destroyed his foundry, stolen some, and ruined the rest of his supply of the raw metal. When Baseer revolted, he would have needed more weapons to subdue his own people, more healing bricks for his troops, using up the little pynvium he'd had left. He had to be running low by now.

Was he also running low on Healers?

He'd been kidnapping and experimenting on them for months, but with all the fighting, he *had* to be using them to heal his troops.

"Do you think Tali is with him?"

Jeatar didn't hesitate this time. "Yes."

"Can we—"

"No, you can't go after her. The Healers will be heavily protected, probably at the center of the army. Most likely guarded by Undying."

The Undying didn't scare me all that much, but the Duke's Healer-soldiers were deadly to everyone else. How could you stop someone who could heal their own wounds, push the pain into their pynvium armor, and keep on fighting? They cut through regular soldiers like farmers cut through wheat.

"Nya, we'll find her," Onderaan said softly. "I owe it to Peleven to keep his girls safe."

Papa.

He had also been Baseeri, though I hadn't known that until a few months ago. I didn't like to think about what that made me. Baseer had always been the enemy, but I had Baseeri friends now, Baseeri family. Baseeri blood.

"What do we do?"

"About Tali?" Jeatar said. "Nothing until we know something solid. Same with Geveg. As for the Duke, we'll keep watching and wait to see what his plans are."

I'd never been good at waiting. In Geveg, doing nothing got you killed. You had to find food, find work, find shelter from the soldiers. Keep your eyes open, your wits sharp. You had to move and keep moving, or trouble found you.

But I wasn't in Geveg anymore.

"Perhaps you should stay close to the house for the next few days," Onderaan said. "Just in case people are looking for you."

"I can't. I have food duty." Besides, lots of folks knew me around here anyway. A spy wouldn't need to see me to learn I was here.

"I'm sure Jeatar can find someone to fill in for you." He glanced at Jeatar, who paused and looked at me as if unsure whether or not to agree to that.

I bristled. I *liked* helping out. At least I was doing something useful and not just waiting for news. "There *is* no one to fill in for me. People are spread thin enough as it is. If I'm not there, everyone else has to work harder, and that's not fair."

"Not everyone else is in danger."

I folded my arms. "We're all in danger—mine's just more personal."

Jeatar's mouth twitched, but he stayed quiet.

Onderaan sighed. "Well, as long as you're careful, I guess it'll be okay."

As if I needed his permission. "Jeatar, you'll let me know if there's any more news today?"

"Of course."

"Thank you." I had a picnic to get back to. I'd promised Danello we'd have fun, and I wasn't about to let him down.

Even if having fun was the last thing I felt like doing.

I made it to the kitchen garden before Danello, but I found Aylin cuddled up with Quenji on a bench under the orange trees. Thin shafts of sunlight cut through the branches and brought out Aylin's true red hair beneath the fake black.

I cleared my throat.

They pulled apart and she blushed, but the glint in her brown eyes said I'd get the full story later. At least one of us had gotten kissed today.

"Oh, hi!" She giggled and glanced at Quenji, who grinned. But then he was always grinning. He'd been the leader of a street pack I'd met in Baseer and had risked his life to help us destroy the Duke's foundry there. I think he really liked the danger, since he'd volunteered for every mission to go back and look for Tali. He was a good person to have watching your back, so I was happy to have him along.

So was Aylin, apparently.

"Sooo, how was the picnic?" she asked.

"Short." I told her about the sainters.

"Pfft, nobody pays attention to them," she said, waving her hand. She smiled. "But tell me, *before* they interrupted—anything interesting happen?"

"Not as interesting as I'd have liked." I glanced at Quenji. Potential kisses weren't something I wanted to discuss in front of him. "Onderaan's trying to tell me what to do again."

"He means well," Aylin said.

"He's annoying."

"Nya, he doesn't know how to act around you. He was probably just as shocked to find out about you as you were about him."

"Well, maybe." I didn't like this conversation any better. Weren't best friends supposed to side with you no matter what? I changed the subject. "Jeatar says the Gov-Gen might be dead."

"Does that mean we can go home?" Aylin turned to Quenji before I could reply. "You'll love Geveg! It's on the lake, and there are beaches and warm breezes and the best coffee you've ever had."

"And soldiers," I said, surprised to see how eager she was to go back. To leave before we found Tali. "Don't forget about the Baseeri soldiers beating people up just for fun."

She flicked a hand at me again, as if she could brush off the idea of soldiers as easily as sainters. "If the Gov-Gen is dead, then the soldiers are next. They'll probably be gone by the time we get there."

"We don't know what it means yet."

"Nya!" She gaped at me. "It means Geveg is fighting back, just like you always wanted. I bet they're kicking the Baseeri out as we speak." She jumped up and pantomimed kicking people one at a time. Quenji applauded.

"I've never been to Geveg," he said. "I'd love to go."

"But—"

"Go where?" Danello said, slipping up behind me.

"Home!" Aylin cried.

"Really?" He stared at me with hope in his eyes. "When did this happen?"

I held up both hands. "No one said anything about going home. I'm not even sure if the rumor is true."

"What rumor?" Danello looked confused. "You went to see Jeatar while I was gone, didn't you?"

"Yes, but just for a minute." I sighed and explained the whole thing. The transport ships, the Gov-Gen, not being able to go after Tali.

Aylin plopped back onto the bench. "So we're not going home."

I'd never realized how much she wanted to. So did I, but not without Tali. Home was wherever my sister was, and without her, Geveg would be just another city.

"Not yet, but we will, I promise."

"If there's a home to go back to," Danello mumbled.

"What?" Aylin said.

"I want to go back, too," he said. "My da's still

there. And Halima and the twins ask about him all the time."

Danello's little brothers and sister stayed pretty close to the farmhouse, and I'd never seen them out past the main gate. After what they'd been through, I couldn't blame them. Kidnapped, almost killed by Undying, running from Baseer with the rest of us. They deserved to go home and be with their father again.

"Well, listen," Danello said, taking my hand. "We have a picnic to finish."

"We'll see you this afternoon, right?" Aylin said.

"At the north gate as always."

We left through the kitchen and out the back door, but Danello didn't head for the pond again. Instead he led me toward some trees near the front of the farmhouse.

"It's not as secluded," he said, "but it's shady and mostly out of the way."

"What did you mean when you said, 'if there's a home to go back to'?"

He winced. "Nothing."

"If it was nothing, you wouldn't have changed what you said to Aylin."

He rubbed the back of his neck. "It's just, well, if someone in Geveg really did kill the Gov-Gen, and there really is a strong rebellion there, and the Duke is suddenly moving troops, then he might be going after Geveg."

"That's what Onderaan said."

He pulled out the blanket again and spread it under the trees. "You're not the only one missing family, you know," he said softly.

"I know." Shame warmed my face. I'd been so focused on Tali, I hadn't thought about what he and his brothers and sister were feeling. Their father was out there somewhere too. Maybe he was safe in Geveg, but maybe not, especially if the city was in revolt.

I took his hand and rested my head against his shoulder. "We'll get them all back, I promise. We'll get *everything* back."

He nodded, but he knew as well as I did that wasn't true. We'd never get his mother back, or my parents. The people the Duke had already killed were gone forever. All we could do was hold on to what little we had left and hope we could make something out of it.

I guessed we wouldn't have any fun today after all.

We met Aylin and Quenji at the north gate midafternoon, standing near a dark-brown horse with the wagon loaded with food. The horse nibbled grass, tearing it out of the ground with quick twists of its head. Ellis sat on the driver's bench in that brown uniform that all Jeatar's guards wore. We'd met in Baseer when I'd saved her life after a pynvium raid had gone wrong. She'd been one of the Underground's guards then, had fought with us against the Undying, and even held shifted pain for us. She'd been promoted to captain a few weeks ago, but she still liked to help out with the food, same as I did.

A second guard appeared and waved hello to Danello.

He waved back. "Afternoon, Copli."

"Do you know *all* the guards?" I said.

"The ones who come to practice." The rapier he carried wasn't just for show. Danello drilled with the guards a few hours every day, working on his skills. "The rest I play cards with."

"You really should socialize more, Nya," Aylin said. "There are a lot of people on the farm."

"Enough people know me already."

Quenji chuckled. "You can never have too many friends."

"Come on," I said, climbing into the wagon beside Ellis. "We have hungry people to feed."

Folks turned our way when we rolled through the outer camp. Families sat on small stools or on the grass, faces turned down, staring at the camp-fires. Not every tent had a fire, and those seemed the saddest of all.

Some of the people looked Baseeri, a few entire families with black hair and sad blue eyes, but we met a lot more folks with strong Verlattian features and clothes, and farmers with blond hair who could have been from Geveg.

I'd seen similar faces after the Baseeri threw us out of our homes. Sad, scared, lost. My guts churned, my own memories tumbling through my head.

"Nya, where we gonna sleep?" Tali had asked, tears on her cheeks, fear in her eyes. No seven-year-old should ever be that scared.

"I don't know, but I'll find us someplace safe. I promise."

No tents for us back then. Just hard ground under scratchy bushes. I'd wrapped my arms around Tali to make her feel safe, but it was years before either of us felt—well, not safe, but safer.

Ellis guided the wagon through the campsites. Folks were already moving toward us when we stopped at a large fire with a heavy cook pot hang-ing over it. A community pot just like the ones I'd eaten at in Geveg. People brought something in the morning, it cooked all day, and everyone shared it that evening. There'd been days when I'd eaten only because I'd sneaked a few handfuls of flour from the mill to thicken the stew. Wasn't much, but it satisfied the rules.

Today's stew simmered, bits of sweet potato and rosemary sticking out of the thickening broth. Cook glanced over at us, his face tough and lined from the sun. He smiled and waved.

"Just in time," he called. "We could use some bread to go with the stew."

"We have lots of that," I said, a little guilty as I climbed off the wagon. None of it was as good as the bread Ouea made. No fruit or nuts, no spices. Just basic bread. But no one seemed to care. Food was food.

The children raced right for Aylin, holding out their tiny hands. She always filled one bag with treats—sugar nuts, candied fruit, even a few bricks of sweet brittle.

"News of the day?" Ellis asked while people lined up. Dinner wasn't all you got at a community pot. Folks got to talking when they had no place to go.

"Nine new carriages rolled into Little 'Crat City," Cook said.

Ellis chuckled. "You really shouldn't call it that."

"Bunch of aristocrats set up camp and keep everyone else out? What would *you* call it?"

"Rude." She smiled and handed him another sack. "Want me to look into it?"

He shook his head. "Nah. No self-respecting Baseeri wants to bed down there anyway."

Ellis glanced at me and winked. Wasn't too long ago I thought no Baseeri *had* any self-respect, and she liked to remind me of that.

"Oh, you might want to send the Healers round," Cook said.

"Is someone hurt?" I asked.

"Might not be serious, but three families came in an hour ago, and they look like they barely made it here. I told 'em to go up to the house, but they insisted they were fine. I said they didn't have to pay, but it didn't change their minds."

"I'll let Jeatar know." We didn't have many Healers, and most of them were apprentices or first or second cords only, but that was more than most folks had access to these days.

We finished up and headed closer to Jeatown and the nicer camps. Carriages, bigger tents, more dark-haired families. Baseeri aristocrats, even a few rich merchants. Dozens of servants still wearing their house colors hovered about, waiting on orders.

Joke or not, it really *was* Little 'Crat City. Just like in Baseer, they'd closed off their territory, using the carriages like a wall around the camp. They even had their own guards protecting it. Of course, the guards moved out of our way pretty quickly. Ellis had taught them the first day who gave the *real* orders around here.

They had their own community fire, but you'd never catch them sharing food, just gossip and opinions. We parked the wagon, and the servants lined up while the aristocrats stayed in their comfy chairs. I couldn't imagine how they'd managed to get them out of Baseer, but I suspected more than one servant had hauled furniture out on their backs.

"You don't know what you're talking about," a woman in red and blue silk scoffed. She sat around the fire with a few dozen others as well-dressed as she. They didn't look at us or the food. "Was the Saints themselves. They reached down and crushed the palace with their hands. No living soul did what I saw happen there."

My stomach twisted. They were talking about me. No good ever came of Baseeri aristocrats talking about *me*.

"Don't be daft—it was an attack. Verlattian retaliation, probably."

"I heard it was a girl," said another man. "One of those quirkers."

"The Shifter?"

"That's right. Part of a Gevegian kill squad to assassinate the Duke."

I was *what*? Danello slipped a hand to my shoulder and leaned close. "Easy, ignore them. It's just gossip."

Easy for him to say—they weren't calling *him* an assassin. I glanced at Aylin and Quenji, both surrounded by children as they handed out the sweetcakes and cookies. She looked back, worry in her eyes, but Quenji had a sly smile like he approved of the story. Quenji liked to tell his own tales. On the streets, a good story told at the right tavern could get you a meal.

"She's as bad as the Undying," a woman said, her voice cracking. "They killed my husband. He wasn't doing anything wrong! Just trying to bring the carriage round." The young girl beside her started crying. She looked like the girl from Baseer. The one I couldn't save.

"Fenda, no!"

Metal clanged against metal, then a girl screamed in pain.

"She's just a child!" the man cried. *"How could you?"*

Anger chased away some of my fear. I wasn't *anything* like the Undying. They'd murdered an innocent girl who'd only been trying to protect her father.

"We traded my wife's jewelry for a gate pass."

A man grunted. "I had a soldier ask me for my *wife* to get through."

Some folks chuckled, but most looked around as if unsure if he was joking or not.

"Well," a woman said, "we're better off than those left behind."

I pictured Tali and my guts twisted.

"I don't know what that flash was, or who caused it," she continued, "but things aren't right in that city. They haven't been right since Bespaar—"

Angry shouts came from behind the tents, then repeated orders to stop. Ellis jumped up onto the driver's bench, her sword out a heartbeat later. Danello drew his rapier.

"What's going on?" Aylin whispered. The children who had gathered around her moved closer, their blue eyes wide and scared. Quenji stepped in front and nudged them back.

"I don't know," he said, "but it doesn't sound good."

Three men burst out from behind some tents. Two were blond, one dark haired. All wore old clothes and masks covering the bottoms of their faces. One man had a bag clutched against his chest, but it wasn't one of ours.

"Thief!" someone cried, and the camp guards appeared, chasing down the bandits.

Ellis swore and hopped off the wagon. She went after the thieves and Danello followed right behind her. The thieves ran like chickens, darting this way and that, knocking things over, throwing them at whoever was close. Folks ran everywhere, just as wild, just as scared, no one paying any attention to where they were going.

Elbows jabbed me, jostling me farther out into the crowd. A man slammed into my shoulder and spun me around. The second wagon guard, Copli, was on the driver's bench protecting the food but looking like he wanted to chase after Ellis and Danello. Quenji had his arms around Aylin, keeping her tight against the wagon and blocking her from the panicked mob. The children ran into the crowd, between legs and stomping feet, caught in the chaos.

I struggled through the bodies and grabbed a boy by the hand, yanking him back before a panicked woman ran him down. He clung to me, trembling.

I looked for another. Saw one of the thieves instead.

He pulled out a knife, then dodged back and thrust it at the guards. Several people screamed, but only one body stumbled, then fell to the ground.

"Stop right there," a tall Baseeri said, waving something at the thieves. I almost missed the glint of blue metal.

Pynvium. He had a pynvium rod. A good one, too, the metal pure enough to shine a rich blue.

The aristocrat pointed the rod into the crowd full of scared people—and children.

"Wait, no!" I yelled.

Whoomp.

Pain flashed from the rod, the familiar prickle of blown sand stinging my skin. People all around me screamed and collapsed—guards, thieves, children. Even the horse shrieked and bolted, sending bags of food flying off the wagon and Copli toppling off the bench. Those at the edge of the flash stumbled and fell, tripping over those on the ground. The boy I'd grabbed dropped and lay by my feet.

I stood in a circle cleared by the pain, exposed and alone.

THREE

D id she just—?"
   "Quirker!"
"The Shifter's here!"

Cries raced through the crowd, then fingers
pointed and hands waved, all in my direction. Saints!
I should have fallen, faked being affected, but it all
happened so fast. I dropped to one knee and took the
hand of the unconscious boy at my feet. My hand
tingled as I *drew* in the pain overloading his senses.
He woke and looked around, whimpering.

"Go find your mother," I said, scanning the rest
of the people on the ground. *Danello, where's Danello?*
There! Lying near Ellis and one of thieves. People
gasped when I ran toward him, backing away like I

was going to hurt them.

"Get her, stop her!" the Baseeri with the pynvium weapon called.

I knelt and wrapped a hand around Danello's wrist, the other around Ellis's. *Drew* in their pain and held it in the empty space between my heart and guts. It simmered there like I'd eaten something that had disagreed with me.

Danello jerked awake, hands out. Ellis woke right after. I let go of them and looked for the guard who'd been stabbed. He'd have real pain—pain I could use if one of these aristocrats tried to—

Someone slammed into me, knocking me to the ground.

"I got her!" a man yelled, practically in my ear.

"Get off of her," Danello said. The weight vanished, and he dragged me back to my feet.

Unconscious people were still on the ground and probably would be for a while. The others surrounded us, fear and anger on their faces. Except for a woman with the boy I'd helped. They looked at me with gratitude.

Be nice if you told your friends to leave me alone.

"Everyone settle down," Ellis said, sword out. Copli was on his feet again, a gash across his forehead. Danello stayed near me, but still close enough to the others to back them up.

"But that's the Shifter," a woman said.

Ellis shrugged. "So?"

"She tried to kill the Duke!"

"No, she didn't. He almost killed her and she defended herself. So unless you want to see what happens when she feels threatened, I suggest you all *calm down*."

Not exactly what I would have said to accomplish that, but they did take another step back. I moved toward the injured guard. He'd been hurt bad, and too much blood pooled beneath him. Dark blood, which meant a pierced organ.

One of the aristocrats jerked and pointed. "What's she doing?"

"Helping him, you idiot," Aylin said, "What do you think she's doing?"

"If I don't stop that bleeding, he's going to die." I reached the fallen guard. No one else tried to stop me, but quite a few fidgeted as if ready to jump on me if I tried anything they didn't like.

He'd been stabbed low on the side, over his liver. I placed one hand on his wound, the other on his forehead, felt my way in. Winced. Lots of damage, like the knife had sliced sideways and not just stabbed. I focused on closing the tears, sealing the holes. I *drew*, and pain flowed from him to me, sharp aches that spread through my middle. He groaned and opened his eyes.

"You're going to be okay," I said softly. So would I once we got back to the farmhouse and found a Healer who could take the pain from me.

He stood, swaying a bit, and I steadied him. Murmurs slid through the crowd, though they shouldn't have. Wasn't like aristocrats had never seen someone healed before. They were the only ones who could afford it these days.

"What did she do to him?"

"Saved his life."

"She's a criminal," the same man said.

Ellis smiled. "No more than you."

"But she's—"

"Oh for Saints' sake," the woman with the boy said. "She's a *child*. Do you really believe everything the Duke says?"

"I believe what I just saw."

"So do I. She saved a life while you hurt my son and other people's sons and daughters. Over what? Petty theft?" She shook her head and pulled her son closer. "You're more criminal than she is."

A few muttered in what sounded like agreement. Ellis reached behind her with one hand and pulled strips of rope out of a back pouch. She tossed them to Aylin. "You and Quenji, bind the thieves' hands before Nya wakes them up. We'll take them back and let Jeatar deal with them."

"They robbed us," a woman said hesitantly. "It should be up to us what to do with them."

Ellis shook her head. "This isn't Baseer and it isn't your property. You want to stay and keep getting fed, you follow our rules and do what we say."

No one else said anything else, but many watched us with narrowed eyes.

"Wake them up."

I did, drawing more pain into the throbbing around my middle. The thieves woke, gaped at us, but didn't try to escape. Quenji hauled them to their feet, and we slowly made our way out of the camp. Ellis and Danello brought up the rear, looking more worried about the Baseeri than the thieves.

The aristocrats followed us to their "gate" but came no farther. The man who'd used the weapon glared at us as we walked away.

Ellis shot me a look that said it was my fault, even if she clearly felt bad about it.

I wasn't worried about a few trinkets getting stolen or that one camp was preying on another. That would sort itself out. But these were Baseeri whose allegiances we didn't know, and they knew I was here. Some even thought I was a criminal, an assassin, but everyone here was supposed to be against the Duke. They were all supposed to be on Jeatar's side.

So where did that put me?

I followed the others to the farmhouse, fresh dread churning my stomach.

Ellis and Copli took the thieves to the barracks. The rest of us went to the room Jeatar had set aside for an infirmary. We'd had more Healers when we'd fled Baseer, but most of them had left, returning to their families or just running farther away to where the Duke couldn't get them again. Only two remained— Lanelle and Tussen. I'd saved both from the Duke and his weapon.

Lanelle was on duty. Aylin immediately turned around.

"We'll meet you after, okay?" she said, dragging Quenji out.

Lanelle looked hurt for a moment but covered it fast. I couldn't blame Aylin for not wanting to be here. I'd have preferred it if Tussen had been on today. Lanelle had helped the Duke with his experiments, "taking care" of Tali and the other apprentices who'd been locked in the spire room and filled with pain.

Lanelle had been part of his next experiment, too, but this time as a victim, one of the Takers he'd chained to the weapon. It had surprised me when she'd volunteered to stay on the farm and help heal the refugees, but she probably didn't have anywhere else to go.

"Is that your blood?" she asked, rising from a chair. She set down the book she'd been reading.

"No, a guard got stabbed in one of the camps."

"He's okay?"

"Yes."

She glanced at Danello, standing stone-still behind me, then held out her hands. I took them. A faint tingle ran up my arms and swirled around my middle, and the pain was gone.

Lanelle made a face. "More than just a stabbing. You could have warned me."

"Sorry, it was only a few flashes."

She walked over to a cabinet and pulled a key from around her neck. "To you maybe, but for us regular Healers, that hurts just the same." She unlocked the cabinet and pulled out a battlefield brick of pynvium. Pure metal, and worth a lot more than anything those aristocrats had in their camp.

She placed one hand on it, pushing the pain into the metal. She usually gave me a sly grin when she did it, taunting me that she could sense pynvium when I couldn't, but not today. Maybe she was finally getting bored with it. I might not be a "regular Healer," but that didn't bother me nearly as much as it once had.

"There are some folks hurt in the outer camp," I said. Probably some in Little 'Crat City, too, but I wasn't worried about them. They'd march right up the farmhouse and demand healing if they needed it. "They might need some looking after."

Lanelle nodded. "I'll head over when Tussen comes in."

"Make sure you take some guards."

"Always do." She put the pynvium brick back into its cabinet and relocked it. "You hear about Geveg?"

She couldn't mean the Gov-Gen. Jeatar hadn't confirmed that, and even if he had, I doubt he'd tell Lanelle about it. "Hear what?"

"They're chasing out the Baseeri." She shrugged. "At least, that's what I heard."

"From who?" Danello asked. He sounded suspicious.

"People in the camps. They *do* talk to me, you know."

"There's a lot of talk in the camps," I said, "but

47

you can't believe half of it." Still, if Gevegians really were chasing the Baseeri out, maybe the Gov-Gen rumor was true.

Lanelle huffed. "All I know is that there's a lot of homeless Baseeri around, and not all of them are from Baseer. They want to go home as badly as we do."

Strange to hear Lanelle say she wanted to go home.

"Anyway," she said, rubbing her eyes. I hadn't noticed the circles under them before. "I'll take care of the people in the camps."

"Thanks." We left Lanelle alone in a room of cots. I shivered, picturing the last room she'd over-seen. The cots there had all been occupied. A room filled with suffering.

I sighed. "When did everything go so wrong?"

Danello paused. "The day you helped me."

"What?" Did he blame me?

"No! I didn't mean it like that," he said quickly. "It wasn't *you*, it was just that day. The ferry acci-dent. All those people hurt. That's when it started."

I exhaled, but my heart was still racing. "Okay. That's when we found out about the Duke's experi-ments, but you know, I think it started before that." I looked at him, and understanding flickered in his eyes. Sadness, too.

"Five years."

I nodded. "Five years."

When the Duke took over and invaded our homes. And until he was gone, nothing would ever be right again.

"Nya," Aylin whispered sometime in the hours before dawn. "You awake?"

"Yes." The wind had woken me a while back, gusting against the farmhouse like waves on rocks. No forests or mountains to stop it, I guess. Just open farmland.

I missed waves. And water. The caw of lake gulls riding the wind.

Aylin shook me. "Are you listening?"

"I'm sorry. What?"

She blew out a sigh. "I asked how long you were going to look for Tali."

"Until I find her."

"What if you don't?"

I didn't want to think about that. Or talk about it. Silence stretched in the darkness.

"I'm not trying to be heartless or anything," she continued, "but if the rumors are true, if Geveg belongs to Gevegians again, well, going home would be a good thing wouldn't it?"

I swallowed, but my mouth was dry. "Yes."

"And I know Danello wants to, though he'd never tell you that. He worries about his father. So do Halima and the twins. They really miss him."

"Maybe you should go without me." It hurt to say, but how could I keep them all here, knowing they wanted to go home?

She snorted and thumped me on the arm. "I'm not saying that. I'm just saying, maybe you should start thinking of ways to find Tali that don't involve putting yourself in danger all the time."

"How?"

"I don't know. Hire a tracker? I hear Vyand is good."

I swatted her with my pillow. "Aylin! How could you even suggest—"

Something thunked against the outside wall, harder than just wind. Aylin popped up.

"What was that?" she whispered.

I slipped out of bed, careful not to rustle the covers or squeak the frame. Jeatar had good furniture, so it rarely made a sound. I was equally quiet on the carpet as I made my way to the balcony doors.

Another thunk, then scraping like metal on wood.

I tugged back the curtains just enough to peek out. Moonlight lit the balcony, reflecting off . . . a grappling hook?

A hand slapped the railing, then a leg. I turned to Aylin.

"Someone's there," I said. "Get out of—"

Glass shattered behind me, then hot pain pierced my back.

FOUR

I yelped and dived forward, away from whatever had clawed me. I hit the floor, but something else landed beside me. Small, and it moved, skittering back toward the doors. It snagged on the doorframe but broke through and caught on the balcony rail.

A second grappling hook.

"Aylin, get out of here!" I scrambled back to my feet as the first intruder kicked open the doors. More glass cracked, and a piece grazed my arm. It didn't sting nearly as much as my back.

"Leave her alone!" Something flew past me. *Was that a chair?* Wood cracked against flesh and a man grunted. Aylin leaped from the bed, the blankets in her hands. She tackled the man and tangled him in the cloth, knocking him down.

The second man charged in and kicked her. Aylin cried out and flew back with an *oomph*. She slammed into the mirror, and glass shattered. I lunged at him, hands out, looking for flesh. I grabbed sleeves instead.

Skin, skin, I needed skin.

We struggled, my back stinging. He twisted and his arm slid back, down, then—skin.

Got you.

I *pushed*, the pain surging up through my shoulder and out my hands. He sucked in a pained breath and staggered back, tripping over his partner and sending them both back to the floor.

Light brightened the room, and I squinted, turning away. "Aylin?"

The lamp on the desk next to her was turned up full, all the shutters open. "I'm okay," she said, but she didn't *sound* okay. She also had one arm pressed against her side.

The door to our room burst open. Aylin screamed and I pivoted, readying myself to dive at whoever was attacking us now.

Danello stood in the door wearing nothing more than sleeping britches and his rapier. He moved in fast, putting himself between us and the two men who were now back on their feet and holding weapons of their own. A knife for one, a short sword for the other.

Sword-man attacked, thrusting the blade at Danello. He parried it, the scratchy *ziinng!* of metal against metal raising the hair on my arms. Knife-man hung back, his face tight with pain. He had to be the one I had shifted into.

"Go find Jeatar," I said to Aylin, nudging her toward the door.

She ignored me and grabbed a statue of a prancing horse off the desk. She threw it at Knife-man. He gasped and dodged sideways. Agile, but not as surefooted as Danello. Nor as graceful as Aylin. Who in Saea's name *were* these men?

Both had dark hair, but they didn't look like Baseeri soldiers. Well-made clothes, good boots. Clean-shaven, so not refugees. Trackers? Aristocrat guards?

Danello fought Sword-man while Aylin kept throwing whatever she could grab at the other. I scurried past Danello to the other side of the room, where there was more to throw. I flung a water pitcher. It glanced off his head and dented the wall.

Danello lunged forward, piercing Sword-man's leg. He screamed and went down on one knee.

Danello stabbed at the other leg, and he collapsed.

Fast steps thudded in the hall outside our room, many feet racing up stairs. Guards in brown uniforms stormed in, swords drawn. Sword-man rolled over and held out both hands, fury on his face. Knifeman ran back toward the balcony. Danello and the guards followed, but he was over the side and sliding to the ground before they could grab him.

"You got this one?" one of the guards asked Danello, tilting his head toward Sword-man on the floor.

"Yeah."

The guards turned and ran out of the room. Danello stood over Sword-man, the tip of the rapier hovering above his throat.

"Don't even think about moving," he said. "Why did you break in here?"

Sword-man just glared.

"Are you okay?" Danello asked me without looking away.

"I'm fine." My heart felt like it was about to thump out of my chest, and I wasn't sure my knees were going to keep me standing, but both would pass.

"Aylin? Are you all right?"

"I think so." She was still holding her side.

"I think not." I hurried over, took her hand, and

felt my way in. "Two broken ribs."

She grimaced. "No wonder it hurt so much to throw those things."

I *drew*, mending her ribs. Mine started aching.

"You're really handy to have around, you know that?"

"Nya?" Jeatar slid to a stop outside the door, two steps ahead of Onderaan. Men with armor and swords were right behind them. Two came in and hauled Sword-man to his feet, then out the door. I don't think his boots even touched the ground. Jeatar didn't say where they were taking him but the scowl on Jeatar's face said I really didn't want to know.

Jeatar looked us over, his scowl turning to worry as he took in my ripped nightshirt and the blood smeared on my arm. "Who's hurt?"

"I was, but not anymore," Aylin said. "But there's a man with a knife out there who's probably not happy."

"We'll find him, don't worry." Jeatar looked like he hadn't been to bed yet, but Onderaan kept rubbing his eyes, his hair sticking out on one side. He came over and squeezed my hand. I squeezed back, pretending he was Papa.

Jeatar stayed by the door. I'd never seen him look so scared before. Or so mad. Hopefully the mad part wasn't at me.

"Tell me what happened," he said.

"Someone tried to kill Nya!" Aylin described the whole thing, yelling and waving her arms. She was scared too.

"We'll post guards outside," Onderaan said softly, patting my hand. "No unauthorized visits to the house."

"Okay. Thank you."

I took a deep breath and looked at the broken mirror. Dozens of my own face stared back at me from the jagged glass. I turned and checked my back. A new scar ran along my shoulders, worse than the ones on my legs and chest.

Shifting was different from healing. I had time to think about the wound when I healed, and make sure it closed properly. With shifting, I didn't think about it, I just did it. I'd shifted into so many. The prison guard. The foundry soldiers. The Undying.

And every shift had left its scar.

Jeatar moved us to a room with no windows at the center of the farmhouse, and we had to go through two other doors just to get to it. There hadn't been any guards when we got there, but they were posted now. Lanelle had complained about them hassling her when she'd come to take the broken ribs I'd healed. Aylin ignored her the whole time, making a show out of talking with Danello.

"Who do you think they were?" I asked after no one else had shown up for a while. The guards had orders not to let me out of the room until they had the perimeter locked down. Which seemed to be taking an awfully long time.

"The Duke's men?' said Aylin.

Danello shook his head. "More likely sent by that aristocrat from Little 'Crat City. The Duke's men wouldn't have been so sloppy."

I shivered. Never thought I'd be grateful for *amateur* assassins. "Think they caught him yet?"

"He had a decent head start," said Danello. "It might take them a while."

"Does that mean I'm stuck here until they do?"

"You should be happy about that." Aylin shuddered, wrapping both arms around herself. "I can't stop thinking about it. I mean, I know people have tried to hurt you before, but not like this. Those were always fights, it wasn't—*personal*."

I knew what she meant. It wasn't a soldier defending a foundry, or men guarding a room no one was supposed to see. These had been assassins sent specifically to kill *me*.

"It's got to be breakfast time by now," Danello said. "Want me to go down to the kitchens and get you something?"

Aylin jumped up. "You stay, I'll go. I need to get out of this room anyway." She left, giving me a wink as she shut the door. Where would she go first—the kitchen or to see Quenji? I was a bit surprised he hadn't come by yet, but maybe the guards were keeping everyone away.

Danello smiled at me, but he was worried, too. "Good thing you're not easy to kill."

No, I was just easy to hurt.

"Healers are always hard to kill," I said. "In the war, the soldiers would aim for their eyes or their hearts—kill them quickly before they could heal themselves." You could always tell a Healer's body by the wound that killed them.

Danello scooted closer and put his arms around me. I leaned my head on his shoulder. "I know the last few months have been awful," he said. "Saints, the last five years have been awful, but we'll get through this."

"Promise?"

"Promise." He pulled back and took both my hands. "Because we have each other."

He smiled in a way that made it suddenly hard

for me to breathe. He leaned in close, hesitating a whisper's length away, then kissed me. A hot tingle ran down to my toes, like a flash all over my skin, but a *good* flash. It was suddenly hard to think too, but I was tired of doing that anyway.

"Wherever you go," he breathed into my ear, "I go."

Aylin returned much faster than I'd have liked, not even bothering to knock first. Her hands were empty, but her eyes were full of fear.

"Something's going on and I don't think it's about you," she said, not even giving me a sly grin after Danello and I jumped apart. This was serious.

"Any clue what?"

She shook her head. "People are running all over, Ouea doesn't have *any* food set out, and I swear the servants are packing." She paused, then gasped. "Oh! And the guards outside your door are gone."

"They're gone? Without telling us?" I rose. That couldn't be good. "Did you see Jeatar?"

"No, but there were people coming in and out of the library."

"Let's go find out what's going on."

It was morning already, and sunlight poured through the windows. Servants were indeed running around with crates and carrying objects wrapped in tarps. Faces were tight, pale, and worried.

Jeatar stood at the big table in the library, maps spread out before him and soldiers around him. Ellis was there, but I didn't see Onderaan.

". . . down through the plains so we can stay ahead of them," he was saying, running his finger along something on the map.

I stepped into the room, Danello and Aylin close behind me. "What's going on?"

Jeatar looked up. "The Duke's army is mobilizing, and it looks like he's coming here."

I went cold.

"We received a message from Baseer. The Duke is ferrying troops over to the west side of the river. He's moving supplies, support staff, everything he needs for an extended march."

"How many soldiers?" Danello asked.

"Rough estimates—between ten and fifteen thousand."

"That's too many."

A brief smile flickered on Jeatar's lips. "It is. He's going to hit us, but we can't be his only target."

"You're sure he's coming *here*?" There was no reason to attack us. I'd caused him a mess of trouble, but you didn't send a whole army after one person.

Shiverfeet raced down my back.

Not unless that one person could destroy everything. Someone you thought you'd *already* killed.

"Yes, I'm sure." Jeatar looked over at two men entering the room. He held up a finger, and I waited while he spoke to some of his guards. They hurried back out, shouting names. Jeatar turned back to me. "There's no strategic reason for him to cross the river. The road from Baseer leads to both Verlatta and Geveg and is much more suited to travel. The only things of value on this side of the river are the aristocrats ready to stand against him."

That wasn't true. Jeatar was here. And I was pretty sure he was the rightful heir to the throne of Baseer. If I was right and the Duke had figured it out, he'd come after him fast.

"What about the people?" Aylin asked.

"I'm evacuating everyone to Veilig," Jeatar said. "That should get them out of the Duke's path and away from the fighting. He won't chase us."

"He will if he's after you," I said. The Duke had burned an entire city to get to Jeatar's father and the rest of his family. Everyone who could have claimed the throne instead of him. I didn't know how Jeatar survived, but he had scars he kept covered up.

For the first time, I could read Jeatar easily.

He was scared.

"He's not after either of us," he said evenly, his blue-gray eyes boring into mine. "This farm is where people who want to see him stripped of power are gathering. I knew we couldn't stay a secret for long. Some secrets you can't hide forever."

Like his secret? Did he suspect I'd guessed? I could ask him right here, right now, and everyone would know who he was. Our resistance could finally have the leader it deserved, one who was strong enough to keep the aristocrats in line and get everyone working together.

But that would make Jeatar the biggest target in the Three Territories.

If the Duke knew he was behind the rebellions, he'd destroy every town he suspected Jeatar of being in, just like he'd destroyed Sorille.

I couldn't put all those people at risk. Not until we were ready to fight.

"Is he going after Geveg?" I asked.

Jeatar let out a held breath and nodded. "That's a reasonable guess. He'll want to make Geveg an example, quell the other rebellions, and eliminate any support the aristocrats have gained."

More guards came in and Jeatar turned away again.

If the Duke was going after Geveg, then the rumors about the Gov-Gen had to be true. Maybe all of them were. Geveg was fighting back, kicking out the Baseeri. Once they were gone, Gevegians would regain control of the pynvium mines, reclaim what was stolen from us.

The Duke would never allow that. He'd do anything to keep those mines, keep the pynvium. Even destroy us.

And when he was through with Geveg, he might go after Verlatta. Then there'd be no safe place to run to in the Three Territories. There wouldn't even *be* a Three Territories anymore. I tried not to picture it, but the images came anyway. Flaming pitch arcing through the air, splattering against roofs and buildings, fire spreading through the city.

Geveg might not even know the Duke was coming. Someone had to warn them.

Someone like us.

Which meant abandoning Tali again. Stopping my search for her. *If you stop the Duke, you can get her back for sure.* The odds of that were just as slim as finding her with no idea where to look. But Tali was probably with his army, and his army was headed to Geveg.

"We have to tell Geveg they're in danger," I said to Danello and Aylin. "They can't possibly know the Duke is coming."

Aylin gaped at me. "You want to go home *now*?"

"She's right, we have to," Danello said. "The more time they have to prepare, the better chance they'll have of defending the city."

She hesitated, lips tight, then she nodded. "Okay, I'll tell Quenji. Knowing him, he'll love the idea of running into certain death."

"Are you going to tell Jeatar?" Danello whispered.

I glanced over at him, deep in conversation with his soldiers. "I'll tell him before we leave. He has more important things to worry about right now."

"I want to go with you," said Lanelle, cornering me in the dry-goods storeroom.

"Go with me where?" I'd been running around like everyone else on the farm, gathering supplies. I'd sent Quenji after a horse and wagon, since he was the most likely person to actually find one. I did warn him against stealing it from someone who needed one, though.

"To Geveg."

I nearly dropped a bag of goat jerky. "You do know it's about to be invaded?"

"They'll need Healers."

Even ones who'd betrayed them? Maybe Lanelle saw this as her chance to redeem herself.

"I'm sorry, but—"

"Please, Nya." She grabbed my free hand. I fought the urge to yank it away. "I can help, I really can. I know people, and I know things about the League you don't. The Elders talked around me, even about things they shouldn't have."

Because she'd helped them. But she did have a point.

"You're not going to get over there and join the other side?"

She actually looked hurt. "No, swear to Saint Erlice I won't. Baseeri lie—I know that now."

Not all of them, but it was a step over the right bridge.

"Please, Nya?"

I sighed. Aylin was going to kill me. "Okay, you can come."

The heat from the forge wrapped around me as soon as I turned the corner. Hammer strikes of metal on metal rang out, mixed with duller thuds and some impressive swearing. I still hadn't come up with a story as to why I needed pynvium, but since I'd stolen it in the first place, I figured some of it was mine.

Smiths banged away, no doubt trying to get the last of something made before we had to leave. Weapons maybe, or tools. Maybe just metal ingots that would be easier to carry. Onderaan worked in one corner off to the side. I cringed. I'd really hoped he wouldn't be here.

"Onderaan?"

He turned, frustration on his face. He seemed surprised to see me. "You shouldn't be wandering around alone."

The forge was on the farm grounds, but it wasn't connected to the house.

"I know but I, uh, needed some pynvium."

"I think the weapons have already been packed, but I'll see what's here. There might be some pain-filled scraps left."

"Any healing bricks?"

"Bricks? Why would you need—oh, Nya." He sighed, rubbed his eyes. "What are you going to do?"

"Warn Geveg. I know it's dangerous, but I—"

"You sound like your father."

"I do?"

"Not the warning part," he continued, "but the going-where-it's-dangerous part. Going to *Geveg*

67

where it's dangerous, specifically." He sighed and sat on a corner of the unfinished forge. "But you need to go, just like he needed to go."

"He went to Geveg?" I'd always thought he'd been born there. I should have known that wasn't true as soon as I'd learned he was Baseeri.

Onderaan nodded. "When he was nineteen. Our grandfather was governor then, and his ore finders had just discovered a huge pynvium vein in the mountains. Geveg needed enchanters to smelt it, and Peleven wanted to go help. I asked him not to leave, but he didn't listen."

"Why didn't you want him to go?" Geveg was safe back then—no Baseeri soldiers on the streets, no Duke telling them what to do.

"It was a *lot* of pynvium. Mountains of it, and Verraad was already making a fuss out of claiming it for Baseer, trying to get his family to listen."

Verraad. The Duke, before he was Duke. Was that when he first started thinking about killing his father and brothers?

"It made Bespaar nervous, and when *he* was nervous, our father was nervous. Bespaar knew too much about what his family argued over, how different their politics were. Your father should have been nervous too."

"Who's Bespaar?"

"The heir."

I glanced around. The other smiths were out of earshot, the bellows and hammering drowning out anything we'd say.

"You mean Jeatar's father?" It was a guess, a risk, but I needed to know who the man who should have been duke was.

Onderaan's eyes widened. "Who told you?"

So it *was* true.

"No one. Jeatar has the Duke's eyes and lots of money, and he keeps trying to help people without anyone knowing he's doing it." I'd figured that out not long after we'd left Baseer. "And I saw his burn scars when he pulled me out of the Luminary's office. He was in Sorille when the Duke burned it, wasn't he? Plus little things he's said and done. It all filled the same bucket."

Onderaan smiled at me the way Papa had when I'd done something well. "You have a way of seeing what no one else does."

My face warmed and I looked away. It wasn't anything special, just what you had to do to survive. "Does anyone else know?"

"Ouea. She's been with his family since he was your age. A few others, loyal supporters of his father's, but they're all over the Territories now."

"Causing rebellions?"

"Gathering support for when the time is right to move against the Duke."

"But that's *now*!"

He shook his head. "No, it isn't. We have no army, no defensible base."

"So we'll tell everyone who Jeatar is and we'll get their support. We build the army, we march back to Baseer and take over, save Tali, then free Geveg and Verlatta. It's a good plan."

Onderaan looked at me, a sad smile on his face. "Nya, that's not a plan, it's a wish."

"Maybe not."

We could do it. How hard could it be to raise an army? The Duke did it, and no one even *liked* him.

"Nya, one day we *will* stop the Duke, but not now." Onderaan stood and looked around the room. "Let me get you what pynvium I can. No bricks, but I think there are some orbs left."

"What about Jeatar?"

"I'll tell him you're leaving after you've gone. He won't be happy about it, but he'll understand. Once we get the refugees settled in Veilig, I'll come meet you in Geveg."

"How will I find you?"

He paused. "Be in Analov Park at sunset in six days. Right under Grandpa's statue."

We decided to leave at night. The man who'd attacked me still hadn't been found, and we agreed it was safer to travel when no one was watching. Quenji found a horse and wagon—which I suspected Onderaan had something to do with by the way the wagon was stocked—and had it tucked away at the edge of the woods down the road.

"Why can't we come with you?" Jovan asked. His twin brother, Bahari, had been the one asking all afternoon, but he'd given up. Or they were taking turns.

"Because it's not safe," Danello answered, same as he'd done all day. He hadn't snapped, hadn't yelled, hadn't done any of the things I might have done if my little brothers had been pestering me for hours. "Stay with Ouea. She'll take care of you until we're done in Geveg."

"And then you'll come back for us?" Halima asked, twisting one blond braid around her finger.

"Promise." He knelt and hugged her tight. "I'll always come back for you."

Was being able to say good-bye harder or easier than just losing someone? I didn't know if I'd have had the strength to let Tali go, knowing I might not ever see her again.

"Find Da," Bahari said, hugging him when Halima was done. "Bring him back with you."

"I will, I promise."

We all got hugs too, and Ouea herded the little ones back inside the house. I took Danello's hand. It trembled, and he grabbed mine tighter.

"They'll be okay, right?" he whispered.

"Safer than we'll be. Ouea won't let anything happen to them. And Quenji's pack is staying, too, so Zee and Ceun will look after them as well." So much more than Tali ever had.

He took a shaky breath and nodded. "Okay, let's go."

"We're all loaded up," Quenji said, smiling from the driver's bench of the wagon. "How far to Geveg?"

"Two or three days."

He made a face. "Sounds boring."

We climbed in the wagon and took seats on the wooden benches on both sides. Not the most comfortable ride to Geveg, but we'd manage.

Quenji snapped the reins, and we rumbled down the road, everyone quiet save for the occasional cough. I watched the farm fade away in the night, unable to shake the feeling I was leaving family behind.

FIVE

We rolled into Dorpstaad, one of the few places in the marshes big enough to be called a town. It sat on the edge of the lake, with blue-reed marshes on one side and rich farmland on the other. Wasn't much more than a few dozen trader posts, but it did have the ferry dock to Geveg Isles, a traveler's house, and one coffeehouse—a welcome sight after two days on the road.

Beyond the buildings the lake sparkled, but Geveg was hazy, and thin tendrils of smoke curled above the rooftops. Fires.

"Jeatar did say they were rebelling." Danello sounded calm, but he had to be worried about his father. "Doesn't look too bad though. No worse than the riots a few months ago."

It had to be worse than that if the Gov-Gen had been killed. But I knew hope when I heard it.

Quenji parked near the stables and arranged for a paddock and a place to store the wagon. It was too expensive to ferry them across, and there were few places to store them in Geveg if we did. Between what Quenji had no doubt stolen and what Danello had won from the soldiers playing cards, we could afford a few days' keep.

I stretched my sore muscles. "Let's find out when the next ferry is."

The ferry dock was empty. Not even the usual beggars crouched by the pilings or resting under the mangrove trees. The ferry itself sat empty at its berth at the far end of the dock.

"Maybe it's not running?" Aylin shielded her eyes with her hand and gazed over the water. It was flat today, barely any breeze to stir the surface.

"Or they're not letting it dock at Geveg," Danello said. "That's the easiest way to keep people from leaving the city."

"Or coming *into* the city," I added.

This would be a problem. Without a boat, we weren't getting into Geveg. A few fishing boats were docked at other berths, plus one skiff that looked fancy enough to belong to an aristocrat.

"If you know how to sail it, I can steal it," Quenji said, following my stare.

I'd had enough of jails and cages for a while. Besides, we needed to draw as little attention to ourselves as possible. "Let's see if someone is willing to take us across first."

Lanelle snorted. "No one is going to risk their neck to help *us*."

"Us, maybe," said Aylin, "You, no."

"Let's look around." I sighed. You'd think after two days of baiting each other they'd be tired of it.

We left the dock and headed for the main street. People were out and about, but the town lacked the usual bustle. No one was looking for work, and no day vendors had set up carts on the streets. It made sense if no one could get out of Geveg, but it was still eerie.

The scent of coffee lured us to the coffeehouse on the opposite side of the block, down near the traveler's house.

"Anyone hungry?" Danello said.

My stomach rumbled. Breakfast had been a long time ago—and not much of it at that. "Sounds good. We might be able to find a fisherman there too and ask about paying him for passage."

Aylin linked her arm through Quenji's. "I haven't had good Gevegian coffee in months, so let's—"

A soldier in pynvium armor walked out of the coffeehouse.

Lanelle gasped. "Undying!"

"Be still." I looked away fast, keeping my face down. My heart raced, and my feet wanted to follow, but running would get me noticed.

A regular soldier in Baseeri blue walked out next, and a boy in Healers' League green followed.

Soek? He was one of the apprentices Vinnot had been experimenting on in the spire room along with Tali. He'd helped me escape, even tried to help free me when the tracker captured me, but we hadn't seen him since that day.

The same day I'd lost Tali.

Soek stared at me, his eyes full of fear; then he looked away and shot a nervous glance at the soldiers escorting him.

What were they doing to him? He had to be a prisoner; he'd never help the Undying or the Duke. But why here and not the League?

Folks stepped aside, their heads down, and let them pass. The Undying walked with the same arrogance I'd seen in Baseer, as if he knew nothing could hurt him.

For a moment I wondered if there was any pain

in that armor of his. If so, *I* could hurt him plenty.

"Eyes down," Danello whispered into my ear. "You're glaring at him."

Was I? I looked away, face flushed, but I couldn't help peeking again.

Soek and the soldiers walked to the traveler's house. Soek glanced helplessly at me once more before following them inside. A plea.

People started moving again, and I caught a few loud sighs of relief. We darted into the coffeehouse and grabbed a table in the back where we could watch both the door and the dining room.

"Was that Soek?" Aylin asked, keeping her voice low.

I nodded. "We have to save him."

"No, we don't," Lanelle said, face pale. "We have to get out of here right now. There are *Undying* here."

I leaned closer. "We knew there was a chance we'd see Undying," I half lied. I'd figured we'd see them once the Duke got there, but not this soon. Had he sent some in advance? "It's just one, and he doesn't seem to be doing anything but guard duty."

"Who's Soek?" Quenji asked.

"A friend of ours. He was an apprentice at the League. Nya, he looked really scared," Aylin said to me.

"He did."

"You think he's the only one here?" asked Lanelle.

"I don't know. The League comes out to the marsh farms once a month for heals. They could be here for that." I used to join Mama on those trips. Folks would ride in from all over Geveg proper for a chance at real healing.

The server headed over and we fell silent.

"Excuse me," I said after he set our plates down. "Did I see a Healer leave here a few minutes ago?"

The server hesitated but nodded. "There's a League group at the traveler's house. Been here a few weeks, ever since things got bad over there." He tipped his head toward the Isles.

"What *is* going on over there? I noticed the ferry wasn't running."

He glanced around and leaned a little closer. "I hear the whole city revolted, Baseeri *and* Gevegians. Each of the Geveg islands belongs to a different group now. The commander, the dockworkers, the aristocrats. Anyone willing to grab a sword and guard a bridge could take an island."

"What about the Governor-General?" I asked, fishing for more information. "Isn't he doing anything to stop it?"

"They say he died the first day. That's what set off the riots."

But why would Baseeri revolt against the Gov-Gen or the Duke?

"Are there a lot of those soldiers in that blue armor?" I said. "I've never seen them before."

The server gulped. "Just the one. He came over with the Healers. That was the last ferry out of the Isles. Lots of smaller boats docked after that, but nothing since last week."

Danello looked puzzled. "The Healers are just staying here?"

"Seems like it." He shrugged. "They're making good money, and it's not safe to go back to the Isles."

I'd met plenty of folks who'd take advantage of such a situation and see it as a way to earn some fast money, but not Soek. Maybe the soldiers were forcing him to do it.

"Is there any way into Geveg?" I asked.

"Not unless you wanna swim." Another customer called, and the server hurried off.

"Did you see his face when you asked about the Undying?" Aylin shuddered. "I think finding someone willing to take us over there just got harder."

We'd be fools to wander in blindly. We had no idea which isle belonged to who, or who we needed to speak to and warn them about the Duke.

"We need more information about what's going on over there," I said.

Danello nodded. "How do we find out?"

"Soek? We need to rescue him anyway."

Everyone looked at each other as if they hoped someone else had a better idea.

Danello sighed. "Yeah, we can't leave him there. And he'll probably know what's going on better than anyone else here."

"We'll need a boat too," I said. "Quenji, see if you can trade the horse or wagon or both for one, even for a day or two."

"Can't we steal one?"

"As long as it's not a fisherman's boat. He can't support his family without one."

Quenji rolled his eyes but nodded.

"How do we talk to Soek?" Danello asked. "They've got him guarded pretty well."

Aylin huffed and added more sugar to her coffee. "He's a Healer. We hurt somebody."

"Help, I need help!" Danello carried me into the common room at the traveler's house, blood running down my face. I groaned and feigned delirium. My scalp stung from the cut Aylin had made, but heads bleed easily, and we needed to put on a good show.

People gasped and pointed. A woman behind the bar called out to a boy who was washing mugs.

"Go get the Healer, hurry."

Patrons cleared an old couch near a window and Danello set me down. He paced, wiping his upper lip and brow like he was afraid I was about to die right in front of him.

"I can't help if you won't let me through," Soek grumbled.

He shoved through the gathering crowd, shooing them back with a sharp twist of his hand. He looked at me and his eyes widened, but he covered his surprise quickly. "What happened?"

"She fell," Danello said, waving his hands about as he spoke. "I told her not to walk on the fence, but she did it anyway and she slipped and fell and hit her head on, oh, I don't know what but it was hard. Her head made this awful cracking noise."

"That's bad." Soek turned to the crowd. "Stop gawking at her. Go back to doing what you were doing before she got here."

The Undying was also in the room but standing back watching the crowd. I didn't see the other soldier or anyone else.

"Now, let's take a look." Soek pulled over a chair and sat down beside me. He put one hand on my wound and the other on my forehead. My scalp tingled and the cut hidden in my hair closed, but he frowned.

"She cracked her skull," he said. "Some brain bruising there as well. You're lucky you got her here in time." He turned to the Undying. "I'm going to need the brick for this. The orb won't be enough."

The Undying hesitated, glancing at his pynvium armor as if debating whether or not to use it rather than go back upstairs. It was either full or he wasn't allowed, because he sighed and headed for the stairs. "I'll be right back."

Soek nodded, then turned back to me, dragging one hand through his red hair. "Saints, Nya, you gotta get me out of here," he whispered.

"We will. What's going on?"

He took a deep breath. "I was over here on a farm run when the fighting started. The soldiers wanted to go back, but Keeper Betaal wouldn't let us. She's selling heals at twice the cost and pocketing the money. She's paying off the soldiers, so I don't think she plans on going back." He swallowed. "Or letting me go."

"Who's Keeper Betaal?"

"One of the Luminary's new 'administrators.' Glorified thug is more like it."

"Is anyone else with you?"

"No. Just soldiers and Betaal. When I questioned her, she said she had an Undying and wondered if she really needed *two* Healers." He gulped. "I stopped asking questions."

Thumps sounded on the stairs. "He's coming back," Danello said. The Undying appeared. A woman followed him, also in Healer's green, but not a uniform I'd seen before. Two additional soldiers walked behind her.

Soek's expression changed to grave concern like any good Healer's. He took the battlefield brick of pynvium and placed his hands back on my head. No tingle this time with nothing to heal, but he made a show of it anyway. He pretended to push the pain into the pynvium and handed the brick back to the Undying.

I fluttered open my eyes and sat up, swaying a bit.

"There you go—all better now." Soek stood and stepped away from me.

"Wait," the woman in green said. I held my breath. "She didn't pay."

I looked at Danello. I didn't know how much he had, but if heals were double now, it couldn't possibly be enough to cover what Soek had pretended to heal. It probably wouldn't even have covered healing the actual cut.

"It was an emergency," Soek said. "She would have died otherwise."

"Then you should have let her die."

"Keeper Betaal—"

"You know the law, Soek, and I'm tired of you bending it. This stops right now." She folded her arms and scowled at me. "Taking a heal you can't pay for is stealing—and punishable same as any other theft."

SIX

Danello fumbled through his pockets. "I have some money, not a lot, but you can have it all." The gratitude in his voice was utterly faked.

Keeper Betaal glared at him. "A pittance won't buy your way out of this. Arrest them," she told the two soldiers.

The Undying was still holding the battlefield brick, and odds were it held lots of pain. Could I reach it before the Undying stopped me?

Flashing that pynvium would alert the Duke I was here. So would shifting. He was on his way anyway, so it might not matter, but if more assassins were looking for me, they'd find out exactly where I was. I had no idea if Quenji had a boat yet, so we might not be able to escape even if I did flash it.

"Keeper Betaal, please," Soek said. "She was dying."

"So? She would have died if we weren't here. And now you've wasted pynvium on a freeloader, so someone who could afford it won't be able to get the help they deserve." She sneered. "You probably just cost someone else their life."

The soldiers grabbed Danello and me. They checked us both for weapons, took our knives, then hauled us out of the traveler's house and toward a small brick building sitting by itself not far from the docks. Bars lined the windows. It was probably the only jail in the marsh farms. The farmers tended to take care of criminals in their own way.

Lanelle was sitting outside the coffeehouse. She rose when we approached, but I shook my head. She stopped, watching us with worried eyes.

The soldiers took us into the guardhouse. One guard sat at a worn table, eating lunch. Shaggy hair a bit too long, worn uniform. Perhaps a local, one of the farmers' sons. He glanced up, then looked again and jumped to his feet.

"Afternoon, sir."

The soldier holding Danello's arm frowned. "Prisoners."

"Yes, sir." The guard hurried over to a rack by

the door and pulled a key ring off a peg. A reward poster hung on the wall next to it. *My* reward poster, the same one Vyand had nailed up in Geveg to flush me out. It wasn't the best drawing, but it was accurate enough. Heart pounding, I angled my face away and let my much shorter and blacker hair fall across my cheek.

What if they recognized me? What if they'd been told to look for me?

The soldier glanced around the room, his lip curling in distaste. "Where's the other guard? Betaal told you to maintain two at all times."

"And I keep telling her we only *have* two." He unlocked the cell and stood to one side. "She wants to send some of you soldiers over to help us out, I'll be happy to take a day off."

The soldier grunted and pushed Danello forward. He stumbled into the cell, a typical ten-foot-square box with two cots. The soldier on my arm let me go, and I walked inside. If they saw that poster and looked at me closely . . .

"What did they do?" the guard asked, his gaze on my bloodstained shirt.

"Theft."

A puzzled frown. "What'd they steal?"

"Healing."

"You arrested them for—"

The soldier stepped close to the guard. "That's the same as stealing pynvium."

The guard gulped. "Yes, it is."

"Stay with him," the soldier told the other.

"Yes, sir."

I sat on one of the cots, my back to the soldier and guard. Danello sat next to me. The guards had no reason to look at that reward poster. It was at least four months old. As long as I didn't do anything foolish, we could bide our time and wait for a rescue.

By now Lanelle had told Aylin and Quenji what had happened. The cell lock would be easy for Quenji to pick, but getting him inside and the guards outside wouldn't be. All three were probably studying the jail right now, looking for weaknesses, ways to get inside, tricks to play on the guards. Well, maybe two. Lanelle was probably trying to get them both to run.

I took Danello's hand. This time it was up to Aylin to come up with the plan.

Unless Lanelle didn't tell her.

I jerked, every muscle tense. What if Lanelle *had* run? What if she hadn't even tried to find Aylin or Quenji? They might not even know we'd been arrested.

My guts twisted. Were our lives really in *Lanelle's* hands?

Saea have mercy on us all.

Rumbling of dozens of wheels broke the silence. The light had left the windows hours ago, and an orange sunset lit the trees I could see. The soldier rose and looked outside.

"What's going on?" asked the guard.

"Horses. Go see what's going on."

"Me?"

"Or stay here and deal with whoever attacks if that happens to be a distraction."

The guard rolled his eyes. "I'll be right back." He slipped outside.

The soldier stood by the door, hand on his sword. Mere feet from the reward poster.

"Doesn't sound like the Duke's men," whispered Danello. Didn't to me, either.

"Refugees?"

"On horseback?"

Voices rose and fell, not arguing, but more than simple conversation. Maybe the guard was telling them they had to leave.

The door opened a few minutes later and the guard returned. He looked nervous.

"Well?" the soldier asked. His hand still hadn't left his sword.

"Undying," he said, voice quivering. My heart stopped for a beat.

The soldier glared at him, his blue eyes narrowed. "You mean the *Wardens*?"

So the Undying had an official name. I was surprised I'd never heard it before.

The guard nodded. "Wardens, yes, that's what I meant. Six of them, plus a dozen soldiers."

Saints, no. If Lanelle hadn't run, she sure as spit would now.

"What did they want?"

"They didn't tell me, they just demanded to see my commander. I sent them to the traveler's house."

I looked at Danello. Hoped I didn't look that scared.

"What do we do?" the guard said.

The soldier frowned and glanced over at us. "We follow orders and guard the prisoners."

Sunset turned to dusk. I couldn't see what was going on outside, but the noises came and went. After a while, the door opened and another soldier came in, sergeant bars on her collar. The guard leaped to his feet; the other soldier rose casually.

"We have trouble," she said. "Looks like the

Shifter might be in the area."

Shiverfeet raced down my back.

"Coming after the Healer?"

"Wouldn't be the first Healer she's killed."

Danello squeezed my hand. They thought I was here to kill Healers? What in Saea's name had the Duke said about me?

"She didn't kill them, she saved them," the guard said. Both soldiers turned their gazes on him. He stepped back. "Well, that's what I've heard."

The woman snorted. "Tell that to the dead."

The guard said nothing. I wanted to say *something* to defend myself, foolish as it was.

"The Wardens told Betaal that the Shifter was seen at a farm a few days' ride from here," the woman said, "but the place is abandoned now. They're convinced she came this way."

They must have arrived at the farm right after we'd left. Someone must have told them I was there, one of the aristocrats who'd seen me. A spy in Little 'Crat City with some message birds maybe. They couldn't have gotten there so fast otherwise.

"I'll keep my eyes open. What am I looking for?"

"A girl, short black hair, sixteen or so." She paused, then reached over and yanked the reward poster off the wall. "Like this, actually. Memorize this *face*, but do *not* approach her on your own."

"She's really that dangerous?"

"Ask Gemid. She almost killed his whole squad."

"Of *Undy*—I mean, Wardens? I thought they were invulnerable."

"No one's impervious to everything." She glared at him and slapped the poster against his chest. "You see this girl, you find us. Clear?"

"Yeah."

She raised an eyebrow.

"Yes, Sergeant."

The guard sank onto his stool the moment the door thunked shut. "I like my sergeant better," he muttered.

Danello looked over, but his it's-all-going-to-be-okay smile didn't make me feel any better. The guards had looked at the poster. As soon as they looked at me again, they'd recognize me.

I had no pain to use unless we hurt ourselves. Even if we did, they might see me before they came close enough for me to shift it. And if one of them got away and told the others . . .

Hurry, Aylin, hurry.

⌐•⌐

Dusk turned to dark. Nervous murmurs and the occasional scream drifted in through the window. The Undying were probably questioning everyone in the town. Folks had seen me in the coffeehouse and when we'd gone to see Soek. If they told the Undying about a dark-haired girl who'd been arrested . . .

"I can probably handle the soldier if I catch him by surprise," Danello whispered. "Can you take out the guard?"

"Maybe. Definitely if he stabs me."

"Are you allowed to play cards?" the guard asked the soldier. "Or will your sergeant disapprove?"

"You got coin?"

"Enough."

"Deal then."

On the third hand of cards, the door flew open. The soldier was on his feet in seconds, his sword out. Aylin jumped and squealed, her surprise faked. The guard nearly fell out of his chair.

"I saw her!" Aylin cried, flapping a hand out the door. She was dressed as nice as a merchant. Where had she gotten the clothes? "The Shifter, she's out by the blacksmith's, doing something to the forge, I think"

The soldier looked her over—her black hair, her

fancy dress. I doubted she'd have his attention if she looked like she normally did. "Are you sure?"

"Yes, she looks like that poster they're showing everyone."

"Did you see anyone with her?"

"Maybe a man and another girl. Come on, I'll show you."

"No, stay here." The soldier turned to the guard. "You, too."

"Don't have to tell me twice."

The soldier raced out. Aylin glanced out the door, concern wrinkling her brow for a moment, then it was gone. She heaved a sigh and dropped both hands onto the back of one of the chairs.

"You really saw the Shifter?" the guard asked.

She nodded fast. "I did! Nearly scared me to death. It was the flames that made me look over there. Blue, can you believe it?" She gripped the chair back.

The guard made a face. "Blue?"

"Blue as the sky. Look—" She tipped her head toward the window next to her. "You can see them from here."

The guard went to the window. Aylin lifted the chair and smashed it down over his head. He groaned and slumped to the floor.

"Hurry, we don't have much time," Aylin said, stepping over the unconscious guard. "It won't take that soldier long to figure out there's no one by the blacksmith's."

"Do they even *have* a blacksmith?" I said.

"I have no idea, but I figured farmers have horses, and horses need shoes, right?" She pulled out some lock picks and knelt by the cell door.

"When did you learn to pick locks?"

"Quenji taught me."

The lock snicked open.

"You're both geniuses." I slipped to the guard's side and placed a hand on his arm.

Aylin pushed her hair back. "I didn't hurt him much, did I?"

"He's fine. He'll have a headache and some bruising, but it'll heal on its own. Where are the others? Is Lanelle still here?"

She rolled her eyes. "Barely. They're at the docks. Quenji got us a boat."

"What about Soek?"

"He's in a building full of soldiers. I don't think we can help him."

"We can't just leave him here."

Danello put a hand on my arm. "Nya, she's right. We have to warn Geveg. We can't lose any more time. If we stop the Duke, we save everyone." He picked up the guard's sword and cracked open the door. "No soldiers, but there's a lot of people out there. They look pretty angry."

"The Undying hurt someone," Aylin said, "an older woman. People are complaining."

The familiar dread came back. Undying didn't care for those who complained.

"Keep Nya between us," said Danello, slipping out. "Less chance of her being spotted that way."

We stayed close to the buildings and out of the yellow circles of the streetlamps. The marsh folks were gathered in front of the traveler's house, yelling and shaking their fists.

A woman cried out, and the crowd parted not far ahead. Soldiers emerged, their eyes scanning faces as they passed. Behind the soldiers, an Undying. Danello and Aylin closed tighter around me.

"Everyone line up over there," the Undying said, pointing against the side of the market building.

"We don't have to listen to you," one man shouted.

The Undying drew his sword and marched toward him. The man held his ground, but apprehension flickered across his face.

"You'll move, *now*," the Undying said.

"I'll move when someone who *isn't* eating from

96

the Duke's table asks me."

The Undying backhanded him, sending him flying into the crowd. People screamed, some shouted, others charged the Undying. He braced himself but toppled under the surge of bodies.

The soldiers drew swords and charged into the mob, blades slicing randomly as they cut through. More screams, and the Undying rose out of the pile, his sword dark with blood. He thrust it at the closest person, a woman who'd been trying to help another. A man with her plunged a knife into the Undying's hand, but the Undying yanked it out and stabbed him with it. A moment later the Undying's wound was gone, healed and pushed into his armor. More Undying stalked into the crowd. One was huge, towering over the heads of everyone. Another was small, cutting through the crowd with quick sword swings.

"They're going to kill them," I said, slowing.

Danello tugged me along. "Nya, we have to get you out of here."

"But these people!" Like when I was little. People running, soldiers chasing, blood spilling. All because one man said no to someone in blue.

"We can't do anything about it—come on." Danello yanked my arm and I stumbled a few steps, but I couldn't look away.

I could do something about this. I let go of Danello's hand.

"Nya, what are you doing? Aylin!" he shouted.

If they were here looking for me, then the Duke already knew where I was. It wouldn't matter if I shifted or flashed. I could stop the Undying, help these people, and free Soek.

Let's see how much pain is in your armor.

I stepped forward into the mob and slipped behind one of the smaller Undying. I slapped my hands onto the armor and pictured dandelions blowing in the breeze.

Whoomp!

The flash echoed as the Undying screamed, high-pitched, feminine, and familiar. She turned as she fell, as everyone around us fell. Our eyes met.

Tali.

SEVEN

N^{o!} I dropped to the ground beside her. She lay on the street unconscious, blood splattering the pynvium armor she wore.

An Undying.

Tali was an *Undying.*

Jeatar's words flooded my mind. *"You've seen the Undying. You know what they do. Few want to suffer all that pain or inflict it on others. But the commanders make them. They twist minds and bend wills and create the weapons the Duke wants. How long do you think Tali can last in there?"*

Not long enough.

"How could they do this to you?" I whispered.

I ached to pull the flash from her, wake her up, find out *why*—but she'd been killing like the others. If I woke her, I might have to hurt her again.

Anger churned my stomach, heated my skin. It was *their* fault. They'd done this to her. Twisted her, made her into a killer. I rose, fists clenched. I opened them. I'd need my hands.

"What did you do to her?" I yelled, heading for the next soldier.

The huge Undying turned and lifted his sword. I kept walking toward him.

He lunged the last few steps and plunged the sword through my belly. I gasped, my skin on fire around the wound, and fell into him. He stared at me, a smug grin on his face. I reached up and cupped both his cheeks with my hands.

"Not smart," I said.

He looked puzzled for half a heartbeat, then paled. "Shifter," he whispered.

I *pushed* the pain into him.

He cried out and staggered to one knee, but was on his feet seconds later, his pain healed. "It's the Shifter!" he yelled, and the other soldiers turned.

He charged me as the other soldiers ran closer. I stepped into the charge and slapped both hands against his chest plate.

Whoomp.

Pain flashed, the tingle of blown sand tickling across my skin. The huge Undying screamed and collapsed. The advancing soldiers staggered and fell. The crowd stood frozen a moment, then cheered.

"Run!" I cried. "Get away from here."

They didn't listen. Some darted forward and grabbed the fallen swords. They attacked the soldiers, cutting them down as ruthlessly as the soldiers had done to the marshfolk. They turned on the Undying, and the Undying vanished beneath a wave of anger and fear.

Tali!

I ran back to her. No one had come after her yet. Danello appeared beside me. "Nya, we have to go."

"It's *Tali*."

"What?" He looked down, paled. "Oh no."

"Get her to the boat." I wasn't done here. More shouts in the street, and the last of the Undying charged out of the traveler's house, followed by Betaal and her soldiers.

"Nya, wait!"

I raced toward the Undying. Soldiers yelled, blades cut my skin, but I didn't stop. They would all pay for what they'd done. Every last Undying.

The soldier from the guardhouse stabbed me in

the shoulder. I pivoted and grabbed his wrist, *pushing* the pain into him. He cried out and fell back, just like all the others. Another Undying, another flash echoing in the night, another sting of blown sand. More pain sliced my skin, behind me this time. I dropped, rolling toward the person who cut me. A *push* and he was down.

I looked for more.

I'd lost my sister. They'd stolen her, ruined her. She was supposed to be a *Healer*, not a killer.

They'd stolen everything from me. Tali, Mama, Papa, Grannyma. The life I should have had, the family I should have kept. They'd made me do things I'd promised I'd never do.

I grabbed the last pynvium-armored man. He screamed next, but no one else. They were all lying on the street, in blood, in pain.

"Nya?"

I spun, hands out. Danello stepped back, hands up.

"It's just me!"

"Danello?"

"We have to go."

"But Tali—"

"Is waiting for you on the boat, just like I promised. You can't help her if you get caught." Someone groaned and he jumped. "We need to hurry."

I nodded, suddenly too exhausted to speak. We ran along the dock. Few lamps were lit, barely enough for us to make our way. It was quiet, just the swish of waves curling around the pilings and the creak of wood from the boats. Quenji stood on the dock ahead next to the fancy skiff decorated in green and gold.

A League skiff.

I jumped in.

Aylin raised the sails as Quenji tossed off the bowline, and we drifted away from the dock. Canvas flapped and took hold, and we were moving, out across the dark water and into the night. Dangerous, sailing at night, but it was safer than staying in town.

I sat on the bench and cradled Tali's head in my lap. Lanelle stared at her, her face twisted in fear and pity. Soek sat next to her.

"How did you get here?" I asked Soek.

"I ran when Betaal and the others went after you. Danello saw me and I helped him get Tali to the boat."

I smiled. "Thank you for that."

"We shouldn't take her with us," Lanelle said, still watching Tali like she was going to jump up and try to kill us.

"Tali stays with me."

"Nya, I've seen what being an Undying does to people. When she wakes up she'll—"

"Shut up, Lanelle," Danello said. Not mean, not angry, just a quiet order.

She looked at him but stayed silent.

Danello took the rudder while Aylin worked the sail. The lights of the dock fell away until I couldn't see Tali's face anymore.

I moved to her side and started removing Tali's armor. Moonlight caught the underside, which glittered silver, and not from the moonlight.

Every piece was lined with silvery metal. What had the Duke called it? Kragstun. The same metal he'd used to make the cuffs that had forced Takers to do what he told them to do. Made *me* do what he told me to do.

Was that how he made the Undying? Forced them to kill?

Tali gasped and jerked upright, arms swinging. She lunged off the bench right at Lanelle.

"Ahhh!"

"Tali, no!" I cried, diving for her.

Lanelle threw herself sideways, and the skiff rocked. Soek grabbed Tali, held her around the waist as she kicked and screamed. He staggered,

Tali writhed, and they both fell to the deck.

"Grab her, get her!" Lanelle pointed, jumping around like we'd turned snakes loose.

Quenji and Soek grabbed Tali again and held her down.

"Tali, it's me, it's Nya." I tried to get close but she was struggling so hard. "Tali!"

She ignored me, or didn't hear me—maybe didn't even know who or where she was. I kept trying, my throat hoarse by the time she wore herself out.

"Can you hear me?"

She stared at me, eyes shimmering. There was nothing in them but moonlight.

"She doesn't know who I am." I could barely get the words out. She was gone. Really gone. My heart felt just as hollow.

I wanted to hug her, tell her it would all be okay, but that was a lie. She wouldn't let me hold her, clearly didn't even want me to touch her, and it might not ever be okay again.

I'd failed my sister.

"You need to tie her up so she doesn't hurt . . . herself," Lanelle said softly. "If she goes overboard, she could drown."

I squeezed my eyes shut, blocking the tears. Tie up my sister? Hadn't enough been done to her already? I took a deep breath and slid closer, one hand out. "Tali—"

She shrieked and swung at me. One hand smacked against Quenji, and he yelped but didn't let go. I pulled away.

"Do we have any rope?" I hated myself for asking.

"I'm sure there is." Aylin got up and went looking. After banging around some, she came back with strips of rope, the ends freshly cut.

I tied Tali's hands and feet. She shrieked again, struggled again, but Soek and Quenji held her down. She lay on the deck whimpering like a trapped animal.

Aylin put a hand on my shoulder. "Nya, I'm so sorry. We'll find a way to help her—we will."

You can't unbreak an egg.

No one said anything for a while. We drifted, the skiff bobbing, the sail creaking.

"What do we do now?" asked Quenji.

The pynvium armor glittered on the deck. I took a deep breath and picked up a piece. "Look at this." I showed them the metal lining the inside. "I think this is what made her . . . act that way."

Lanelle shuddered and pulled her knees up to her chin. "Vinnot had some of that where he was experimenting on us. He argued with the Duke over it a lot."

"Argued about what?"

"Wasting it. He said they couldn't get any more. The person who made it was dead."

"Who?"

"Zerten or something."

Zertanik.

The pain merchant, the enchanter. The one who'd offered me pynvium scraps in exchange for shifting pain for his rich clients. He'd had glyphed pynvium in his town house, the same kind used in the Duke's weapon. He must have made the kragstun, found a way to mix it with pynvium and make it affect the mind.

I gazed across the water. Rows of lamps along Geveg's docks lit the night, evenly spaced in what looked like berth width. Darker shapes bobbed in front of them, making the lamps flicker bright and dark. Boats on the water around the docks. A blockade? We had to get past those boats. Past the soldiers, and the people fighting, and whatever else was going on in Geveg.

"We're going to Zertanik's town house," I said. "If he made the kragstun, then there might be something there that can tell me how to fix Tali."

Quenji looked confused. "Who's Zertanik?"

"He was a pain merchant who tried to steal the

League's pynvium Slab," I said. I didn't mention what I'd done to him, though I couldn't help but picture the red mist on the broken stone walls of the League. "We were hiding out in his town house for a while, until we had to leave Geveg."

"He didn't mind?"

"He's dead."

"Oh." Quenji paused. "You stole a whole house?"

He sounded impressed with that. I sighed.

Danello nodded. "The town house it is. Do you think my da might be there?"

Danello's father had stayed with us after the soldiers had come after him, looking for us. He'd left Geveg shortly before we had, trying to arrange a place for us to stay in the marsh farms. He'd probably been worried sick about Danello and the little ones.

"It's possible."

"How do we get past the blockade?"

I'd worked enough fishing boats to learn a few tricks. Not all of those boat captains wanted their Baseeri bosses to know how much they'd caught that day. I doubted those spots were being guarded, even if the docks were.

"Head for the warehouse district. I know a few places we can land without being seen."

Canvas rippled as we changed course, the warm breeze tickling through my hair. We cut up the shoreline and headed around the docks.

"Keep the channel marker bells on our right," I said. "There's a landing beach on the north side, near the warehouse row."

Danello frowned. "Where they sank the old docks? I thought there was too much wreckage to take boats in there anymore."

"There's a hidden channel through the underwater debris."

Quenji smiled. "A smugglers' bay. Nice."

"We can go through a crumbled lakewall," I said. "It's steep, but you can get a boat in there and tie it off. We'll need a sounding stone to get to it. There's got to be some on board."

"I'll check." Aylin got up and started searching the neatly tucked away compartments all boats seemed to have.

"You can lead us through?" Quenji asked.

"Yes, I've done it before," I said.

Of course, I'd never done it at night, and I'd only tossed the stone, not guided the boat based on what it found. I'd also never tried it on a boat this big. The currents ran hard along the north shore of the isles, and we had a lot of hull to run aground if we timed the tide wrong.

We sailed through water dark as ink. My eyes had adjusted by the time Aylin found the stone, but I still strained to make out details in the silvery blackness. The skiff was a dark mass, the passengers moving blurs. I watched the shore, looking for landmarks to get my bearings.

Anything to keep from looking at Tali tied up in the corner, staring at nothing.

The Healers' League dome glowed brightest, marking the city's center. Spires from the Sanctuary on Beacon Walk shone directly behind it, so we still had a long way to sail. We needed to position the boat so we were in front of the Sanctuary. Then we'd line ourselves up with the dock lights glowing on Coffee Isle and make our way in.

My skin started itching. I plucked at the dried blood on my ruined clothes, sliced and ripped from my fight with the Undying and other soldiers.

"Where's my backpack?"

"In the cabin," Quenji said. "I tossed them all down there."

I went inside and changed. I hadn't brought much, and I was already down one set of clothes. Aylin brought me lake water to wash with, and my fingers brushed over the hard lumps of new scars.

"I'm so sorry, Tali," I whispered, sinking to the

floor. Tears came hard and I let them fall, sobbing quietly in the dark.

It felt like we'd been out on the water for hours by the time we reached the hidden channel. Aylin dropped the sail, and Quenji and Danello went below and grabbed the oars. Soek stood at the top of the stairs, ready to call out directions.

"Lanelle, grab the rudder."

She did, and I hurried forward with Aylin, the sounding stone in her hand. I unspooled the twine and tossed the stone forward. It sank with a *plop*.

"How narrow is the channel?" she asked as I reeled the stone back in.

"Twenty feet maybe."

She frowned. "No room for mistakes."

"None at all." The old dock pilings were still down there, and they'd rip a good-sized hole through our hull if we hit them.

"We'll find the old breakwater first," I said. "Then we'll move around it, keep sounding until we get to the channel opening."

I tossed the stone again. It sank deep without hitting anything below the water. I gave Soek the signal, and he called to ease the boat forward.

Bloop—splash.

We drifted closer. The water sounded quiet, no

hard waves splashing against the lakewall. Good luck with the tide then.

Bloop—splash.

The wind gusted and a sour smell wrinkled my nose. The tannery. Smelled strong, so we were in the right place for sure. Not far from the bridge between the warehouse and the production districts.

Bloop—thunk.

The stone hit something hard.

"Hold it!" I waved at Soek, and the oars creaked, pulling the boat back.

"A little to the right," I said, pretty sure that we were higher along the old breakwater than we needed to be.

I tossed the stone. It thunked again.

"Drift more right." The boat sidled down the sunken breakwater wall.

The stone sank deep this time. Clear water. I threw the stone out a few more times, gauging the center of the narrow opening into the channel. Danello and Quenji maneuvered the boat inch by inch until we were lined up, then slid us through.

Seemed like even more hours before the break in the lakewall came into view, but it was probably minutes. I grabbed the bow railing and held tight as we ground across the sand and up onto the thin strip of beach.

I threw the anchor and it dug into the sand. Aylin jumped out, light on her feet and barely rocking the boat.

"Will anyone see us here?" she asked.

"Not unless someone cut down the hedges that run behind the boardinghouses." They used to be warehouses, reached by the dock that was now underwater. I couldn't remember what had happened to the docks, but no one had bothered to rebuild them, and the warehouses had all been converted to low-ceilinged rooms with few windows. I'd never lived in them, but I'd heard the rent wasn't nearly cheap enough for what you got.

I leaped down and shoved the anchor deeper into the sand. It was damp above the edge of the water, higher than where the waves hit it. The tide was going out. I pictured the skiff on its side in the sand, the water ten feet beyond the stern.

"Someone needs to stay behind and keep moving the anchor back."

"I'll do it," Lanelle said.

Aylin crossed her arms. "I have no problem with that."

"I'm not surprised," she shot back.

I sighed. "Stop it, both of you."

"When you're done searching this Zeranzik's house, then come get me."

Danello cleared his throat. "What about Tali?"

"She comes with us."

"Nya, that's a bad idea," he said. "We can't control her."

"I'm not leaving her behind again." Especially with Lanelle.

He looked into the dark. Even this late, you could hear people yelling and the occasional clang of metal on metal. Someone was fighting not too far from here. "One scream and she gives us away."

"So gag her," Lanelle said.

Aylin gasped. "It's bad enough we had to tie her up—you want to gag her, too?"

"I don't *want* to do it, but it's the only way Nya can bring her and keep her quiet."

"She's not gagging her sister."

Lanelle smirked and crossed her arms. "Then give her another option."

Aylin didn't. She clearly wanted to, was struggling to think of something, but there wasn't a better idea.

"Aylin's right," I said. "I'm not gagging Tali. She's been mostly quiet since she woke up."

114

"You could leave her here where it's safer," Danello said again.

I glared. "I'm *not* leaving her behind again. If that means we get caught, then we'll get caught together."

I tied a rope to her wrists like a leash, looping it around my hand. *I have a pet sister.*

"We'll be back by dawn," I told Lanelle. "We can cast off and see what's going on around the isles in the daylight. Maybe we'll be able to tell who controls what isle."

"See you at sunrise."

I tugged Tali's rope, and she plodded along beside me, staring at the ground, her hair dangling in her face.

Danello paused at the foot of the bank that led up and into Geveg. "Ready to go home?" he asked me.

"Let's go."

EIGHT

Gravel slid beneath my feet as I climbed up the bank. I tried to steady Tali, but she whined and jerked away from me when I touched her. Danello followed close behind, making sure she didn't fall.

The hedges at the top of the bank were still there, neatly trimmed into flat rectangles. The windowless rear wall of the boardinghouse rose up two stories, casting a darker-on-dark shadow on the ground.

The street was black, except for a few lights glowing like eyes in the distance. I hesitated, but the lights didn't seem to be moving. So not a patrol. Maybe a guard post? We had no idea which side this isle belonged to, so anyone could be friend *or* foe.

We stayed to the side of the street, masking our

silhouettes against the buildings. A smoky smell mixed with the stench from the tannery, but not quite strong enough to have been a recent fire. I scanned the rooftops anyway. No orange embers smoldered, no signs of fires new or old.

Trash was piled outside the doors, debris caught in the corners. Just as many broken windows as boarded-up ones. Worse than when we'd left Geveg after the last riots.

No, not left. Been kidnapped and hauled away. Or arrested like Danello and Aylin.

And Tali.

My gaze slid to the Healers' League dome. Tali should have been there learning to heal, and she would have been if the Duke hadn't used Geveg's League and its apprentices for his twisted experiments. He'd ruined everything he'd ever touched. Even his own family.

"Um, Nya?" Aylin whispered, tugging on my sleeve. She pointed inside one of the buildings, the window broken but not boarded. Candles flickered on a small table against one wall. An offering bowl sat between them—under the reward poster with my face on it.

"Is that a *shrine?*" It couldn't be. Not here, not in Geveg.

"I guess the sainters didn't stop just at the farm."

And they weren't going to stop spreading their belief in me. But folks here *knew* me. They knew I wasn't sent by anybody to do anything. Saints, most of them wouldn't even *hire* me, so how could they— I glanced back at the shrine and swallowed. *Worship* me? It was wrong in every sense.

Worse, it might make the Saints mad.

"Let's hope that means the people here are on our side," I said, moving away from the window.

I slowed when we got closer to the bridge, staying behind whatever cover I could find. Even when there wasn't a war, the bridges were usually guarded, plus they made convenient ambush spots. I peered through the darkness. Nothing but stone and shadow, though a good ambush wouldn't appear as anything else.

Water swished under the bridge, splashy pops and gurgles that sounded like no one had hired leaf pullers in a while. The canals must be clogged with water hyacinths. Getting around in a pole boat was probably impossible.

Someone near the bridge coughed. I held up my hand and crouched. The others dropped behind me. So there *was* an ambush waiting for us. I could barely make out square shadows, like some kind of barricade at the foot of the bridge. Zertanik's town house was in a Baseeri neighborhood, so it was probably controlled by Baseeri soldiers. We'd have to find another way there.

I signaled a retreat and we crept away from the bridge, hiding in the shadows behind a building.

"Think all the bridges are guarded?" Aylin whispered.

Danello nodded. "Probably. They're natural choke points, easy to defend."

"Any other way in?" Quenji asked.

"Yes," I said, "but we'd have to cross three bridges and go through League Circle to do it. I'm sure they have the League well guarded, probably by Undying."

Soek looked up. "Rooftops?"

"Tali would never be able to make it. What about lower?" I pointed to the canal. "There's a pole boat dock not far from here. We can slip into the water there, swim across Grand Canal, and climb out on the other side. Those soldiers at the bridge won't even see us."

"That's better than climbing?" Danello asked.

"She won't fall and break her neck. She's always been a good swimmer."

"You'll have to untie her hands."

I hesitated.

"You could wrap the rope around her waist," said Soek. "She can swim and you can keep a hold of her."

"That could work."

"What about crocodiles?" Aylin frowned. "Don't they hunt at night?"

"Crocodiles?" Quenji said. Soek looked just as concerned.

"They'll be in Half Moon Bay or along the farm isles where the animals are." Unless the water hyacinths made good hunting grounds. I glanced at the plants covering the dark water. We wouldn't even *see* a croc if it were in there. Not until it had one of us in its jaws.

"I don't know," Soek said. "Maybe we should take the boat? There has to be a place to dock on that isle."

I shook my head. "Not through these plants. They're too thick."

"I guess we get wet then." Aylin sighed. "These were new sandals, too."

We slipped around the buildings and along the lakewall to an overgrown dock. The jewelry shop above it had been closed for a while, even before we'd left Geveg. No Gevegian could afford jewels, and the Baseeri who could would never buy them from a Gevegian shop.

I tied the rope around Tali's waist. She just stared into nothing, not even trying to run. I took a deep breath and untied her hands. They flopped to her sides. I shoved the rope into my pocket.

"We're going for a swim, Tali, okay?"

She looked at me. Still no recognition, but another spark. Maybe being home again was reminding her who she was.

"I'll go in first." I slid into Grand Canal. Cool water soaked my clothes but not enough to drag me down. The water hyacinths scratched my arms, their dangling roots tickling my skin. My feet didn't touch bottom.

"Now your turn." I held out my hand like I used to when we were little, playing on the beach behind our villa.

She stared at the water, head cocked, and jumped in. The splash echoed off the lakewall, getting louder after Tali bobbed to the surface and started thrashing. I slipped in behind her and wrapped an arm around her.

"I got you, it's okay."

She writhed and I loosened my hold, tipping

her so she could float on her back. She'd always loved floating. She calmed, staring at the stars, arms out at her sides. I tugged her along and she moved easily.

"We're good."

Danello slipped in next, then Aylin, then Quenji. Soek hesitated, wiping a hand across his mouth. He closed his eyes and slipped in. He held his chin high, paddling like a dog. I guess he'd never done much swimming, but at least he knew how.

The lakewall rose above us, casting the canal in shadow. I kept one hand on Tali while I swam, pushing the plants aside with the other. It was dark enough to get lost down here, swimming in circles, never finding the wall just beyond your reach. Getting more and more tired until something brushed against your leg and—

Stop it.

I shoved the thoughts away and swam harder.

The current rippled around me as we reached the cross canal between the warehouse district and North Isle. I pulled my fingers away from the curve of the wall and swam straight as I could, focusing on a faint reflection of moonlight on metal ahead. A lamppost, maybe. The flames were out like all the rest.

The reflection slid sideways and the current nudged me farther into Grand Canal. I kicked harder, knocking the twisted hyacinths aside.

A gurgle and a soft splash came from behind me. I stopped and trod water, nerves tight, though I couldn't say why. Tali was fine, still floating. Another gurgle, like someone drinking too fast.

Drowning. Someone was drowning.

"Who's in trouble?" I called back.

"What?" Danello asked.

"Stupid plants," Quenji said.

"I'm okay," called Soek.

Aylin didn't say a word.

"Find Aylin, now!"

I swam toward the voices, the dark shapes on the water, dragging Tali with me.

"Aylin?" Where was she? Had the current swept her away? Was she back by the wall? Images of Aylin cold and still rolled through my mind.

"I can't find her," Quenji said, voice frantic.

I kicked something soft under the water. Sank down and found an arm. I yanked hard, dragging myself under, but hauling her closer to the surface. I let go of Tali, praying she'd stay afloat. I kept pulling, kept kicking. Aylin's face broke the top of the water and she sucked in a breath—and some water—and started coughing. She flailed at me as if trying to climb *me* out of the water.

"Stop struggling or you'll sink us both." I wrapped an arm around her chest just like I'd done with Tali and slipped under her, keeping her afloat. "I got you—rest, breathe, it's okay."

I reached for Tali while Aylin hacked up water. She was still floating, and I pulled her closer to me.

"Nya," Quenji whisper-yelled. "I see torchlight coming this way."

Guards.

"Go under," I said. Heads submerged, even Aylin's.

"Tali, we have to go under. I need you to take a deep breath and hold it. Can you do that?"

She ignored me.

"Inhale, now!"

I let us sink a little, and Tali sucked in a breath. I tucked tight, making us heavy, and dropped below the water. Tali struggled, fighting me, clawing back to the surface. I held on, kept us both under.

I'm sorry, Tali, but be still.

How long could she hold her breath? Long enough for the guards to look and leave?

Tali clawed at me, drawing blood. The gouges in my arms stung. Her fingers grew tighter and tighter on my arm while I counted the seconds. *Twenty-five, twenty-six . . .*

Light shone above, smeared and flickering through the water. The guards must be looking over the lakewall, holding the torch out to see into the canal. The pale glow hung there.

Thirty-two, thirty-three . . .

Tali flailed. I held on tighter. The light was still there.

Thirty-seven, thirty-eight . . .

Tali slammed her head against my nose, and bright pain filled my head. She broke out of my hold and started for the surface. I grabbed her leg, dropped my weight, *drew* just in case I could heal drowning. My chest tightened a little, but it didn't seem to make any difference. She kept heading up.

The light vanished. Tali broke the surface. I popped my head out of the water a heartbeat later, sucking in a quiet breath. Tali was gasping, but not coughing. Maybe the heal had done some good after all. Or maybe some part of her knew she had to stay quiet.

"I'm so sorry, but we had to hide," I whispered. "The soldiers would have captured us. You don't want that again."

She backed away from me, breathing too fast,

whimpering. She was still on the edge of panic. I wasn't too far from that edge myself.

"I'm sorry, Tali, I had to."

Danello and Soek surfaced, their heads rising out of the water like turtles next to us. Quenji and Aylin were already up, close to the wall.

"We gotta get her out of here," Quenji said.

"This way, I think."

Tali wouldn't let me touch her. I couldn't find the rope around her, but it had to be there, dangling below, possibly tangling up her legs. *We should have risked the soldiers.*

I swam toward where I'd seen the light. "This way to the dock, Tali."

For a moment she glared at me, but she swam forward and followed. The others moved in around her, keeping her between us. Soon the lakewall emerged from the shadows.

Darkness broke ahead, and I spotted steps leading up. My fingers found the flat surface of a pole boat dock. Still no lamps lit, but the stone reflected enough moonlight for us to get our bearings. I climbed out and helped Aylin up, and she collapsed on the dock.

"Climb out, Tali."

Tali stared at me, then felt her way around the

dock edge and pulled herself out. She flopped down and sat there, head low. Soek and Quenji crawled out and dropped beside us. Quenji slid a hand over and took Aylin's. Danello came out last.

"When this is all over," Aylin said, "I'm moving to a mining town. No water anywhere."

"I'm with you there," Quenji said.

We caught our breaths and wrung some of the water out of our clothes. I wanted to help Tali, but she flinched away every time I reached for her. I managed to get the rope, but that was it. No retying her hands. But maybe I didn't need to. She hadn't screamed or tried to get away.

"Are you hurt?" Soek whispered.

I looked at my arms, covered in deep scratches. "Tali got scared."

"Want me to heal it?"

"No, I'll be okay." I didn't want to waste our pynvium on a few scratches. Even if they did sting. I sucked in a breath. The pynvium! I'd left it on the skiff in my backpack, which was still tucked away in the cabin. I looked at the others. No one had their packs.

Danello crept to the stairs and peeked over the top.

"See anything?" This dock was public, so there

were no buildings to hide behind. Just an open square framed with benches and a few palm trees, their fronds rustling in the breeze.

"Seems quiet. If that torch was a patrol, they're gone now."

I stood. Tali didn't. I tugged the rope. "Time to go, Tali."

She shook her head. My heart soared. She'd responded!

"Just a little farther, then you can sleep. Come on, you can do it."

She shook her head again.

"Tali, get up."

She got to her feet, moving as if she hadn't slept for a week. I hoped we wouldn't have to run.

We crossed the too-high grass to the street, staying in the shadows again. At Beacon Walk we turned right, heading away from the Sanctuary, the only light on this isle that I'd seen so far. Well, aside from the patrol.

Zertanik's town house was halfway between the Sanctuary and his pain merchant shop close to the League. A residential block for those with money but not wealthy enough to afford the aristocrats' district or the terraces. Folks who had enough to be paranoid about holding on to it.

Most of the first-floor windows along the street were boarded up, a good thing for us. No allies lived in these buildings. A few gates were barred, heavy boards across them. No sounds of fighting, no sounds of any kind, really, just the soft tap of our footsteps on brick. My pace quickened the closer we got to the town house.

"There it is." It was more overgrown than we'd left it, with trash in the courtyard like all the other buildings we'd passed. No lights shone in any of the windows. None were boarded up.

Danello hurried forward, but I caught his shoulder. "Easy. Anyone could be in there."

He nodded and we moved slower, checking the shadows and the likely places someone might be hiding if they were guarding this building. The places *we'd* watched from when we were hiding here.

No sign of anyone. The front door wasn't locked, and the entrance room looked as abandoned as the courtyard. Drawers and cabinets hung open, and it looked like everything worth having was gone.

We stepped farther inside, the occasional creaks sounding loud as screams. No doors opened, and I didn't hear anyone moving around on the upper floors.

"Soek and I will search upstairs," Danello said. "Quenji, Aylin, you take the bottom floor. Nya can guard the door with Tali."

Tali was looking around, her eyes wide, her mouth open a little. Did she know this place? Did she remember? I sat on the stairs and talked to her, but she ignored me like she had all night. Like a good little soldier, she only listened when I gave an order. I wiped my eyes.

Danello and Soek returned shortly after Aylin and Quenji were done.

"There's no one here," Danello said. "It looks safe."

"So we start searching?" Quenji asked.

Soek shrugged. "If there's anything left to find."

"Nya said the owner was a thief," Quenji said. "Thieves hide stuff. I found jewels inside a table leg once."

A fuzzy image popped into my mind, of bookshelves and something hidden behind them that made my skin itch. What *was* it? The image cleared. A small locked box I'd found hidden behind some books months ago when we were living in the town house. We'd been looking for valuables to sell, but the box had bothered me so much, I hadn't wanted to open it.

"There might be something in the library," I said.

"Let's see if it's still there," Quenji said.

I nodding, praying it was and that it held some clue to helping Tali.

NINE

Danello made a torch out of some ripped fabric and a broken table leg while Quenji found some flint in the kitchen. It took a few strikes of the flint to light the torch, but it gave us enough light to see by. I just hoped it wasn't bright enough to be seen from the outside.

Tali had curled up in a chair, her eyes closed.

"I'll stay here and watch her," Aylin said softly. "Soek can guard the door."

"No one gets in," he said, hefting another table leg.

I smiled. "Thanks." I hesitated, then turned back to Aylin. She'd almost drowned, and I hadn't even said anything. What kind of friend *was* I? "Are you okay?"

"I'm fine. Shaky, lungs hurt a little, and I don't want to go anywhere near water for a long time, but I'll live."

I hugged her, then hurried up the stairs. The library was in shambles like the rest of the town house, but the looters had ignored the bookshelves completely. The heavy tomes were dusty, but the same as we'd left them.

"Feel anything?" Danello asked.

I stepped closer to the shelves, my hand out. At a few feet away, my stomach started quivering, just like it always did when I was near glyphed pynvium. "Here."

Danello handed Quenji the torch. He dragged the books away and set them on the floor in piles. The small box with the lock was still there, tucked in the alcove. My skin crawled, the sense of over-whelming wrongness just like before.

Danello took it. "Heavy. Could be the box, though. Do you sense anything else?"

"Not with that thing so close."

He took it into the hall. "Better?"

The quivering stopped. "Yes, thanks."

"See what you can find," Danello said, setting the box down and coming back inside. "I'll clear the rest of the books. If he hid one thing back there, he might have others."

I walked slowly around the room, running my hand over shelves, checking drawers that had been yanked out and tossed on the floor. No quivers. Not even a flinch.

Whoomp.

Danello cried out a heartbeat before the prickling of fine sand blew across my skin.

"Danello!" I ran to his side, fighting the instinct to draw away his pain the instant my hands touched him. He was woozy, but conscious.

"I'm okay, no need to heal me," he said, groaning. "Hands sting a bit, that's all."

"What did you touch?"

"The books. I was reaching for them, but I wasn't really looking at them."

"That flash is a good sign," Quenji said, grinning. "You don't ward things unless they're worth a lot. Danello, see if anything else flashes."

He grimaced. "I think it's your turn to check."

I scanned the books above where Danello had collapsed. One spine poked out a finger width from the rest of the books. Dark leather, worn binding, the title so faded I couldn't make out any words. Thin blue strips of pynvium ran along the edges of the spine, looking like decorations. Until you touched them.

"Step back." I reached out and ran my finger down the spine.

Whoomp.

Sharp pain washed over me, stronger than the typical muted flash. I pulled the book off the shelf. No flash this time.

The entire front edge was covered with a leather flap, with locks at both the top and bottom corners. "It's locked."

"Forget valuable," Danello said. "Whatever is inside there has to be important."

"Let's see what it is." I set the book down on the floor and motioned Quenji over. "Don't open it, just unlock it. Odds are something else will flash."

Quenji gulped but started on the lock anyway. It took him longer than any other lock I'd seen him pick, but he eventually got it unlocked. He stepped back and ducked around the corner. "Your turn."

"I think he has the right idea," said Danello, joining him in the hall. "That hurt before."

"Yeah." I braced myself and lifted the cover. No flash. But the pages were filled with enchanting glyphs and notes and drawings that made my fingers itch. And my heart race. "It's some kind of enchanter's book," I called over my shoulder.

"Worth anything?" said Quenji.

"To me, everything. This might tell us how to fix Tali."

"How?" Danello asked.

"I don't know, but there must be something in here that says how the kragstun works."

"Do you read enchanter?"

"No, I don't." My hopes sank, then rose again. "But Onderaan does."

Three days until he was supposed to meet us at Analov Park.

"Keep searching," I said. "Maybe's there more here."

"Told you," said Quenji, rubbing his hands together. "Thieves hide stuff."

We opened every drawer, looked behind every book, looked *in* every book, but found nothing else in the library. I went to the next room, running my hand over everything again, but no quivers and no pynvium.

"Bedroom next," Danello said, pushing open the door. The room had been searched already, long before we got here. Drawers were empty, chairs were knocked over, nothing left on the tables. Even the bedding was gone.

My stomach clenched when I walked in, but not from any glyphed pynvium. This had been

Zertanik's bedroom. I'd killed the man who used to sleep here.

"Let's get this over with." I moved quickly, checking the places that might hold hidden compartments like Quenji said. I stepped into the closet, which was as big as my old room over at Millie's Boardinghouse.

My stomach quivered. "Check the floor. My toes are tingling."

Danello felt around the edge near the baseboards. A knot in the wood had a hole in the center, and he stuck his finger into it. One section of the floor pulled up.

"Another hiding place," he said.

Two bags and one long box sat in a compartment about six inches deep and two feet square. The box was locked.

Danello picked up a bag. It clinked. He looked inside and sighed. "Only jewels," he said.

"You say that like it's a bad thing." Quenji grabbed the bag from his hand and poured gems into his palm. "Look at all this! We could live like aristocrats with these."

Shame we hadn't found those back when we were living here. That one bag alone would have been enough to get every last one of us out of Geveg and someplace safe. I sighed. I'd been a fool not to search the town house before. To avoid rooms I really hadn't wanted to go into. If I had, maybe we'd have escaped in time and Tali wouldn't have . . . been changed.

"Nya?" Danello rubbed my shoulder. "You okay?"

"I'm fine. Quenji, unlock the box, then stand back again, just in case."

Quenji worked on the lock until it snicked, then joined Danello in the hall. I reached for the long box. Lifted the lid.

Whoomp.

I winced, the blown sand prickle stinging this time. Zertanik created strong enchantments, stronger than anything Papa had ever made. Zertanik might have been a thief and a traitor, but he was a talented enchanter for sure.

"What's inside?"

"Glyphed pynvium. Long strips of it, about two inches wide, maybe a quarter inch thick. They look a little like rulers." A single column of glyphs ran down the center.

"Are they weapons?" Danello called.

"I don't know. We'd have to trigger them to find out, and they might only have one flash." I pulled over the box from the bookshelf, my stomach doing flips. I took a deep breath and opened it.

Whoomp.

Same sting, same sharp pain. If I were a thief, I'd run the second I touched one of these things.

"It's clear," I said, reaching inside the box. Something the size and shape of a battlefield brick was wrapped in cloth. I unwrapped it as the boys gathered around.

"That looks expensive," Quenji said.

A cylinder of ocean-blue pynvium sat in my hands, glyphs carved deep into four vertical strips of silvery-blue metal.

Kragstun.

"What is *that* for?" Danello whispered. Something about that cylinder made me want to be cautious, too. And run as fast as I could out the door and hide. I held the cloth carefully, not letting the cylinder touch my skin.

"I don't know." But I was sure it had something to do with the Duke and his weapons.

Zertanik had been working with the Duke to help create his pain-cycling device, and maybe more than just that. The Duke's pynvium weapons had flashed several times—and they'd flashed hard. Had Zertanik made those? Had he made the pynvium armor? The lining?

I guess Vinnot hadn't been the only one doing experiments.

I put the cylinder back in the box, feeling better the moment the lid closed. Zertanik probably hadn't wanted anyone to find these things. Maybe not even the Duke. He was, after all, planning on robbing him. Selling his enchanted items would have no doubt made him more money than anything the Duke had been offering.

I slipped the boxes into a makeshift bag made from scraps of curtains and wondered if killing Zertanik hadn't been a bad thing.

There was no way we were going swimming again, so getting back to the boat was going to be tricky.

"Is there another way around the bridge guards?" asked Aylin. She'd curled up on a chair next to Tali. Quenji sat on the arm, his hand in hers.

"Going around them is even more dangerous. The ones closer to the League will be the Duke's men."

"We could lure them away," Quenji said, worried eyes on Aylin. "The pack used to do that to get into guarded windows."

"A distraction?" she asked.

Quenji smiled. "Part of it. What good is getting rid of the guards if they catch you? You also gotta trick them."

"We could try talking to them," said Soek. "I know it sounds crazy, but what if they're on our side?"

Danello nodded. "We wanted to make contact with someone in charge and warn them about the Duke. We'll have to talk to someone to do that."

Guilt washed over me. I'd forgotten about the army, the danger to Geveg. "If we're going to try talking, should we wait until morning?"

"They'll be more people on the streets," said Quenji. "That could go either way for us."

The clock tower chimed, deep bells ringing out one after other. Tali gasped and jerked awake, head swiveling, eyes panicked. She shrieked and lunged at Quenji, sitting above her on the arm of Aylin's chair.

"Tali, no!"

She knocked him to the floor and pummeled him, swinging wildly. I grabbed one arm, Danello grabbed the other, and we dragged her off. Quenji scrambled away, his nose bleeding.

"Saints, what got into her?" he said. Aylin had both arms around him, watching Tali warily.

141

We held Tali down. She screamed, trying to get to me and Danello, flailing about with fists and feet.

"Shh, Tali, it's okay, please be quiet or someone will hear you."

Her shrieks bounced off the bare walls, sounding loud enough to wake every person on the isle.

"Tali, *quiet!*" I hummed a lullaby Mama used to sing to us, the one about clouds and fish that dreamed of flying. She fought us all through the first verse but settled down on the second. I started over, and finally her body went limp and she dropped back to the floor.

Danello let go of her, his hands hovering above her arms a few seconds before pulling away.

"Soek," he said softly, "any movement outside?"

Soek peeked out the window. "Doesn't look like it."

I didn't know whether or not to be relieved or bothered that a young girl screaming in the middle of the night was ignored.

"Sorry she hit you, Quenji," I said.

"She didn't mean it. And look"—he stuck his nose in the air, turning it to each side—"the bleeding's already stopped."

Tali rolled over and pulled herself up, her knees shaking. She crawled into the chair and curled back into the same ball she'd been in before. I wanted so much to hug her and let her know it would be okay.

"Do you think it was the bells?" Aylin said. "Or just that she woke up scared?"

"I don't know." My guts said it was fear. I'd woken up in a panic before, almost every night the first month after the soldiers had thrown us out of our home. I had to find a way to get her back, make her Tali again.

For once I was actually looking forward to seeing Onderaan.

We left the town house shortly after the clock tower struck one. Tali jumped when the chimes started, but didn't attack anyone. I kept the rope around her waist, left her hands free. The street was quiet as a grave, but I still felt watched. Even in the shadows it felt out in the open.

No one said a word while we sneaked along the buildings and climbed over low walls. Aylin carried the bag with the enchanter's book, pynvium, and jewels close to her chest, keeping it as silent as we were. We stopped near the bridge behind some gardenia bushes, their white flowers sickly sweet.

I scanned the street ahead. I counted four soldiers, all sitting. They'd built a barricade, crates piled high, tied together with rope. More crates were stacked across the street at the foot of the bridge. They wouldn't be easy to get over.

"So what do you think?" I whispered. "Distract them or talk to them?"

If they didn't want to talk, Danello had his rapier. Quenji no doubt had at least one knife on him. Aylin and Soek had thick table legs from the town house. The soldiers had swords. Probably no pynvium weapons.

"Won't hurt to try and talk, right?" Aylin said. "But just in case, you'd better take this." She handed me one of the ruler-shaped pynvium strips out of its metal box. Soek had checked them earlier and discovered they did indeed hold pain.

My skin started itching as soon as I touched it. "Right. Never hurts to be prepared."

"I'll go first," Danello said, giving Aylin a quick grin. "Just in case."

He slid out quietly and slipped around the bushes. Quenji and Soek went next, then Aylin. I followed her, Tali right behind me. We crossed the open distance, fifty feet, seventy-five.

One soldier turned, glanced away, then snapped back to us. He cried out and his partner turned our way as well. They both stepped forward, swords out. Hard to tell in the moonlight, but both looked fair-haired.

"Hold it right there!"

"We're Gevegian," Danello said, hands out to his sides. "We need to speak to whoever is in charge of the rebellion. The Duke's army is on the way."

"Don't care who you are, and on this isle, *we're* in charge."

"But the Duke is coming!"

"So?" The man tipped his head at the bundle in Aylin's arms. "What you got there, girlie?"

She gripped it closer. "Nothing of yours."

"It's *all* ours here."

Saints, they were looters. They weren't fighting for freedom—they were trying to steal what they could while everything was a mess.

"We don't want trouble—we just want to pass," Danello said, hand on his rapier. Quenji pulled out his knife and Soek hefted the table leg.

I pressed my fingers against the pynvium strip and angled closer. I had no clue what the trigger might be, but it was usually just a flick of the wrist. My guts said it would be a strong flash, just like all Zertanik's weapons, but the other two men were still back a ways and could be out of range.

"Give us the bag and you can pass."

"No." Danello drew his rapier.

"Better know how to use that shiny sword then." He charged forward. I flicked my wrist.

Whoomp!

The two men in front screamed and went down. Other men hollered, shouting orders, swearing, yelling at each other. More stepped out from the barricades they'd been hiding behind, swords drawn. A *lot* more.

"They got pynvium!"

Tali's rope yanked out of my hand. She shoved me aside and dived for one of the swords lying on the street. Grabbed it in one hand as she somersaulted back to her feet.

"Tali!"

She sidestepped Danello, spinning right and sinking the blade into the stomach of one of the looters. Kept moving, graceful as a dancer, the sword flying from man to man. Danello gaped at her, then stumbled back, parrying an attack.

What was she *doing*?

Aylin swung the table leg at a looter's head. It cracked against his skull and he went down. More men appeared from the shadows. There had to be a dozen, maybe more now.

"Two on your left," I called, trying to watch Tali

and the looters at the same time. She moved through them fearlessly.

A looter thrust his sword at me. I threw myself right, but not fast enough and the tip cut through my side. I grimaced, rolling the moment I hit the ground. He came at me again. I held my ground and my breath, then darted for his wrist as he struck. Skin met skin and I *pushed* the wound into him.

He tumbled forward, hand pressed against his side. "Shifter! It's the Shifter!"

I cringed and scrambled back to my feet. I had to get Tali, get them all, and get out of there.

"Across the bridge, hurry!" Danello shouted.

Aylin smacked a soldier with her club and ran for the crates blocking the bridge, the bag tucked under her arm. A looter lunged at her. Quenji jumped between them, taking the blade in his shoulder. He gasped and stumbled sideways.

"Get away from him!" Aylin flailed with the table leg, nearly smacking Quenji with it as she hit the looter.

I darted between shocked-looking soldiers, protecting Soek's back and heading for Quenji. A looter got past Danello and came at me, his sword slicing my thigh. Sharp pain pinched my leg, but he jumped back out of reach before I could touch him. Danello swung his rapier around and stabbed him.

Tali was still a blur of blades and anger. Quenji backed away, protecting Aylin as they moved across the bridge. A looter charged out of the darkness and kicked Danello behind the knee. He collapsed onto the bridge, and the man kicked him again, catching him across the temple.

"Danello!"

Two other men lunged at me, grabbing my arms and pinning me to the railing. I struggled, writhing against the warm stone, trying to break free.

"Let me go!"

Soek raced over and smacked one in the head with his club. The grip loosened, and my arm wrenched free. Quenji appeared, running right at me. He leaped at the man holding my other arm, and they both toppled over the side of the bridge and into the canal, dragging me over the rail with them.

"Quenji!" Aylin screamed.

I clung to the railing, my feet dangling. Two splashes below—the looter and Quenji. Then a third splash, and a raspy growl that chilled me.

Crocodile.

TEN

Quenji screamed, thrashing wildly. I caught a glimpse of flailing arms before the water churned and his scream was cut off. The croc spun, twisting Quenji round and round, then sharp snaps that I prayed were hyacinths, but they sounded far too much like bones breaking.

Please, Saint Saea, help him.

My fingers clung to the stone railing, but my arm muscles were already shaking. I couldn't hold on much longer. Part of me wanted to drop, grab the croc, and see if shifting worked on animals.

Another raspy growl, more splashing. The same croc, or had another arrived to finish off the looter?

Oh, Quenji.

"Hang on!" Soek grabbed my wrists. Aylin seized my shirt. They both pulled, dragging me over the railing and back onto the bridge.

Shouts and screams all around me. Terror from below, fear from above. The looter in the water clawed at the lakewall as if trying to climb it.

I glanced at where Quenji had vanished, the water's surface dark again.

Was there blood? Anything that said Quenji was down there?

"We can't just leave him," Aylin said, and I realized we were moving. Soek had us each by a hand, pulling us across the bridge. Danello was on his feet, blood running down his face. He had Tali's rope in his hand and was leading her away from the fighting.

"He's gone. We have to go," Soek said.

Aylin slapped at his arm. I stopped. Her arms were empty. Her bag was gone.

"The book! Where's the enchanter's book?" I couldn't lose it. I let go of Soek's hand.

"Nya, we don't have time, come on!" Soek looked ready to throw us both over his shoulder and run, but Quenji had died helping me get that book so I could find a way to save Tali. He *wasn't* going to die for nothing.

I spotted the bag. Some of the looters were on their side of the bridge, hauling their friend out of the canal. The others were racing toward me. I snatched the bag and ran back to Soek and Aylin, the looters right behind me.

"No, please," Aylin cried as we ran. "What if he's still alive?"

Danello reached the other side of the bridge first. Dark shapes moved from behind another set of stacked crates, but they didn't come forward. Maybe they were on our side, or maybe they'd seen the fight and didn't want to take us on.

"The boat," I gasped. "Get back to the boat."

Torchlight flared ahead. Shouts from behind.

Danello cut down a side street heading deeper into the isle. We plunged into shadows again, the close buildings masking most of the moon's light. A putrid smell hit me, rotting food, or maybe dead animals.

Aylin tripped and the smell got worse. She squealed, shaking her foot.

"Ah! Get it off, get it off!"

"Shh, what is—" Danello stopped. I followed his gaze.

A body. Dead several days from the bloat.

"Keep moving," I said, trying hard not to look

for more. Had it been a soldier or some poor person trying to get home?

Orange torchlight flickered on the side of one of the buildings.

"Are they still after us?"

"I'm not staying to find out."

No boarded-up buildings on this street, just broken windows and shattered doors. Trash and wood littered the ground, slowing our steps. More dark shapes slumped on stairs and on porches; some smelled, others didn't. We didn't linger to see what—or who—they might have been.

Danello took streets haphazardly, cutting back and forth, putting as many turns between us and the looters as possible. The clock tower struck two, its sorrowful bell like a howl over the dark city.

"In here." Danello slipped through an open door. I couldn't make out much in the room, but it looked like some kind of shop. Counters, shelves—all bare now. We huddled behind a counter, panting. Tali stared at the bloodied blade in her hand, turning it over and over.

"Tali, give me that, okay?" I held my hand out, ready to yank it away if she came at me.

She stared at me, then back to the sword, and tossed it on the ground.

I exhaled and slowly pulled it out of reach.

No footsteps raced by outside, but faint shouts floated in on the breeze. Not close, but not far enough away to risk leaving yet.

Aylin sobbed, pressing her hands over her face. Her whole body shook.

"It's going to be okay," Soek said gently.

Her hands fell. "No it's not," she snapped. "Quenji's *dead*. He got *eaten*—how is that ever going to be okay?"

"It's not. I'm sorry." He looked away.

No one spoke. I had no idea what to say or even what to feel. Quenji was dead. He'd come here to help us and now he was dead.

"How, uh, close do you think the boat is?" Danello asked, not looking at anyone.

"Eight or nine blocks?" With no light and everything in and around me in shambles, it was hard to get my bearings. "Where are we now? See any signs or anything?"

"Not from here." He got up and crept to the door. "I'll see if I can figure out where we are."

Aylin continued to sob. I held her, stroked her hair. A dozen things to say rushed into my mind, but nothing I said was going to make her feel any better.

I watched Tali while Aylin cried. Hard as that was, it was easier than thinking about Quenji. She leaned against the wall, wiping her bloody hands on the floor. Nothing about her right now suggested she could have done what she just had.

She'd fought like Danello, maybe even better. Moved as gracefully as Aylin. She was so small, the looters probably didn't even see her darting between them until it was too late.

What *had* the Duke done to my sister? She'd killed men, and it sure as spit didn't seem like she'd given it any thought. She'd just gone wild, as if triggered, same as any other pynvium weapon.

"Why did he have to die?" Aylin said. "It's not fair!" She buried her head in my shoulder.

"People die easy," Tali said.

She spoke! Her words chilled me, but she'd spoken.

"Tali? Do you know where you are?" I asked.

She didn't answer, just stared at the blood still on her hands. "Too easy," she whispered.

I shivered, my skin hot and cold at the same time. It was just too much. Quenji gone, Tali killing, the Duke coming to destroy everything I cared about. I never should have come home. We should have stayed with Jeatar and gone with the others.

But then you'd never have found Tali.

I glanced over at her. Heard her words again.

People die easy. Had I found her? Or had I found only what was left of her?

Light footsteps outside, then Danello slipped back into the shop. "I think it's clear."

"Where are we?"

"I'm not sure, but I can see the lakewall from here, so we can't be far from the water."

"He thought this was so exciting," Aylin said to no one in particular. "An adventure he could talk about for years. He never thought he could get hurt." She looked at me. "Did any of us? I know we talked about the danger, but did we *really* think we could *die*?"

I'd expected to die every day for the last five years. It never occurred to me *not* to worry about it. But was worrying the same as thinking it could happen?

Aylin drew her knees up to her chin and wrapped her arms around them. "Danello, you might never see Halima and the twins again. *Ever.* Soek, you could fall off the next bridge and die. Tali could attack the wrong person and lose. And Nya—how many people are trying to kill *you*? How long do you think you can stay ahead of them?"

"I don't know."

Danello sighed. "This is our home. What else can we do?"

"Leave!" she said. "Take the skiff and dock at one of the river towns. Find your family and go somewhere the Duke *isn't*."

"And let Geveg be destroyed?" I asked.

She scoffed. "Like we can stop that? This is war, *real* war, with *real* soldiers and *real* swords and *real* people dying *real* deaths. We can't do anything about that. We're *nothing*."

"That's not true."

"Yes, it is! You found Tali, you got the enchanter's book. Let's *go*."

Leave Geveg? Abandon it? Grannyma's words drifted into my ears. *Eggs should never fight with stones.* Was Geveg doomed no matter what we did?

Aylin stared at me, her frown growing deeper. "What is it with you? It's a *city*. It never cared about you, so why do you care about it so much?"

"It's *my* city. My family helped build it."

"And the Baseeri killed it five years ago. In a few weeks, they'll finally bury it." She got up. "I don't want to be here when that happens. Do you?"

I didn't want it to happen at all.

"Is that what you want for Tali?" she asked.

I looked at my sister, still sitting quietly on the floor, staring at blood. I wanted her to be safe. To be *herself* again. To never worry about soldiers or experiments or people who wanted to hurt her just because they could.

Even more than seeing Geveg free?

My family might have built Geveg, but Tali *was* my family. She had to come first. I'd ignored that once, and look what had happened to her. I could never let it happen again, no matter what the cost.

"Let's get to the skiff." I picked up the bag and the end of the rope. My heart ached, but I'd lost so much already—I couldn't risk losing Tali again. Saints knew I'd never get her back if that happened. I'd been lucky too many times.

We left the shop. No one said a word, but Aylin sniffled a few times. We walked single file, following Danello through the trash and the broken furniture and the occasional body. Warm breezes blew the stench away when we reached the street along the lakewall.

I looked around. If this was the edge of the warehouse row, then the boat was about six blocks down on the left. "That way."

We stayed close to the buildings, in the shadows and behind whatever cover we could find. Froze at every sound, even when it was nothing more than the trunks of palm trees rubbing together in the wind. Once or twice we heard shouts, saw torchlight up ahead, and held our breaths until it was gone.

It was chaos here. It *was* foolish to stay, much as part of me wished we could. We'd leave, find somewhere safe, start over. Onderaan probably hadn't left Veilig yet. It would take several days at least to get the refugees settled and find supplies. We could probably get to him before he left if we started there by morning.

And tell him you abandoned your home?

Home was with Tali. With Danello and Aylin. It might even be with Onderaan. I owed it to Tali to find out.

The row of converted warehouses appeared ahead, huge black hulking boxes along the lakeside. We cut across the street and hurried along the wall to the break in the neatly trimmed hedges. Slid down the path to the beach where the—

The anchor rope lay on the ground, one end cleanly cut.

ELEVEN

Danello drew his rapier and scanned the beach. I stared at the cut anchor rope, guts churning.

"She *left* us," Aylin said, voice tight. "I *knew* we couldn't trust her."

Lanelle had taken the skiff? How? Why? It didn't make any sense.

"I don't think she took it." Danello picked up the rope and ran a finger along the edge. "Look, the rope is cut. Why cut the anchor instead of just picking it up and putting it back on the skiff?"

"Because she was in a hurry to betray us." Aylin folded her arms. "I bet she went for her knife as soon as we were out of sight."

Danello shook his head. "But *why?*"

"It's Lanelle. She'd betray us for a hot meal."

My heart believed Aylin, but my guts sided with Danello. There was no reason for Lanelle to take the skiff and run. "I don't know. She practically begged me to take her with us. Why do that just to run now?"

"Someone offered her a better deal."

"I agree with Aylin," Soek said. "Lanelle only cares about herself. I was in the spire room, remember? You didn't see her cataloging symptoms and preparing bodies for dissection. She knew what was going on, but she didn't care. Working with the Duke helped her, so she did it."

He was right about that. She'd betrayed us to the Luminary as well. Told him about me and my abilities, which might have even led to the Duke sending trackers after me. "I'm not saying I trust her," I began, "but she's had plenty of better opportunities to betray us and she hasn't yet, so why now?"

Danello walked to the edge of the water and knelt by a v-shaped trench in the sand where the skiff had been. He reached down and picked up something.

"It's a tooth."

"A what?" I asked.

"There's still blood on it." He brought it back to us. "I think it's Lanelle's."

Soek and Aylin looked at each other, uncertainty wrinkling their brows.

"Why would anyone take Lanelle?" I said, gazing over the water.

"Exactly my point," said Aylin.

"I don't *know* why." Danello tossed the tooth away. "But whoever did it might still be around. We should go look for her."

"What?" Aylin and Soek said in unison. Soek shook his head. "No, we shouldn't."

"She's obviously in trouble."

"So?"

Danello gaped at the both of them. "You want to just leave her?"

I put my hand on his arm. "If we knew where she was or who took her, then maybe we could go after her. But we have no idea where she is, and those looters are still out there. We need to get someplace safe."

"There is no place safe anymore," Aylin muttered. "We're trapped here."

Danello looked at me and frowned. "You too?"

"I'm not risking everyone's life for someone who helped the Duke kill Healers. I know she thought she had no choice, and maybe she didn't, but Lanelle grabbed her own thorns. She probably stayed behind tonight because she didn't want to risk her own neck by helping us."

Danello hesitated. "Okay. What about my old apartment? I know folks there who would help us."

Aylin shook her head. "We'll have to cross another bridge. What if there are more of those looters?"

"We'll use a pynvium strip right away this time." I pointed to the bag Danello was holding. "I'll flash it and we'll run past them. No stopping to fight, no stopping to talk."

She closed her eyes, her lashes wet with fresh tears. "I just wanted to go home. I wish we'd gone with Jeatar."

"Aylin, we have to keep moving. I'm scared too, and I want to curl up and cry, but we can't. Not yet."

She looked down at the bloody tooth in the sand, then nodded. "Okay. We'll go to Danello's."

I led us back up the bank and around the outside of the isle, following the street that ran along the lake. The waves would help mask any sounds we made, and if the breeze blew right, we might even hear the bridge guards talking. Or snoring at this hour. Somehow I doubted we'd be that lucky.

We ducked behind a row of hibiscus bushes. Another barricade was up ahead, with some kind of gate in the middle, and only two people. I scanned the street for places additional guards might be hiding, but the area around the bridge was open.

"I think it's just the two." I could handle two. The strips flashed hard enough to take both out easily. And if one got past me, I still had the cut in my leg to shift.

Danello peeked over the bushes. "Two guards seem like a weak defense against the looters."

"Unless they're working *with* the looters," Soek said.

Great. One missed guard, one shout, and who knew how many people might show up to rob or kill us.

"We'll have to risk it," I said. "I'll go out alone with the pynvium. You all stay back. Even if more show up, stay—"

"Are you coming out or are you planning to hide all night?" someone shouted from the bridge.

We looked at each other. "Is he talking to us?' Danello said.

"The longer you hide, the more nervous you're making us."

They had to be talking to us. "They don't sound like looters," I said. "Maybe we should go out there."

"I'll go. Be ready to run if they try anything."

Danello rose and walked slowly toward the bridge. "Who are you?"

"Why don't you tell *us* first."

Danello paused. "We're Gevegians trying to get home. My family's apartment is on that isle. On Market-Dock Canal."

"Your name?"

"Danello del'Sebore."

Soft mumblings for a few seconds. "What about the others?"

Danello waved us over. We left the bushes, staying close together. I nudged the pynvium strip up my sleeve, an easy drop back into my hand if we needed it.

"My friends. It's been a long night. We just want to get someplace safe from the looters."

They seemed satisfied. Then one man stepped closer. "Why is that girl on a rope?"

I winced. "She's my sister. She's, uh, a little off. I didn't want her to wander away."

"There's a lot of blood on you two." He moved a hand to the sword on his hip.

"Looters attacked us and killed our friend," Aylin said, her voice raw and sad. "We barely got away."

His hand came away from the sword. "I'm sorry about that. They've been a problem for weeks now, but there's not much we can do about them." He gestured behind him, and a woman walked out and opened the gate. "Come on through."

"Thank you so much."

My chest loosened the moment we got off the looters' isle. There were honest Gevegians here, folks we might even be able to trust.

"Better get home quick as you can," the woman said. "We have patrols out, but it's hard to protect the whole isle. It's really not safe at night."

"We noticed," said Soek.

We hurried past the blockade and followed Danello toward his old building. The streets were just as dark, but occasionally cracks of light seeped around boarded-up windows on the lower floors.

"That's it there," Danello said, pointing at a wooden building with a brick foundation. Unlike a lot of others, his had shutters, and all of them were closed.

The building door was open, the stairs up even clear, though not clean. Danello practically ran to the third floor and down the hall. He tried the door to his old apartment.

"Locked," he said. I wasn't sure if he was glad about that or not. His voice sounded odd—shaky and hopeful at the same time. Maybe he thought his father had come back here when he didn't find us at the town house.

"So knock," I said gently. "Unless you still have the key."

"Lost that a long time ago." He took a deep breath and rapped softly.

No answer.

He knocked harder. Someone coughed and a bed squeaked, but I couldn't tell which apartment it came from.

Danello knocked again, rattling the door. Soldiers knocked like that. Plenty of sounds down the hall this time: chairs dragged across the floor, voices murmured, soft cries.

"Who's there?" A gruff voice, thick with sleep. Didn't sound like Danello's da though.

"I'm looking for Master del'Sebore," Danello said. "Is he here?"

"Don't know any del'Sebore."

"Please, sir, is he here?"

The door behind us cracked open. If I hadn't been standing right against it, I'd never even have heard it. I turned. A single eye peered out through the crack.

"He's looking for his father," I whispered.

The crack widened enough for an old woman to

appear, her face thin, her eyes scared. "He's with the soldiers," she whispered back.

My heart clenched and I reached for Danello's arm.

"He was captured?"

"Nah, *our* soldiers."

"Saama!" Danello said. The door opened all the way, and the thin old woman held out her arms. Danello fell into them for a hug. "Do you know what happened to my da?"

"He was looking for you a long time, but then when things got bad, he went and joined the resistance." She let go of Danello and pulled him inside, then motioned for the rest of us to follow. "Come in already. Not smart standing out there in the hall."

She ushered us in, raising a curious eyebrow at Tali and the rope, but didn't question me. The apartment reminded me of Danello's. Warm and homey, even though there wasn't much to it. One main room with old furniture that used to be nice, a side room with a small bed. A tiny kitchen.

"You look like you've had quite a night," she said softly.

Danello nodded. "It's been rough."

"Are the little ones safe?"

He took a shaky breath. "I hope so. I left them with a friend to watch until we got back."

Saama looked at the rest of us and gasped. "Saints, child, is that blood?"

I checked my leg where the looter's sword had cut me. The bleeding had stopped, and I was too tired to pay any more attention to the throbbing.

"I got cut before."

"You sit down and let me treat that." She pointed to a kitchen chair. I sat. "Goodness, Danello, you didn't even think to get the girl some help?"

"I, uh," he began, but she cut him off.

"Go get me a bowl and some water from the pitcher there." Saama opened a cabinet and pulled out a reed basket that looked older than I was. "I've got a salve here that'll fix you right up."

A *salve*? "No, I'm fine, really," I said. There were always one or two herb sellers hanging around near the League, selling their homemade potions and claiming they healed you just fine. Sheer foolishness, Grannyma used to say. Mixing a bunch of flowers and weeds together didn't do a thing to help healing. In the summer, the League had a lot of folks come in with infections and blood sickness from those "treatments."

"That's a deep cut."

"Once I wash and wrap it, it'll be fine." I took the bowl from Danello before she could and started washing my leg. It stung where the water hit it, but I'd endured a lot worse. The cut was clean and would heal well on its own, probably barely even scar.

Saama gave me a look. "Never known someone to turn down healing before."

"That's not heal—" Folks who couldn't afford the League did what they could, and offending Saama probably wasn't the best idea. "—really necessary. It looks worse than it is. And I heal fast." That last part was true.

"It's fine, Saama," Danello said, taking the basket out of her arms. He peeked into the basket and pulled out some long strips of cloth. "Here, wrap it with this."

I did, tying the ends off and tucking them under the edge.

Saama gave me one last incredulous glance, but she didn't force the salve on me. "What are you all doing here? In the middle of the night no less." She settled herself in a chair bigger than she was. It was the only thing in the room that didn't fit her.

"We came to warn the city that the Duke's army is on the way," Danello said. "He's coming after Geveg."

Saama's eyes darkened. "I figured it was only a matter of time. Better get you to Ipstan at first light then. I don't get out much, but one of the girls who helps with my shopping can run a message for me."

"Ipstan?"

"*General* Ipstan." She rolled her eyes. "He leads the resistance, such as it is. Bunch of fools playing soldier mostly, but their hearts are in the right place. Not as organized as the 'Crats though."

"The aristocrats have an army?" I asked.

"I wouldn't go that far. They have soldiers who took on the Gov-Gen, and at least one of them was responsible for the man winding up facedown in the canals."

"Wait, Baseeri *aristocrats* killed the Gov-Gen?"

"They did. The Duke demanded too much too often from them, just as he'd done to us all those years ago. They finally said no, same as we did."

Amazing.

Danello sat on the arm of a chair. "Saama, what's been going on? We've heard some news, but not enough."

"We've been away for a while," I added. No need to say why or doing what.

Saama nodded. "Were you here when those Healers were arrested?"

170

"Um, I don't know." Did she mean when Vyand had captured us?

"You'd know if you'd seen it. Some tracker was hauling them through the streets like they were a prize catch. Made folks mad, and they joined up and freed them. Gave those trackers a good what for too."

She *did* mean us. "That we saw. But nothing past that."

"Then you got out before it went bad. The whole thing started people talking, and then complaining, and then talking about doing something about the complaints. Wasn't anything serious at first—a few places got torched, some folks roughed up. The blue-boys put a stop to it before it got too far."

"Blue-boys?" I said.

"Soldiers still loyal to the Duke. Not as many as there were, a few thousand, but still enough to cause trouble."

Danello frowned. "How did the Baseeri get involved?"

"The Duke's new laws. He demanded money, men, food, pynvium, Healers. They complained to the Gov-Gen about it, and he ignored them like he ignored us. They didn't take too kindly to that. Once his body was found, the whole city went mad.

Blue-boys tried to get control again, but with half of them working for the 'Crats, and a good chunk of the 'Crats angry as we were, it didn't go so well."

"So the aristocrats are working with us?" I asked.

Saama cackled. "Saints no, child. I think if they could chase us off the isles as well, they'd do it. They've got themselves tucked away in the Aristocrats' Isles and the terraces, probably the Gov-Gen's estate by now too. The looters control North and South Isles, which is probably the only thing keeping the 'Crats from coming after *us* next." She sniffed. "Well, that and the blue-boys at the League."

I looked at Danello. That wasn't good. We'd have trouble defending against the Duke if *everyone* fought. If we had to watch our backs as well as our fronts, we didn't have a chance of winning.

"The Duke's soldiers are at the Healers' League?" said Soek.

"The whole lot of them is holed up there. It's why we can't do anything about them. They've got the bridges and Upper and Lower Grand Isles locked down on our side, and the looters control the isles on the other."

"Maybe you should leave Geveg," Danello said, frowning. "Head into the mountains and find somewhere safe to hide."

"These old bones wouldn't make it. This is my home. I was born here and I plan to die here." She shrugged. "Didn't think that'd be so soon, but the Saints do what the Saints do."

No one said anything for a bit. Saama's eyes fluttered, and Aylin looked about ready to fall asleep herself.

"Is it okay if we stay here until morning?' Danello asked.

"Of course! Can't let you sleep in the park. Easiest way to get yourself kidnapped these days."

Danello jerked straight. "Kidnapped? A friend of ours was waiting for us on a skiff, but both she and the boat are gone. It looks like someone might have taken her."

"Oh dear, sounds like she was plucked for ransom then."

"Why? Who would they ransom her to?" I said.

"I don't know, but those looters started grabbing rich folks right after the riots. If they took her, they must have thought she was from a rich family."

"But how—" We'd stolen the League's boat. If that didn't say rich, nothing did. "It had to be the skiff. They must have thought she was from the League." I sucked in a breath. She might not be from the League, but Lanelle *was* a Healer. The League would probably pay good money to get a few more of those back. She could wind up right back with the League Elders and in the Duke's experiments.

"What happens if no one pays the ransom?" Soek asked.

Saama shrugged. "Don't know. They might kill her, or they might just toss her out."

Aylin looked at me, her bloodshot eyes clearly saying she was okay with taking that chance.

I couldn't leave Lanelle to the League. Maybe she deserved it, but she'd already paid that price once. "Do you know how to contact them to pay the ransom?" We had that bag of jewels we found in Zertanik's town house. A gem would certainly cover the ransom.

"I only hear the rumors. Bridge guards might know. They deal with them folks more than most."

Aylin sighed. "Does this mean we're going to go get her?"

"She didn't leave us or betray us. We can't *not* help her just because we don't like her."

"Nobody's going anywhere else tonight," Saama said, standing. "I've got extra pillows and blankets. Most of you will have to bunk down on the floor, but

174

you'll be safe. You can go get your friend when the sun comes up."

"Thank you," I said.

Aylin curled up in the big chair and pulled the blanket under her chin. Soek grabbed a blanket and a patch of floor. Tali had already fallen asleep on the floor under the kitchen table. I draped a blanket over her, praying that she'd be more like herself in the morning.

"Get some sleep." Danello tossed a pillow down on the couch and nudged me toward it.

He blew out the candles and sat on the floor beside me, leaning back against the cushions. I put my pillow behind his head, then lay down, stretching my hand until it rested against Danello's shoulder. He reached up and laced his fingers through mine.

"My da's with Ipstan," he whispered, his words heavy with hope.

I nodded in the dark. "Think he'd come with us? Your da, I mean."

"Why wouldn't he?"

My parents had stayed and fought. Danello's mother had fought. "I don't know. He might want to help defend the city."

"He'll want to leave with us. We'll tell Ipstan

everything we know, then we'll get another boat and go to Veilig."

"Okay."

I stared at the ceiling. Faint streaks of moonlight slipped in past the shutters. I tried to imagine starting over with Tali and the others in Veilig, leaving Geveg and the Duke behind, but all I could picture were people dying and soldiers in blue.

And me, walking away from them.

TWELVE

I woke to bells. Loud, insistent, the kind of bells
that rang when something was very wrong. Then
came a sharp bang, wood scraping across the floor,
and a soft whimper.

Tali!

I jerked around. The table had moved and the
candles on top had fallen over. Tali was up against
the kitchen cabinets, hands out, her gaze darting
back and forth. It settled on mine, and for a heartbeat something flickered in them, like she knew me.

"It's okay—it's just the clock tower," I said. "Go
back to sleep." She looked at me, then at the window, and settled down again.

"What's going on?" Danello asked, yawning.

"That's the attack bell," Saama said, coming out of her room. "Means the blue-boys are making trouble for someone."

"Better wake the others," Danello said.

Soek was already up when I turned around, but I had to shake Aylin a few times.

"Hmmm? What's going on?"

"Soldiers are coming."

"Oh, not again."

We opened the shutters and huddled around the window. Men and women ran past carrying weapons, heading for the bridge on the far side of the isle by Tannif's Coffeehouse.

"Been happening a lot the last week," Saama said. "Soon as Ipstan started openly organizing folks, handing out weapons and armor. The blue-boys attack fast and hard and then run back to safety."

We watched the streets while the sun rose, its gentle light reflecting off swords and bits of armor as more and more people raced past. It was all so familiar, like nightmares come to life.

"Wait, I see something," Danello said. "And I definitely hear fighting."

And running, feet slapping against brick. Folks fled past us, their clothes and faces bloody. They ran as if they didn't care where they were running to. Panic.

Two soldiers walked down the street, their swords dark, their armor blue.

I gripped the curtains, every inch of me hot. "Undying."

Danello moved closer, blocking my path to the door. "Nya, don't."

"It's only two. I can handle two."

Saama looked at me as if I'd lost my mind. "You can't kill *those* blue-boys. Why do you think they've been able to keep us down and licking our wounds?"

"I can stop them." I'd done nothing while the Undying turned my sister into a weapon. Just watched when they killed that poor girl in Baseer. I wasn't going to do nothing again.

"They're coming inside," Soek said. "One here, the other across the street."

Wood banged against wood, a door being kicked open. People started screaming. Tali gasped and dropped to floor, arms around her knees. I hated to see her scared, but that was a more Tali reaction to screams.

"Let me go." I shoved against Danello, but he wouldn't budge.

"No. You don't know how many more might be out there."

"It doesn't matter. I can stop the one in here."

"Nya, you—"

I put my hands against Danello's cheeks. "Move, please."

His eyes widened a little, like he wasn't sure if I was asking or threatening. I wasn't sure either.

He stepped aside. I raced out the door and down the stairs, ignoring the ache in my leg. I'd be rid of that soon enough. I followed the sobbing, the pleading, and found the Undying on the second-floor landing, standing above three men cowering on the floor. Fathers, brothers, uncles. Their clothes were sliced and blood seeped through.

Cold anger settled around me. I thought the folks here had been fighting back. But these three grown men just sat there, not even *trying* to fight. Is this what the Duke had done to us? What the Undying had done?

"Get away from them."

The Undying looked at me, casual, as if he had nothing to fear. Was his armor lined with silvery metal too? Maybe not. He didn't seem blank like Tali. He looked like he enjoyed the killing. So young to be so cruel. This one wore a helmet, but his face was exposed. He smirked the way older boys with too much power always could. "Wait your turn."

"Some Healer you are. Nothing but a pathetic Undying."

His smirk vanished. "Be smart to shut that mouth of yours."

"Murdering thug. Your mother must cry herself to sleep every night."

He climbed closer, blood dripping from his sword onto the stairs. I retreated, luring him farther up, out of range of the men on the floor.

He stopped halfway up the stairs. "Trying to draw me into an ambush? I don't think so."

I took a step closer. Then another. He did a poor job of masking his surprise.

"Coming after *me*?" he said. "Nobody does that and lives."

"I can."

He studied me and his bluster faded. "No, you can't be."

"Can't be what?" Another step.

"*Her.* I know who you are," he said, backing away. "The commander warned us about you."

"Then why aren't you running?"

He stopped two steps above the men he'd cornered before. They hadn't run either, though they should have.

"I'm not running from no quirker."

I smiled. "You mean Shifter."

I dived forward, hands outstretched, aiming for his chest plate, or an arm bracer, or, Saint's willing, his hand. He jerked back and slipped, falling off the step and toppling toward the landing. The men yelled and rolled out of the way. I hit the bottom of the stairs on my side, but not quite close enough to grab him.

An older Undying stepped onto the landing, his sword arcing toward my neck. "Good thing I know how to kill Shifters."

"Yeah," Danello said, "aim for the eyes."

A knife whooshed over me and sank into the Undying's eye. His sword dropped. His body followed. Danello stood at the top of the stairs, his throwing hand still pointing at the Undying.

I scrambled forward and grabbed the younger Undying's hand, and *pushed*. He yelped, but I doubted my sliced leg hurt him all that much. I slapped both hands flat against his chest plate.

"Put it in your armor," I said, crawling to my knees. "I dare you."

"Don't kill me!"

"You can't help us if you're dead." He'd hurt them. He could heal them, one way or another. I held out one hand to the three men. "If you're hurt, grab my hand."

Two men stepped forward. The first slipped a shaking hand into mine. I *drew*, pulling out a deep shoulder wound. *Pushed*, and the Undying yelped louder this time. He merely whimpered as I *pushed* the other man's injuries into him.

"Anyone else hurt?" I asked.

"On the first floor," the oldest man said. "Not sure how many."

"Bring them here."

Danello stood beside me, his rapier tip hovering over the Undying's eye.

"Nice throw back there," I said.

"I was motivated."

The Undying swallowed, his gaze darting from me to Danello and back. I could see the planning going on behind his blue eyes. Could he get me before I flashed his armor? Could he get Danello before he stabbed him in the eye? Could he survive either if he pushed it into his armor fast enough?

People came up the stairs: two limped, three others were carried. Pale, bleeding, moaning. Random victims of the Undying shaking under my hands. How many more innocents were bleeding and dying in their homes? And for what? Why kill random people? They weren't soldiers—they weren't trying to fight—they were trying to hide and stay alive.

"Nya, what are you doing?" Aylin said from behind me.

"Helping people." I reached out for the injured.

"You can't, not like this."

"Sure I can." I *drew* and the pain swirled through me, sharp and biting. I gathered it in the space between my heart and my guts and *pushed* it into the Undying. He sucked in a breath and whimpered again.

"Let me heal them," Soek said.

"No. He hurt them so he has to heal them."

"This is wrong and you know it." Aylin padded down the stairs and dropped beside me. "You're torturing him."

"He did this, he can fix it." I reached for the next person.

"Nya, stop!" She yanked on my arm.

I shrugged her off. She stared at me, pleading. I stared back, but she wasn't going to talk me out of it.

"Healers don't kill. It's time one of them learned that lesson." I'd teach the others as soon as I got my hands on them.

"So this is it now? We're just as bad as they are?"

"For the Undying? Yes."

Aylin backed away.

I healed the next person in line. And the next, and the next. The Undying sobbed softly, glaring at me through the tears.

"Is that all of them?" I asked the old man.

"Yes. Except for the dead."

The Undying had killed them for no reason at all. No, worse. He was probably *told* to, and that was worse than having no reason. "Go see who else is hurt out there. Bring them here."

I unbuckled the Undying's bracer and pulled it off him. No kragstun lining. So he didn't even have that as an excuse. Then the other arm. Shoulders. His helmet. He moaned but didn't fight me. I needed help on the chest piece, but the men he'd planned to kill were delighted to hold him up. I unbuckled the greaves last, pulling them off his legs.

I grabbed his chin and shook it. "Hey." He grunted and opened his eyes. I put the greave in his hand, pressing his fingers against the pynvium. "Heal yourself."

He looked surprised but clutched the pynvium. His color returned, his eyes cleared.

I stood. Danello kept the rapier on him. The Undying stayed on the floor, watching me. So did

Aylin and Soek. Soek didn't look upset like Aylin. He seemed fine with what I was doing.

"Why didn't you kill me?" the Undying asked.

"Because I'm not like you." I turned to the small crowd now gathered in the hall. "Does anyone have any rope?"

Several folks vanished and returned with various lengths. I tied his hands behind him and his feet to the banister. We'd have to figure out what to do with him later, but for now, this was good enough. I knelt in front of him.

"Why are you running around killing people?"

"Like I'd tell you."

I shrugged. "Okay. I'll let these folks have you then."

His eyes bulged. "Wait!"

I waited. He didn't continue. "Listen," I said, "people are going to die when the Duke's army gets here. Innocent people. You don't care about that, but *I* do. If you act like a real Healer and help these people now, you'll get a chance to redeem yourself. Otherwise, I walk away and I don't care what happens to you."

He paused, his jaw working slowly side to side. "Fear," he muttered.

"What do you mean?"

"We were supposed to spread fear. Go building to building, kill people, kill guards, cut through and show everyone that you can't stop us. Soften you up so you'd be too scared to organize."

This had to stop. The Duke couldn't treat us like stock animals. Couldn't kill us whenever he felt like it. "Do we *seem* soft?"

He glanced away. "You did 'til I found *you*."

"How many Undying are here?"

"Eight."

Down to six now. Six Undying could kill a lot of people, especially if they were all spread out in small groups like we'd seen so far. They could kill and kill until their armor filled up. Organized or not, the resistance wouldn't be able to stop them.

But *I* could.

The door opened below, and folks started up the stairs. Ten, fifteen, twenty—growing harder to count as they filled the hallways.

I picked up the greave again, held it out in front of the Undying. "I can either untie your hands so you can heal them, or I can do it and shift into you. Your call."

He paled. "I'll do it."

Two men had picked up the Undyings' swords, and a few women had arrived with rapiers. They pointed them all at the Undying.

"I don't have to warn you about trying to run or trying to hurt these people further, do I?" I said.

"No."

He healed them one by one. I checked afterward, just to make sure he'd done it right. When he was finished, I tied him back up again.

"Now what?" Danello said.

"Kill him," cried someone in the crowd. A few more agreed. Even Danello seemed okay with that.

I shook my head. "No. We need Healers and we need information. We'll keep him here and find out what we can. Maybe heal more injured who haven't had time to reach us yet."

"He's the enemy!"

"We're not murderers." I looked at each person in turn. The ones who glared back I stared at until they looked away. "When more soldiers come, and they will, you'll need him. Would you risk your families to get revenge?"

Shamed faces stared at the floor.

"You heard him. The Duke is trying to soften us up. Break our spirit. There are more of us on this island than them, yet we're the ones hiding. We're the ones fighting each other, looting our homes, and kidnapping our friends."

"How are we supposed to fight *them*?" someone asked. "They don't die."

I pointed to the dead Undying on the floor. "He did."

"You're the Shifter. It's different."

Danello stepped forward. "I killed him, not her. Undying die quick if you hit them in the eyes. They don't have time to heal themselves."

Impressed murmurs ran through the crowd.

"A small blade is all you need. Better if you can throw it. We have those in every kitchen and tackle box in the city."

"Long, thin steel'll work too," said a woman, waving her rapier.

Danello smiled. "It will."

"We can fight back, even against *them*," I said. "Show them that we aren't soft, and if they want what's ours, they'll have to send more than half-trained soldiers in pretty blue armor to get it. And if they try, it'll cost them more than they can afford."

A few folks cheered. The rest nodded, determined gleams in their eyes.

"Gather everyone who can throw a knife well," Danello said. "Those who are fast and accurate with a rapier. Swords are too big and won't work, but those who own them can help defend the others.

Guard the bridges, and when the Undying try to cross, you stop them."

"Yeah, put 'em down!"

"Show the Duke what for!"

"No more hiding!"

Those from other buildings left, heads held high, chins set. So different from the scared folks who'd scurried inside not long ago. The rest went back to their apartments, except for the older man I'd saved earlier.

"What can I do to help?" he asked.

"Spread the word," I said. "The Duke is on his way. We need to fight and we need to protect those who can't. Get them out of the city or into brick buildings, places that won't burn."

He frowned. "The Duke really is coming?"

"He is."

"Guess we'll have to be ready for him. You gonna fight him with us?"

"I've been fighting him my whole life."

He nodded and walked away, a smile on his still-bloody face. "Good enough."

I grabbed the rope and hauled the Undying to his feet. Danello kept the rapier on him. "Soek, Aylin, gather the pynvium armor, please."

They stripped the other set off the dead Undying

and grabbed what I'd already removed.

"We'll keep him upstairs for now, but he'll need to be guarded by folks who won't kill him when our backs are turned. We can hand him over to the resistance once we make contact."

"Nya, this is crazy," Aylin said. "What are you doing?"

"Fighting." Even when we were losing, Mama and Papa fought. Grannyma, too. Now the Duke was threatening us again. He'd broken more than our bodies. He'd broken our spirit, and unless we got that back, we didn't stand a chance.

"I thought we were leaving?"

I hesitated. I had said that, hadn't I? "We are, as soon as we meet with Ipstan and find Danello's da. Oh, and get Lanelle back."

"Then why say all those things?"

"Because we might as well help while we're here."

Aylin and Danello dumped the pynvium armor into a trunk Saama brought out. Heavy stuff, and pretty too, if you didn't think about what it was used for.

Saama recruited the two husky sons of a fisherman down the hall to help guard the Undying. They tied him to a chair and watched him like cats with mice. Tali watched too, her eyes narrowed. I didn't like suspicion any more than fear, but at least she was showing *some* kind of emotion.

"Is that really one of the Undying?" Saama asked.

"He is."

She tsked. "Well Saints and sinners, he's just a boy."

"Young minds are good and pliable," Tali said. The Undying jerked and looked at her. I stepped between them, blocking his view.

"He might be a boy," I said, "but he's still a murderer."

"And now everyone will know how to kill them," Danello added. "They won't be able to terrorize us anymore. We'll be able to make them fear *us*."

The Undying started laughing. "You really think you have a chance against the Duke?"

"We can fight you now. We can beat your army."

"Don't you get it? There won't *be* an army. The Duke is going to sail up and burn every last building to the ground. These little isles you have? Your little soldiers at the bridges and docks, 'keeping us at bay'? You're being herded. He *wants* you there where it's easier to kill you."

"That's a lie."

He smirked. "Why do you think we were here to

scare you, keep you in your homes? You're a bunch of fishermen, with no armor and no real weapons. We could cut you down without even trying, but why risk good soldiers on trash? While you're all dying, we'll be boarding ships at the League and leaving this hunk of rock to burn."

THIRTEEN

I knew there'd been a good chance the Duke planned to burn the city, but hearing it stated so plainly—so coldly—made it all the more real.

"If Geveg dies, you'll die with us," I said.

He shrugged. "Not if I get out first."

He thought he would too. He'd been scared before, but of me, not them. Or maybe this was another way of trying to scare us, part of some plan to help him escape. I'd done similar things before.

But it made too much sense to be a lie. The Duke had the Undying and thousands of soldiers. A city that was split down the middle, with Gevegians struggling on one side and Baseeri on the other, and looters out for themselves in between. Even if we convinced everyone to fight and somehow outnumbered them, what good was an army if there was no one for it to fight?

I turned back to the others. "The city should evacuate, like the farm did."

"There's nowhere to go," the Undying said. "The Duke controls the river and all the roads to Geveg."

The Duke had to be close to Jeatar's farm by now. How long would it take him to destroy it and move on? A day? He had brought his army, so he must have planned on using it somewhere, even if it wasn't on us. Did he plan to take over the river towns? The marsh farms? Or maybe the plan was to crush them and keep on marching. If so, we might have as little as a week before he reached Geveg.

"Put him in Saama's room, please," I said. We needed to talk without him hearing and spinning lies just to prey on our fears.

The two husky boys grabbed his chair and dragged him across the floor and into the other room. They shut the door but stayed with him.

"We should meet with Ipstan right now," I said. "I don't know what we can do, but they need to know all these attacks are part of a trap."

Saama nodded and headed for the door. "I'll

fetch those girls of mine. They'll know someone in the resistance who knows Ipstan."

"What about Lanelle?" Danello said.

I groaned. "She'll just have to wait."

"We'll need Healers if we're taking on the Duke."

"We're not staying," Aylin said quickly. "*We're* not taking on anything."

"But *she* came here to fight." Danello went to the bag and pulled out the pouch of jewels. He picked out a small gem and slipped it into a pocket. "If we're leaving, we can at least give the resistance Lanelle."

Some trade. Us for her. "Then let's go get her."

One of the girls Saama fetched ran off to find someone who could take us to Ipstan. The other took us to the bridge to the looters' isle. Tali stayed with Saama. I hated to leave her behind, but she was safer inside than out where she might attack someone again.

The streets weren't so quiet anymore. People ran back and forth, some carrying baskets, others with old rapiers and bits of armor that needed a good polishing. Preparing for war.

Ten people guarded the bridge now, and four had several knife sheathes on their belts. They'd moved fast as fright to get defenses in place against the Undying. A good sign.

"These folks need to pay a ransom," the girl said as we approached the guards.

"You're her?" one of them asked me, his face full of hope. "You're the one who stopped the Undying?"

"Him too." I pointed to Danello. "We've all fought them before."

The bridge guards stared at me, but no one came close. It was almost . . . reverent.

Danello cleared his throat. "How do we get back the people the looters kidnapped?"

"We'll ask for an exchange," one of the men said. "We've done it a few times already."

He walked to the middle of the bridge and called out. A man from the other side appeared from behind the barricade and took a few steps onto the bridge. He kept his sword ready. They spoke, then both returned.

"He's getting someone," the guard said. "A man named Optel is in charge over there. Sometimes he comes, sometimes he sends a thug."

After a few minutes, two men appeared and walked to the middle of the bridge. One was obviously the thug, big and stocky, a heavy sword in his hands. The other wore fancy clothes that didn't fit him well. Probably weren't even his.

"Lucky you, you earned the boss himself," the

guard said. "Come on."

We followed him across the bridge. More guards came out and stood behind Optel. One for each of us.

"Who do we have that you want?" Optel asked with a smile. His brown hair had blond streaks through it, and his hands were rough and callused. Fisherman probably. Not husky enough for a farmer.

"A girl about my age," I said. "Brown hair, bad attitude."

Optel grimaced and rubbed the back of his neck. "I know that one. I can sell her to you for"—he looked us over, but something in his gaze said he wasn't guessing what we could afford—"say one hundred oppas."

"You've got to be kidding?" our bridge guard said. I hid my relief. It would have been a lot more if they'd known she was a Healer. At least she'd been smart enough to stay quiet about that.

"She's not worth that much," Aylin said. Soek nodded emphatically behind her.

Danello handed me the gem. It was worth more than one hundred oppas, but we didn't have anything smaller. "Bring her to us."

Optel's eyes gleamed when he spotted the gem, but he got his excitement hidden again. He muttered something to one of his guards and he ran off.

"Looks like I'm getting the good side of the deal here," he said.

Optel's guard came back with Lanelle, her hands tied in front of her. Bruises covered her jaw, and one eye was swollen shut. She seemed shocked that I'd come for her. I felt only a little guilty that I'd debated against it.

Optel smiled and held out his hand. "One final detail and the transaction is compete."

I handed him the gem. Lanelle darted between us. I cut her bindings, checked her injuries. Banged up, but nothing serious.

"Thank you for doing business with Optel's Supply and Demand. Let us know if we can be of further service in the future." He laughed and turned away, his guards closing in behind him.

"I should have let you bring some pynvium," Danello muttered, hands tight on his rapier.

"Trust me, I wish I had." But satisfying as it would have been, we'd need all the weapons we could get for the Duke and his blue-boys.

I glanced at Aylin.

No, *they'd* need all the weapons they could get. We'd be gone way before then.

Shrieks reverberated in the stairwell of Danello's apartment building.

Tali's shrieks.

I raced up the stairs, my heart thudding. People stood in the halls, looking worried, but not scared enough for more soldiers to be there. I grabbed the door latch to Saama's apartment, but it was locked.

"Tali!"

The door flew open. Saama waved a hand inside, her face pale. "She just went crazy!"

Another shriek. Tali darted around the room. She sobbed between shrieks, shaking her head, muttering, though I couldn't make out the words.

"What happened?' Danello asked.

"She just went after him!"

The Undying lay on the floor, a knife hilt sticking out of his eye. He was still tied to the chair.

"Sweet Saea, Tali, what did you do?" Fear and fresh anger surged through me. They'd done this to her. Made her this way.

"She *killed* him?" Lanelle said.

"He started talking about how we were all dead. He got real descriptive about it too." Saama shuddered. "Kept saying what the Duke would do to us. She just went for the knife and then for him."

Everyone spoke at once, words falling over each

other. Tali pressed her hands against her ears and squeezed her eyes shut.

"Quiet, all of you." I stepped farther into the room, hands up. "It's okay, Tali, you're safe." I scanned the kitchen. Two other knives stuck out of a block on the counter. One slot was empty. *So that's where she got it*.

"Hurt," she said, still not looking at me.

"Do you hurt?"

"Hurt," she said again. Her hands were clenched. One had blood on it.

"Do you *want* to hurt someone?" I prayed not, but that's what the Undying did. She didn't have the armor anymore, but maybe she still felt like one of the Undying. I shivered.

"Hurt." She barely whispered it this time, a sob coming right after. She pressed her fists against her eyes and sank to the floor.

I went to her, though Danello and Aylin and even Lanelle whisper-yelled for me not to. I sat beside her. Harder for her to attack me from the side.

"I'm here, Tali. You had to do it—I understand. He was a bad person. He killed people."

She cried, tears rolling out from under her fists, but didn't say anything. I scooted closer. Put one arm around her. A quiet hiss came from the doorway as if lots of breaths were being held.

She leaned toward me, just a little. I wrapped the other arm around her and hugged her close. She sagged against me and her hands fell into her lap. No hug back, but it was a start. I fought back my own tears and stroked her hair.

"You're going to be okay, Tali. I promise."

"Don't want to hurt."

"We'll find a way to make it stop."

"Saints, she really *is* back," a boy said. The voice sounded familiar.

"Kione?" Lanelle gasped.

I was just as shocked to see him and more than a little worried what Tali might do when *she* did. He'd been a guard at the Healers' League, had even protected the door to the spire room Tali and the other apprentices had been kept in—the same room where Lanelle had worked. He'd grudgingly let me smuggle in pynvium chunks to save Tali and kept Lanelle out at breakfast long enough for me to heal her. He'd been even more hurt by Lanelle's treachery. I suspected for him it had been a far more personal betrayal.

Kione's eyes narrowed and his hand went for the rapier on his hip. "What is *she* doing here?"

"I'm here to help," Lanelle said softly, real sadness on her face.

"Help who? The Duke?"

Lanelle choked back a cry. "No! I want him dead as much as you do. Probably more."

That I didn't doubt.

Kione turned away from Lanelle, but I caught a flicker of pain in his eyes. "We heard folks saying the Shifter was here, that she killed some Undying." He leaned in a little more and stared into Saama's bedroom. "I guess more than one?"

"Tali killed him," Lanelle said. I cringed. Not information I wanted folks to know.

"Tali?"

Lanelle nodded. "She was—"

"Hurt badly by the Duke's men," I said quickly, shooting her a keep-your-mouth-shut look. "She's pretty upset."

Kione nodded, but he didn't look like he believed me. Or cared that I wasn't telling him the truth. "Yeah, well, the general wants to see you right away."

"Give me a minute to calm her down." Tali had stopped crying, but she still trembled.

"I'm sorry, but we don't have time. You're needed now."

Doubtful. If they knew I was here already, then they also knew why. Hard to imagine my being back was a bigger rumor than the Duke's army being on the way.

"Tali?" I pushed her curls away from her face. Still red, but her natural blond was starting to grow back, same as mine. "We have to go see someone, okay? Can you stand up?"

"Um, Nya," said Danello. "Maybe you should leave her here."

Saama shook her head. "Oh no, she's better off with her sister. Safer for everyone."

I helped Tali to her feet, biting back my anger. She'd only tried to hurt those who had hurt her or were trying to hurt us. She wasn't dangerous. Just confused and scared.

Are you willing to risk Saama's life on that?

"Where are we going?'

Kione glanced at Lanelle. "I'll take you. But not her."

"That's not fair!" she said.

"I'm not putting a known ally of the Duke's in the same room with the general. You're lucky I haven't arrested you already."

Aylin smirked. Neither Soek nor Danello came to her defense. I couldn't fault Kione for the decision.

"Stay here and rest," I told her. "You've had a rough night."

"Nya, I can be trusted, I really can." She seemed so genuine, I almost believed her.

"We'll see. For now, wait here."

We followed Kione out. Like before, people were running around with purpose in their steps. Cover nooks were being built at intersections, places where folks could hide and ambush any soldiers who got past the bridge guards.

"They got organized fast," Danello said.

Soek huffed. "I'd move fast too if the Undying were after me."

There might be enough people to fight the left-over garrison, but not the fifteen thousand soldiers the Duke was bringing. I just didn't see a way to defend against that.

We crossed the bridge to tradesmen's corner, and I spotted the hull of an overturned skiff cresting the water at the end of it, blocking the canal. The docks beyond it were well-guarded.

Tradesmen's corner had people working as well, mostly at critical shops like the butcher's and the carpenter's. Half the buildings here were brick, safer from a fire attack, but so many others would burn. Even some made of brick had wooden upper stories where the shop owner lived. Those wouldn't last long.

Kione cut across a trampled park where some

women tended a large cookfire at the center. Folks were already starting to gather around, bowls in hand, though I didn't smell any food yet. Heads turned toward us—then came the quick double takes I'd grown to hate. Fingers were pointed, words whispered. *Look, it's the Shifter!*

Curse Vyand and her reward posters. If only she hadn't nailed them up all over Geveg. Everyone seemed to recognize me. How foolish to think that just the people who wanted the bounty would remember my face.

Kione stopped at the blacksmith's. The bay doors were open, the *tink-tink clang!* of the hammers rolling out with the heat from the forge. Just a regular one, though. The League had the only pynvium forge on the isles.

We slipped inside and headed up the stairs. Windows lit the upper floor, open now to the midmorning breeze. Several tables had been pushed together, with mismatched chairs around them. One wall had maps of the city pinned to it.

So this was Ipstan's war room. Jeatar had had one like it, but with nicer furniture.

A corner door opened and a man walked in. Tall, broad shouldered, a way of moving that clearly said he was in charge and knew it. Familiar, though I couldn't quite place the face. Kione stood a little taller.

Danello leaned closer. "Doesn't he own Three Hooks Fishers?"

Of course! I'd hauled fish for his boats once or twice. He owned several and didn't sell to Baseeri. He was one of the few Gevegian businesses still *in* business and the closest thing we had to an aristocrat these days.

"So you're Nya," he said. "I've heard a lot about you."

I bet he had, and most of it was probably bad. "Don't believe every rumor you hear."

Ipstan chuckled. "The rumors I ignore, but what I hear from those I trust I believe. We heard what you did in Baseer. We know what you did here at the League. We need someone like you."

Two things I hadn't done on purpose. And two things I'd prefer never to do again.

FOURTEEN

W̶e came here to warn you the Duke's army is on the way." I hesitated, my guts squirming. "But we're not staying. No one should. Everyone should evacuate while they still can."

"Evacuate?" Kione said. "Nya, we need you. You've been back one day and already you've beaten the Undying and given us hope that they could *be* defeated. Our lookouts at Dorpstaad even told us what you did over there. We can't win without you."

My guts said Ipstan wouldn't be too pleased to hear his men talking about me like that. Even on his boats, he was a man who liked being in charge and giving orders. He was the "general," after all.

"I . . . I need to protect Tali," I said. "She's been

through too much already."

"General Ipstan's a good man," Kione said. "He knows what he's doing. He's the one who convinced us all to fight and got rid of the soldiers in the districts. You can trust him."

Aylin folded her arms. Kione wasn't the best judge of character. He'd worked for Vinnot and the Luminary, for Saints' sake.

"Easy, K." Ipstan put a hand on Kione's shoulder. "Family is important, and you can't fault a girl for sticking by hers." He turned to me. "We can start with you telling me what you know about the Duke."

I told him what Jeatar's scouts had seen and what the Undying had said about the blue-boys herding us, keeping us pinned so we'd be easy targets for the Duke's fireboats.

"So we *didn't* win?" Kione seemed crestfallen that they hadn't been the tough fighting force they'd believed.

"Of course we did," Ipstan scoffed. "We chased them out. They're just doing their best to hold what little ground they have left. Don't believe a word that blue-boy said."

I gaped. "You think he's lying?"

"We beat them. They're too scared to try to

retake the isles or they would have tried by now. All they've been doing is sending the few soldiers they have that we couldn't beat. That's changed now."

"But the tactics make sense," Danello said. "The Duke's soldiers have the native population of Geveg penned in one area of the city. You need to take this information seriously."

Ipstan's eyes narrowed. "I don't *need* to do anything. You're forgetting who's in charge around here."

"You're forgetting you have maybe a week before the Duke reaches Geveg."

Kione frowned and stepped closer, like he was all set to jump in and defend his general's honor. Danello tensed.

"Arguing about it isn't going to help Geveg," I said evenly, tugging Danello back. "We all want what's best for the city."

Kione backed down. Ipstan took a deep breath and nodded, but he scowled at Danello once more before looking back at me.

"People say you want to free Geveg, like we do," he said. "They say the Duke is trying to kill you because he knows you can destroy him. You risked your life to save our Healers, you risked your life to save your sister—surely you can take one more risk and at least hear what I have to say."

We hadn't found Danello's father yet, so I could hardly say no, especially when he made it sound so reasonable.

"I'll listen, but my friend's father is part of the resistance. They've been looking for each other for months. Could you send Kione to find him and bring him here? We can talk until they get back."

Danello gave me a grateful smile. Ipstan didn't look so pleased.

"Of course."

Danello gave Kione the name and description of his father. Ipstan pulled Kione aside and spoke to him a moment before he hurried off.

"Now where were we?" Ipstan began, taking a seat at the table and gesturing for us to do the same. "Geveg is divided by more than just who controls what isle. Not everyone wants to fight. Many insisted that fighting was going to get us all killed and we didn't stand a chance at winning. Until this morning, that is. You inspired them, Nya. They want to fight now. They believe we can win, and it's all because of you."

"They just needed to know the Undying could actually die."

He smiled at me, but it was a calculating smile.

"No, it was more than that. You're a hero to many—all of you are—and it's given them hope."

All of us? Aylin was looking at her hands, her fingers laced tightly together. Soek seemed proud and happy to be considered a hero. Danello looked skeptical. I sensed Ipstan wanted more from me than to hear him out.

"I don't know what you expect us to do," I said.

"Talk to people. In fact"—he got up from the table—"why don't you come with me and see what we're doing. See how prepared we are, how we plan to defend ourselves. You'll realize we don't need to run. We can fight back. We just need more hands to hold the weapons."

"I *am* curious," Danello said. So was I. Even Soek nodded. We all looked at Aylin.

She sighed. "I guess it wouldn't hurt to just look. We're safe here, right?"

"Safer than when the Baseeri were in control," Ipstan said.

"Okay. I'd like to see what a Gevegian army looks like too."

I held tight to Tali's hand as we followed Ipstan from building to building, house to house. My guts said he wanted me to talk to as many folks as possible now in case he couldn't convince us to stay.

The more I saw, the more I wanted to.

Ipstan and the resistance *had* been busy. Shops that had once made clothes made leather armor—chest pieces and pants, long heavy gloves, and skullcaps. Seamstresses worked on uniform tunics in dark violet. The blacksmith banged out weapons by the rackful—rapiers, swords, knives. Woodworkers sanded spears to sharp points.

"Wow, how long has this been going on?" Danello said, marveling at every house and shop.

"It started after Nya killed the Luminary and exposed what the Duke was doing to our Healers. To our *children*. We couldn't let that happen again." Ipstan turned to a group of people making boots. "Geveg for Gevegians!"

"Geveg for Gevegians!" they called back. The words were passed down the street, voice after voice picking up the cry.

"This is our city," Ipstan said. "It's time we determined our own destiny again."

"Our home is worth fighting for," I said.

Aylin looked away, biting her lip.

All three of us had said those words not long ago, sitting outside the farm of a family who'd risked everything for each other. So much had happened between that promise and now. So much lost.

How much found?

Renewed hope, like Ipstan said. Renewed purpose. The Gov-Gen was gone; a lot of Baseeri were gone. Things *had* changed. Enough to drift luck in our favor?

"What kinds of defenses are you setting up to keep the fireboats away?" If the Duke really was planning to burn us out, they would be the biggest problems. With their catapults, they could launch fire rocks without ever setting foot on land.

"We made our own fire rocks."

Impressive. Fire rocks weren't easy to make, requiring a white-hot forge and a mixture of pitch and who-knew-what-else to keep them burning. But fling one onto a boat or house, and they burst apart with a sticky flame that set everything it touched on fire. Well, everything that would burn.

"Took some doing to get enough catapults for the boats, but what we couldn't buy, we stole, and what we couldn't steal, we made."

The Duke had bigger catapults and launched fire rocks heavy enough to splatter across multiple houses. A few solid hits could destroy an entire block.

Unless our boats sank theirs before they got in range.

"What about pynvium weapons?" Aylin asked in a quiet voice, as if reluctant to show any interest. "The Duke will have a lot of those."

Ipstan grinned, but there was an edge to it. "We have something special to counter those. I think you'll be very impressed."

Ipstan took us to a warehouse where a dozen women and children sat at long tables, grinding seeds. Baskets of red-veined plants sat in the middle of the table, the pungent, earthy aroma making my nose itch.

"These are our poison makers," he said proudly. "I recruited every herb grower I could find."

Shiverfeet raced down my back. Poison. He was actually making *poison*.

"Are you insane?" Soek burst out. "Do you have any idea how deadly that is?"

"Why do you think we're using it? We need to take out soldiers as fast as we can just to survive. Blades tipped with this mixture can kill in minutes, and a well-thrown spear can hit outside the range of a pynvium flash."

Danello raised one finger. "Um, isn't that a good thing?"

"Not if someone on our side accidentally cuts themselves," Soek said, his cheeks an angry pink.

"Or someone misses and one of those spears is picked up and used against *us*."

"You can't cure poison," I added when Danello still looked confused. "It's the only ailment that ever scared my mother."

Water vipers killed their share of fishermen and leaf pullers every year. So did two kinds of spiders commonly found in crops. Both farmers and fishermen knew that a bite from any of them meant a long and painful night if they were lucky, death if they weren't.

"I know it's risky," Ipstan said, "but we'll need every advantage we can get."

Just like they'd need every weapon they could get. If he was willing to do *this*, what else was he willing to do to win? Was he also after the girl who shattered the League, crumbled the palace, broke the Undying? Was that what he *really* wanted from me?

I didn't want to be that girl.

Or that weapon.

"We're being extremely careful with the poisoned weapons, don't worry," Ipstan said, steering us out of the warehouse. "Only those trained to use them will be allowed to carry them. We'll be taking additional precautions as well, like marking them in red so it's clear which weapons are coated."

Maybe that was what the heavy leather gloves were for. A way to protect the arms and hands when you carried one of those spears.

It turned my stomach, but it would take only a few spears to make the Duke's men terrified of getting close. Seasoned troops understood pain, had little fear of it, knowing a Healer stood close by if they got hurt. But poison would make even a commander run.

"Let me show you the other warehouse." Ipstan headed for a row of buildings with multiple guards posted at all the entrances, and more on the street corners leading up to it.

"What's in there?" Aylin said.

"You'll see."

He cleared us with the guards and escorted us in. Tall shelves marked with various colors lined the room, rows and rows of them. Boxes of dry goods, baskets of fruit, bags of grains and flour. Enough food to last months. Along the walls were weapon racks. Blue for swords, green for rapiers, red for knives. Barrels of spears stood next to them. At the far end of the room near the stairs were ten wardrobes, probably for uniforms or armor.

"Where did you get all this?" I'd never seen so

much food in one spot in my life. I didn't even know Geveg *had* this much food.

"We raided some Baseeri storehouses and bought or traded for the rest. Once we had control of the farms again, we started stockpiling it. I told you we were prepared."

Even Aylin stared wide-eyed at the overwhelming amount of supplies. "Are you giving it away to whoever needs it?"

"It's for the army, so if you fight, you're taken care of." Ipstan walked past the last weapon rack and led us upstairs. "We're not letting anyone starve, even if they don't want to fight. But food isn't all we have."

The second level of the warehouse held just as many shelves and racks.

"Those shelves there are full of seeds," he said. "Those there are bulbs, and some seedlings there by the windows. We're likely to lose a lot of crops on the farming isles during the fight, and we'll need to replant."

Danello whistled. "That's thinking ahead."

"My goal is to see Geveg self-sufficient again, so we need to be ready to replace what we lose in the war." He walked between the shelves, waving a hand at objects as we passed. "Fishing nets, traps, spare sails. Yokes and plows, nails, tools. Even some pots and pans and basic bowls."

Ipstan had done a lot to prepare Geveg for survival. Saama had been wrong. The resistance wasn't a bunch of people playing soldier. They were prepared, not only to fight but to rebuild *after* the fight.

"The one thing we *are* short on is pynvium." We headed back downstairs again. "We didn't have much to begin with, and with the blue-boys in control of the League and the Baseeri in control of the Aristocrats' Isles, all the places where we could have found more are closed off to us. That pynvium armor you got for us this morning was a blessing right from the Saints, but it still won't be enough to last the whole war."

I'd never said the armor was for the resistance, and it bothered me that he'd just assumed it was his. But what did I need it for? Jeatar had all the raw ore I'd stolen from the Duke, and eventually he'd find, or Onderaan would make, a pynvium forge to smelt it.

They could really use that ore here.

Not that we had time to go get it for them.

"What about Healers?" Soek asked. "Are there enough of those?" It surprised me he might be willing to stay and fight. Verlatta was his home, and he'd come here to escape the Duke when Verlatta was under siege. I always assumed he'd go back once he could.

"There're never enough of those in war, but we have a few." He looked up and chuckled. "And there are two of them now."

Two boys around twenty stood by one of the wardrobes. The door was open, and armor pieces lined several of the shelves. One boy laughed when the other struck a pose, hands in front, fingers splayed, like he was about to pounce. It took me a moment to recognize the bracers and the chest piece.

The Undying's armor.

Tali's hand dropped from mine and she moved, fast as fright. She snatched a knife off the closest rack and lunged for the boy in the armor.

"Tali!"

Danello moved a breath later, closer to the Healers than we were. He met her before she reached them, going for the knife. She threw herself forward, right into Danello. The knife blade sank deep into his shoulder.

He cried out but didn't let go of her. They both toppled to the ground. Soek and Ipstan grabbed Tali, dragged her off. She kept kicking and swinging toward the terrified Healer, who was now up against the wall.

I jumped between him and Tali, grabbed her face and forced her to look at me. "Stop it! Calm down. Do you hear me? Calm down!"

Tali whimpered, staring at me with fear in her eyes. She still squirmed but had stopped struggling.

"Get that armor off," I said, not taking my gaze off Tali's. "Put it in the wardrobe where she can't see it."

Shuffling and thumping behind me. Nervous murmurs.

"What in Moed's name is going on?" Ipstan glared at me. Soek had let go of Tali and gone to Danello. Ipstan held her by both arms.

"She doesn't know what she's doing."

"Nya," Soek called, "something's wrong!"

"What is it?"

"Look."

I glanced over. Soek held the knife out, balanced in his palm.

Red. The hilt was painted red. The whole *rack* of knives was red.

Saints' mercy, no.

Tali had grabbed a poisoned blade.

FIFTEEN

I left Tali and dropped to Danello's side. He was unconscious, his face pale and sweaty, his breathing fast and shallow. Soek had healed the shoulder wound, but the poison was still working its way through Danello's system, eating him alive.

"Don't die, please don't die." I pressed my palm against his forehead and grabbed his hand. Felt my way in. Bright spots flared everywhere, damage I'd never even seen before. I *drew* what I could, healed what I could.

Tali started whimpering again. Ipstan cried out, then Tali crashed to the floor beside me, staring at Danello as if she knew he was in trouble.

"She bit me!" Ipstan said. "The little brat bit me."

I ignored him. Prayed she'd stay still, stay quiet, and let me save Danello from the poison every Healer said couldn't be healed.

She watched while I *drew* in another batch of the damage, this time in his lungs. It chewed through my chest and I gasped. Her gaze flicked from him to me.

"Nya, you can't help him," Soek whispered. "I know you want to but you can't."

"Yes, I can." More pain, more damage, shredding his blood, his muscles. I shoved it into the hollow space between my heart and guts. It wasn't so hollow anymore, but there was still room.

"What is going on?" Ipstan yelled, stepping into my field of vision. He sounded more scared than angry. "Why did she attack my Healers?"

I said nothing, my teeth clenched against the pain.

Aylin cleared her throat. "She, um, was kidnapped by a tracker and taken to the Duke. He turned her into an Undying and forced her to fight. To kill. Nya found her and pulled her out of the armor, but it did something to her mind. She's been . . . like *that*, ever since."

"You brought an *Undying* here?"

"I brought my sister *home*." I healed again, *drew*

again. "She needs help."

Ipstan wiped a hand across his mouth. The confidence he'd shown earlier was slipping, as if weighing whether my support was worth my crazy, murderous sister.

"You're going to need pynvium if you insist on healing him," Soek said, "and we don't have any."

"Ipstan does."

Ipstan shook his head. "We don't have enough to spare on someone who's dying."

"Bring me the armor."

Soek took a step toward it, but Ipstan grabbed his arm. "That's our armor."

"No, it's not," I snapped. "We killed the Undying, so it belongs to us. I never said you could have it. You took it from Saama without even asking us."

"I need it for the resistance. You don't need it—"

"I need it *now*."

Soek yanked his arm away and went to the wardrobe. The two Healers were still there, but they backed away.

"He's already dead," Ipstan said, though not unkindly. "You're wasting it trying to help him."

Danello's lungs were failing again. I healed them, following the poison as it ravaged his body. "I'll empty it when I'm done."

"That's not possible."

"It is for her," Aylin said.

Soek came back, a pynvium bracer in his hands.

"No." Ipstan blocked him, hands out. "I'm sorry, but I can't let you waste this when in days we'll have soldiers needing it more who *can* be saved."

"Get out of his way," Aylin said. "You're the one who decided to make those awful weapons! If you let him die, then I'll tell everyone in Geveg that if they get hurt too badly, you'll let *them* die too. That all you care about is the pynvium, just like the Duke and the Luminary."

"That's a lie! I care what happens to Gevegians."

"Prove it. Help save one."

Ipstan hesitated, looking less like a leader with every breath. "You'd better be telling the truth about emptying that." He stepped back. Soek came closer with the bracer. Tali shrieked and dived toward it, swatting it away. It flew across the room and skittered along the floor.

"Tali!" I bit back tears. *Please, Saint Saea, don't let me lose them both.*

Tali stared at Danello, then at me. She put a hand on my arm. The skin beneath her fingers tingled as she *drew*, and the pain in my guts subsided.

"Hurts," she whispered.

"That's right, it does," I said, hope bubbling past the pain in my chest. "You have to get rid of it. Can you push it into the pynvium for me? Soek, bring it back, give it to Tali."

He brought her the bracer again, but she raised her hand and recoiled. Soek backed up.

"Tali, please, use the pynvium."

Soek crouched down and slid the bracer across the floor. It stopped next to my knee. I took my hand off Danello's forehead and pressed it against the bracer. "It won't hurt you, see?"

She scooted closer and put her hand over mine. I slipped mine away and returned it to Danello. He was pale as death now, cold and clammy. The damage was everywhere, moving faster than I could heal.

I closed my eyes and dug deeper, chasing the poison down, trying to get ahead of it. Tali put her hand back on my arm and the tingling returned.

She gripped my arm tight. "Too much," she whispered.

Clothes rustled and someone sat next to me on the other side. Warm hands wrapped around my forearm. Soek's.

"Aylin, we'll need the other bracer," he said.

"I'll get it."

I expected Ipstan to object again, but he didn't say a word. The Healers in the corner murmured between themselves, their voices getting louder, like they were coming closer to watch.

I *drew*, braced against the constant flow of pain. Soek and Tali pulled it out just as quickly. I prayed as hard as I healed, everything Mama and Granny-ma had ever said about poison ringing in my ears. It can't be healed, the poisoned person can't be saved, it's impossible.

But I'd done the impossible before.

Saea willing, I could do it one more time.

We healed for hours. The sun had set, and Aylin brought lamps and food, though I wasn't able to eat. She put a cup to my lips, and I sipped fruit juice when my mouth got too dry to swallow. Three pieces of pynvium armor were piled next to us—two bracers and a greave. Soon we'd need a fourth.

Kione had arrived with Danello's father, who sat near us, his jaw set, his eyes worried, watching his son struggle to live. Ipstan was still there, and others had joined him, gathering like buzzards around a kill.

"How long can she keep this up?"

"Do you think she can save him?"

"What happens when they run out of pynvium?"

I didn't want to think about that. Soek and Tali could try keeping up with the heals while I flashed the armor, but it was taking all of us just to stay ahead of the damage. If I left, the poison would surely kill Danello before I could get back.

"You could help, you know," Aylin had told the remaining Healer somewhere after midnight. He hadn't answered her, but he'd left quickly, the disapproving glares of the others following him out the door.

More pynvium stacked up beside us, an entire suit of armor. Tali trembled, but I couldn't tell if the armor bothered her or just the exhaustion.

Ipstan left. Others arrived. Some brought candles and sang prayer songs. Saama sat with us for a while, helped in by the same two girls who'd run messages for her before. The flow of people was as constant as the flow of pain.

It was like the Duke's weapon all over again. My skin sizzled from within, my throat was raw. I had no feeling in my hands but the tingle that pricked me over and over and over.

Danello groaned, the healing no less painful for him. Probably more so since the same organs were torn and healed again and again.

The clock tower struck three, like the chimes were saying, *Let. Him. Die.*

"Maybe we should . . . I mean, he's in so much pain," his father said, struggling to get the words out. "It might be time to stop."

"No." I refused to let him die. Refused to lose one more friend.

"Nya, he's suffering. We can't do this to him anymore."

Hot tears rolls down my cheeks. "I'm not giving up on him."

Danello, stay with me. You promised you'd stay with me.

Sunrise brightened the warehouse, shafts of yellow cutting through the upper windows like knives. I squinted and turned my face away. Almost two full sets of pynvium armor sat beside us now, the final pieces in Tali's and Soek's hands.

Sweat dampened my clothes, probably all our clothes. Danello lay in a pool of it. I hurt with every breath. Shook with every exhale. I followed the poison, round and round and—

The lungs I'd been healing all night were still healed. I sensed further. So were the heart and muscles that had been shredded and repaired. The poison was fading, the worst of it around Danello's liver.

"He's . . . getting . . . better," I rasped, barely able to speak.

Danello's father sobbed, relief soothing some of the lines in his face.

I kept healing, but the damage didn't return.

By midmorning the poison was all in his liver, fighting to stay, to keep hurting, but Danello's body was finally winning. I *drew* out the last of its damage, dull now, no longer shining bright. It slid through me with hardly a sting, as if resigned to its defeat.

I kept my hands on Danello, searching, making sure it was all gone, all healed.

"We got it." He was going to be okay.

Danello opened his eyes, took a ragged breath. Still too weak to talk, but he was alive. Alive!

I hugged him as tight as my trembling arms would let me. Tali slumped to the floor with a heavy sigh and closed her eyes. Soek looked ready to drop as well. Aylin cried and clapped her hands while the rest of the watching crowed cheered.

"Thank you, Nya," Danello's father said, squeezing my hand with both of his. "I don't know how—I can't repay— Anything you ever need, you tell me. Anything."

I nodded, but I had what I needed. I hadn't lost Danello.

"Is it safe to move him?" His father ran a hand through his hair, looking a lot like his son. "I have a room not far from here where he can rest."

"Yes. I don't think he'll be able to walk for a while yet but—"

"Not a problem." He picked him up as easily as if he was Jovan or Bahari. Danello's father was a lot stronger than he looked.

"You could use some rest yourself," Aylin said. "All of you. Let me find us some rooms." She followed Danello's father toward the door.

Heads turned, watching them leave, then swiveled back to me. Most of the candles had melted to stubs, but they still flickered.

"She saved him, did you see that?"

"It's like she brought him back from the dead."

"If she fights with us, we can't possibly lose."

I sighed. That wasn't true. Nothing I did would stop the Duke's fire rocks from raining down on us. But as Grannyma used to say, running from trouble only left you too tired to deal with it when it caught you. Maybe there was something we could do to help—

"Nya!" Aylin burst through the crowd, but she

didn't looked scared, just puzzled. "You'd better come see this."

I glanced at Tali, asleep on the floor.

"I'll watch her," Soek said. "Too tired to move anyway."

"Thank you."

Aylin helped me up, and we made our way to the door, my legs shaking. The crowd parted, smiling at me and nodding.

Aylin opened the door. More people stood outside the warehouse, lining the streets on all sides. Hundreds of them. Their candles also still burned, and honeysuckle filled the air. Wreaths of it had been tossed on the ground in front of the building, like offerings to a saint.

I stepped into the sunshine. The crowd cheered and applauded.

"Just look at them all," Aylin said.

"What do they want?" Sure, it was nice *not* having people calling me names or trying to kill me, but this kind of attention came with a price. I'd lived on the streets long enough to know that.

Bells rang, the same fast, sharp clangs we'd heard yesterday morning.

Attack bells.

"More Undying?" Aylin asked as the crowd

turned, murmuring to each other but not running.

"Would they send more if two didn't come back?" I said.

Someone shouted at the far edge of the crowd. The murmurs rose to nervous chatter, and the folks on the edge took off running.

"That can't be good."

The shouting grew louder. Kione ran through the crowd. "We're under attack!" he said, finally close enough for us to make out the words. "The blue-boys are attacking in force!"

Aylin griped my arm.

"Nya!" Kione ran straight toward me. "Several hundred soldiers just crossed the bridge to the tradesmen's corner. General Ipstan's rallying a defense, but we weren't expecting this many—we're not ready for it!"

Saints! All those people.

"But what about the trap?" Aylin asked, face pale. "I thought the Duke wanted to keep us pinned and burn us out."

Kione shrugged. "That was before Nya arrived. Maybe they've changed their minds now that she's here." He turned to me. "What are you going to do?"

"Me? How am I supposed to stop a whole army?"

"Pynvium," Aylin said, eyes bright. And a little

scary. "You have two sets of armor full of pain that need to be emptied, right?"

My stomach twisted. Wear the Undying's armor? But there *was* a lot of pain there to flash. Maybe even enough to bring down those soldiers before they slaughtered everyone on the isle. "Right."

We raced back inside. The warehouse folks were gone, but others were there now, grabbing weapons off the racks and armor out of the wardrobes. Soek had pulled Tali to a corner, and both were staring at the rush of people in confusion. She'd listened to him? I said a quick prayer of thanks but didn't have time to be happier than that.

"What's going on?"

"We're under attack," Kione said, telling him about the soldiers marching toward us.

I scanned the floor for the pynvium armor. It was still where we'd left it. "Aylin, can you take Tali upstairs?" I tipped my head at the armor. I had no idea how she might react if she saw me putting it on.

"Got it." She smiled at Tali and held out a hand. "Tali, come with me, okay?"

She took Aylin's hand without a word, and my heart soared again. Maybe she'd recover after all. *If you can keep her from attacking people.*

Soon as they were out of sight, I went to the armor. I grabbed the smaller of the two chest pieces, and Soek and Kione helped me put it on. It dug into my shoulders, heavier than I'd expected. How had Tali worn one of these things?

"Um, I don't think that fits," Soek said. The armor hung on me. "Can you even walk in it?"

I tried. The chest piece slid on my shoulders and dragged me sideways. "Not well."

"You can't do this by yourself," Soek said. "Not without armor."

"What choice do I have?"

"Let me go with you. I'll wear it."

"Soek, it's too—"

"That set will fit me. You'll need protection out there, and I can heal us if"—he gulped—"*when* we get hurt and give you time to get deep enough into the soldiers to catch them all in one flash."

He clearly didn't want to do this any more than I did, but he was right. What good was all this pain if I couldn't get it close enough to reach them all?

"Together then." I went to the wardrobes where the leather armor was stored. It wouldn't stop every blade, but it was better than nothing. "Kione," I said, sweat already dampening my skin, "like her or not, you'd better get Lanelle. If we're going to survive this, we're going to need all the Healers we can get."

"It sounds bad up there," Soek said on the way to the tradesmen's corner. A cord bound our hands together and they trembled as one. We couldn't risk being separated.

Shouts ahead. Metal hit metal, bodies hit stone. I couldn't see much, but it sounded like Ipstan had gotten some of his army together and had met the blue-boys near the bridge. More shouts, warnings, alerts. A horn blew, a single clear note in the morning air.

Fear had chased away some of my exhaustion but the reprieve wouldn't last. Neither of us had the strength to fight for long. If we stumbled or fell and couldn't get back up . . .

I never even got to tell Danello good-bye.

Our soldiers appeared ahead, outnumbered but holding up for now. The fighting split, and a small corridor big enough for Soek and me opened up between the soldiers.

"Run!" I burst forward with Soek, our arms and legs pumping together. We ran toward the narrow opening, the best hope we had of getting past the outer fringes and deep into the attacking force.

We dodged past our people and skirted around a group of theirs. The soldiers ignored us at first, Soek's blue armor disguising us in all the confusion. Then a soldier noticed us, realized we weren't on their side. He thrust his blade at me. I ducked left and it glanced off Soek's armor. A second blade pierced my shoulder, cutting right through the leather, tearing through flesh. My hand tingled and the pain was gone, drawn through my fingers into Soek's.

More soldiers charged at us. I swung Soek around hard, slamming him into a pair of women on our right. He tucked his shoulders, banging against them with the heavy back of his chest plate. The soldiers went flying.

We kept running.

Men with swords closed in fast. Blades came from every angle, stabbing, slicing, jabbing. Pain flowed from me to Soek so fast, my hand stung as if I'd been flashed. My lungs hurt, still raw from healing Danello all night.

We're not going to make it.

A soldier tackled Soek. He went down, dragging me with him. My arm twisted and cracked, and fresh pain shot through me. I flung my other hand across the soldier's back, grabbed his hair, and pressed my fingers against his scalp. I *pushed* and he jerked away screaming, cradling his arm. I scrambled to my feet and hauled Soek up with me.

We kept running, kept bleeding, kept healing. Step by step. Soldier by soldier.

A man shouted orders, his voice deep and oddly beautiful. For the strangest of moments, I wondered if he sang.

A wall of soldiers turned toward us, one in chain-mail armor, with silver commander's marks on his collar. More soldiers were behind him, so thick I couldn't see anything but shadowy blue and steel.

I spun and flattened my hand against Soek's armor. He tensed and squeezed his eyes shut.

WHOOMP! Whoomp! WHOOMP! Whoomp! WHOOMP!

Five bright stings in a row—the chest plate, plus all the other pieces I hadn't even touched. A ring of soldiers ten men deep around us screamed and collapsed. The ones past them tripped and toppled over their bodies. Angry shouts became confused cries. I sank to the street as Soek fell, knocked out by my flash, the skin on his face red. Under the screams, softer sounds reached me, more felt than heard—

Whoomp—whoomp, whoomp whoomp . . .

More flashes, but not aimed at me. People screamed, and beneath the screams, a chain of soft thuds one right after the other. More flashes. From what?

Who cares? Move!

I *drew* in Soek's pain. His face cleared, his eyes opened. I gave him a moment to get his bearings, then yanked him to his feet.

Flashing still rippled away from me like rings on a lake, jumping from soldier to soldier.

And then it was silent.

SIXTEEN

Soek and I clung to each other, swaying from pain and shock.

"Sweet Saea, what did you do?" he asked, gaping at the unconscious soldiers on the street all around us. Hundreds of them. The streets were eerily quiet.

"I have no idea."

"But you *did* something."

The pynvium just, I don't know, chain flashed? Jumping from piece to piece, each flash triggering the next pynvium piece it touched?

But that was impossible.

Soek wiped the sweat off his upper lip. "What do we do now?"

"I . . ." I had no answer for that either. Our people

were also unconscious, lying next to the soldiers on the street.

We needed to move, to act, to do *anything*, but I couldn't stop staring.

"You do realize you took out an army by yourself," Soek said, awed. "Two if you count ours."

Not the full army. Our people were starting to move forward, hazy forms at the end of the flash range. But Soek was right. I shouldn't have been able to flash so much so far. Pynvium had specific triggers to make it flash—it *couldn't* do what it just did.

Only it had.

I walked to the commander. Knelt down and rifled through his pockets. I pulled out a pynvium orb the size of a walnut.

"They had pynvium on them." Personal healing orbs. How many soldiers had them? Officers only, perhaps, but enough orbs to keep triggering from one to the next. They couldn't have all been for healing or they would have been empty. Were some carrying weapons?

"Nya, you are amazing."

I didn't want to be amazing. Who else would want to use me or kill me because of this? I felt more like the abomination the Duke claimed all unusual

241

Takers were. Worse than anything he and Vinnot had tried to make—

He pumped them full of pain to see if they developed unusual abilities. . . .

Wait, is that how it happened? *When* it happened? Vinnot's twisted experiments had proven that pain brought out unusual abilities. He'd pumped *me* full of pain when he'd connected me to that horrible glyphed pynvium device and cycled the pain of dozens and dozens through me for hours.

"We need to get our side awake," I said, bile stinging the back of my throat. "The main flash was strong enough to keep the soldiers at the center unconscious for a while, but the soldiers on the edges probably won't be down long."

Soek held up our still-tied hands. "Be easier with two hands."

I grabbed my knife and sawed through the cord. Soon as our hands were free, we ran from person to person. Kione was sprawled across a Baseeri soldier, his arms cut and bleeding. I knelt and grabbed his hand, *drew* in the flashed pain and healed the wounds he'd taken.

"Wha?" He rolled up, his hand flapping around, probably looking for his sword.

"You were knocked out by the flash."

"What flash?" He got to his feet, looking around

at the bodies as if trying to figure out what had happened.

I found Ipstan in the pile of bodies and Soek healed him. It took him a little longer to clear his head; then he gaped at the soldiers around us.

"What happened?"

"I flashed Soek's armor." I'd have preferred not to admit that, but trying to hide it would be foolish. People were running toward us even now, and some of them had to have been close enough to see what I'd done.

"*You* did this?"

"It flashed stronger than I thought it was going to."

Ipstan got to his feet, excitement on his face. "Get our people moving. We can't waste this opportunity."

I winced. I wasn't an opportunity.

Soek and I ran from person to person, *drawing* away injuries and flashed pain as fast as we could. He paused every dozen and reached for my hand, healing me and shoving that pain back into his armor.

Slowly the resistance rose. Ipstan shouted orders, sending people among the unconscious soldiers. I kept my gaze on the people who still needed healing, trying not to hear the distinctive sounds of swords into flesh behind me.

It's war. You have to kill in a war.

243

Resistance members were looting the pynvium of the blue-boys on the ground. The two other Healers were getting folks back on their feet. Not everyone woke up. Not everyone could be healed.

Some of the faces were red like Soek's had been, like those in the Duke's palace had been when I'd flashed the weapon. But they'd been blocks away from the main flash. They shouldn't have been affected at all, let alone this badly.

Now that Ipstan realized what I had done—what I *could* do—he'd want to lead every battle with me. Throw me into soldiers and blades and pain. He wouldn't want me to leave.

The other Healers pushed their pain into Soek's armor, more for me to flash when the blue-boys regrouped and came at us again. He went with them to treat the last of the wounded.

I dropped onto the front step of an abandoned bakery, too exhausted to take another step. Shame it wasn't open. Food would be good. Almost as good as sleep. Men and women flowed past me, calling out thanks, cheering, stopping to shake my hand or pat my shoulder.

Aylin found me, Tali trailing behind her.

"Are you okay?" She ran a hand over my armor, but most of the blood had been blasted away in the pain flash. Bits remained, trapped between cuts in the leather.

"Tired." It was hard to speak, like my tongue was too big for my mouth. "How's Tali?"

"She's fine. Well, fine for her." Aylin cocked her head and looked at me. "You don't look so good. You don't have any injuries you forgot to heal, do you?"

"No, I'm—"

"Nya!" Ipstan ran toward me, waving his arms around and giving orders to those he passed on the way. "That was incredible! Do you have any idea what this means? We can beat them, *really* beat them."

"A few soldiers maybe," I said, but my words sounded wrong. "They're not the problem. We have to prepare for the Duke."

"I don't—" Ipstan made a face and turned to Aylin. "What's wrong with her? Should I call over a Healer?"

Aylin dropped to a knee in front of me and took my face in her hands. "We need to get her . . ."

Her voice faded away with the rest of the street.

I woke to singing.

At first I thought I'd died and was being welcomed into the afterlife, but the smell of bacon

245

chased that idea away. I doubted they had bacon in the afterlife. Or cinnamon muffins, though the really good ones were at least a possibility.

I sat up. Typical boardinghouse walls surrounded me, a decent-size window—which was open—and a bed that wasn't very comfortable. Voices drifted in from outside, more prayer songs, saying farewell to those who'd died.

"Feeling better?" Aylin was sitting on one of the small chairs around an even smaller table. A slice of bacon dangled from her fingers. A plate of it sat in front of her.

"I think so." I stretched, wincing. Last time I'd felt this worn down, I'd spent three days hauling crab traps out of the lake. But it was still better than I'd felt last night.

Last night. Poison and soldiers and too many friends in trouble.

"Where's Danello? Is he okay?"

"He's fine. About like you, actually."

Thank the Saints. I wouldn't stop worrying until I saw for myself, but breakfast would go down a little easier now.

"Hungry?"

"Starving." I swung my legs over the edge of the bed, and my toes thumped something warm. Tali squeaked and popped up from the floor like some deranged toy.

"Tali! Oh Saints, I'm sorry."

She rubbed her shoulder and glared at me, seeming like her old self. The moment was gone just as quickly, but she did turn and look over at Aylin. "Hungry," she said.

I smiled. Asking for something had to be a good sign. It might not be laughing and talking, but it was a start.

"Plenty of food over here." Aylin set a muffin in front of a chair. "Come help yourself. Both of you."

Tali took the muffin but not the chair. She sat under the window, the sunlight warming the back of her neck. My throat caught. I pictured her sitting on the edge of her bed not long ago, dressed in her Healer's apprentice uniform. A sunbeam had shone over her then too.

"Where's the enchanter's book?" I asked, heart racing. If we'd lost it . . .

Aylin patted something by her feet. "I have it right here, along with the gems and pynvium strips. And that creepy cylinder." She shuddered. "I'm not letting any of it out of my sight."

"Thank you." I took a seat at the table and a handful of bacon. "Any news about the attack?"

She shook her head. "Not much. No one else has tried to cross the bridges. Ipstan's people have been dealing with the bodies since yesterday."

"Yesterday?" I muttered around a mouthful of bacon. "How long was I asleep?"

"About twenty-two hours. Soek too, though I think he woke up around dawn."

I glanced at the window. Midmorning light, same as it was yesterday when the attack bells had rung. I'd lost a whole day.

Wind gusted and the singing grew louder for a moment.

"Can we go ask Ipstan if he can arrange a boat to the shore?" Aylin said. "If we leave before lunch, I bet we can still make it to Veilig before Onderaan leaves. We can afford to hire a carriage now."

I chewed slowly. The sister in me wanted to leave and keep Tali safe, just like I'd promised. But the daughter—the one whose parents had fought to defend Geveg—wanted to stay. Whatever I'd done yesterday had worked. I still had no idea how I'd done it, but it was a better defense than poisoned spears.

"Onderaan might have already left. It's been what—five days since we left the farm? Veilig is only a few days from there. Maybe it's better if we stay for now."

But you promised to leave.

She shook her head. "I'm sure he hasn't left yet. It would have taken a while to get everyone settled, and then he'd need supplies and everything."

"Maybe, but—"

"Ipstan had someone bring us some clean clothes. Was nice of him, wasn't it?"

She went to a basket by the door and tossed me a faded pair of pants and light shirt. She pulled out two more sets just like it.

"Pretty," said Tali. "So many flowers."

Aylin and I turned toward the window. Tali leaned on the windowsill, chin in her hand, staring down at the street.

"What flowers?" I hurried over, eager to see what had brought her a step further out of her shell.

Aylin nudged in next to me. "What is it?"

People lined the street again, just like when Danello was hurt. Some carried wreaths of white violets—symbols of Saint Moed, courage, and protection. Others held candles, flickering in a light sun shower. The fine mist sparkled in the sun as it fell.

"I thought you said Danello was better."

"He is. They can't be here for him—he's not in this building," Aylin said. "He's with his da over on Mangrove. Maybe they're worried about you. You did collapse right in front of a lot of people."

"We should tell them I'm alive and well then." Not that I wanted to go out there. It would be worse than the people last night. The ones who'd watched me heal Danello. *"We can't lose if she's with us."*

What must they think now?

And what will they think when you leave?

I couldn't face that, not yet. "Right after we finish breakfast."

I stepped onto the street and people . . . cheered? I nearly tripped over a pile of wreaths.

"The Hero of Tradesmen's Corner!"

They cheered again, and some tossed flowers at me. More white violets.

"We're ready to strike back."

"May the Saints bless and keep you!"

"We're with you, Nya!"

So many smiles, so many people reaching for me. Light touches on my arms and back as we moved through the crowd. They parted in front of me, closed in behind me. I felt like an island in a lake of reverence.

I gripped Tali's hand tighter, but she seemed more curious than wary, probably won over by the flowers. Tali loved violets of all kinds. Just like Mama.

"What are you going to do now?" a man asked.

"Uh, go see a friend." I wanted to check on Danello, make sure he was okay.

"Do you think we can beat the Duke?"

They were asking *me* that? "I do, if we all work together."

"How are you going to beat him?"

It was a real question, not someone whining about how he was too strong or too powerful to beat. They wanted to know what I was going to do. Like I had the answers.

"I'm working on that; so is Ipstan. We'll figure something out."

"We're behind you—just say the word."

"Thank you, everyone, really. We have to be going now." I waved at the crowd and they cheered again. It was strange, all those folks looking to me for help. No insults, no threats. What had changed their minds? The healing, the soldiers, or both?

The crowd followed us through the misty rain, continuing to call out their support, ask what I planned to do next. By the time we got to Danello's, my nerves were as tight as my curls.

"Okay, listen," I said, turning around and facing

them. "I appreciate your, um, support, I really do, but the Duke is on his way, and we need to prepare for his attack. You should all be doing whatever needs to be done there, not following me around."

They nodded but didn't leave.

"Go ask Ipstan what he needs you to do," I said.

"Will you be there?" someone called.

"After I see how my friend is doing."

Smiles broke out on many faces, heads bobbed, whispers wandered through the crowd. A woman at the front turned around and clapped her hands several times. "Everyone to the square. Wait there for Nya's instructions."

"What? No that's—"

Aylin put a hand on my arm. "Let them go."

"But they misunderstood."

"And they'll figure that out when Ipstan tells them what to do next." She flipped her frizzy bangs off her face. "Unless you don't want them to leave?"

I twitched. "No, leaving's good. Much better than staying."

We headed inside the boardinghouse and hurried up the stairs. I tried not to notice the old bloodstains on the landing. Or the gouges in the wall no one had sanded out yet. Aylin went to a door halfway down the hall and knocked. Danello's father answered.

"Oh good, he was just about to go find you." He stepped aside and let us in. "I told him you both needed to rest, but he was up with the sun."

More flowers sat on the table, but no white violets. Hibiscus, honeysuckle, a few hyacinths. Baskets of food filled the spaces between the flowers.

Danello cupped my cheeks and pulled me in for a kiss. He ended it far too soon. "Are you okay?"

"I was going to ask you that."

"I'm fine, thanks to you." He grinned. "That makes what? Twice you've saved my life?"

I blushed. "I'm not keeping track."

"Well I am." He thumped my nose with one finger.

Danello's father cleared his throat, and my cheeks warmed again. "Danello tells me you're all leaving?"

Aylin sighed. "We were until Nya became the patron saint of Geveg. Now I'm not so sure."

"I'm not—" I took a deep breath. "There was a crowd of people outside, waiting for us."

"For *you*," Aylin said.

"Fine, yes, for me. It's just a misunderstanding, and Ipstan will straighten it all out, but they seem to think I can do something about the Duke and they're waiting for me to tell them what that is."

Danello shrugged. "So tell them."

"But I don't *have* a plan."

"You always have a plan." He glanced at his father, who looked apprehensive. "Nya, people have been coming by since yesterday, dropping off gifts and telling me what you did—both for me and for Geveg. You can't leave them now."

"But *you* can," his father told him. "Your brothers and sister need you."

"No, we all leave together," Aylin said. "*That* was the plan."

"That was before Nya gave everyone hope that we could win. If she leaves now, that hope goes with her."

"So let her stay and you go," his father tried again. "We can't both risk our lives."

"Da, I can't. You never believed in this fight. Ma did, and now so do I. You should go to Halima and the twins. Take Aylin with you, but I'm staying here." He smiled at me. "I made a promise."

I warmed down to my toes. But I'd made a promise too. That I'd protect Tali and keep her safe, and I couldn't do that here. Still, I also couldn't leave when folks were so close to standing up for themselves. They wanted to fight—they were just looking for someone to lead them. No, they had that. Like Ipstan said, they needed someone to inspire them.

We'd never be safe as long as the Duke ruled. To save Tali and all the other families, I had to help stop him. I didn't know what I was—quirker or Saint touched—but I had a weapon that we needed most.

Hope.

Jeatar once said faith was no match for steel, but maybe *hope* was.

"Onderaan is going to meet me in Analov Park at sunset tomorrow," I said, taking Danello's hand. "Master del'Sebore, Aylin—you both can go with him and Tali to Veilig. Jeatar will help you."

They both disagreed at once, talking over each other.

"I can't leave you here."

"We're supposed to stay together."

"This is our last chance," I said. "If we beat the Duke, we win back the entire Three Territories, not just Geveg. Even Baseer will be free again."

Danello's father shook his head. "What if we lose?"

"Then the Duke will destroy Geveg and claim our pynvium mines for himself. He'll have so much, he'll be able to build an army of Undying and make sure there's no one left in the Territories who will ever oppose him again."

Aylin looked away. Danello's father didn't.

"Is stopping him worth our lives?" he asked.

"It's worth mine. You'll have to decide if it's worth yours on your own."

He hesitated. "Then I'd better make up my mind by sundown tomorrow."

SEVENTEEN

I guess they found Ipstan." The crowd was outside the blacksmith's shop, circled around him, passing his words back to those too far away to hear.

"That's a lot of people," Danello said.

Maybe a thousand, filling every street leading to the plaza and the fountain Ipstan was standing on. The rain still misted, but the sun had dipped behind the clouds.

"We struck a blow to the blue-boys," a girl called back, and others repeated it through the crowd. "Now is our chance to stop them," she said next.

"Stop them?" Aylin said. "Does he even know how many there are?"

"I don't know what he knows."

"Armor and weapons for those willing to fight," the girl said. Then she gasped, her gaze stopping on me. "It's Nya!"

The word runners started to send that back until folks around me cheered. Rapt faces turned from Ipstan to me.

"Are you leading the attack?"

"Do you need us or can you take them all on your own?" Folks laughed, but not at me. They laughed as if I actually *could* take on the blue-boys by myself.

"Are you going to cause another Great Flash?"

Oh no, not another sainter. They probably thought what I'd done yesterday was a Great Flash too. Like I could just command the sky to open up and rain down pain.

"Ipstan's the one in charge, not me," I said, but they were asking so many questions, my voice didn't carry far. "I need to get to Ipstan!"

"Get her to the general!" bounced through the crowd. Hands reached out and I was moving, half dragged, half carried from person to person. Tali's hand slipped from mine. My chest tightened. *If she thinks I'm in danger . . .*

Aylin caught her, slipping an arm around her and hurrying along behind me while the crowd swept me forward. Tali watched, her face flickering between delight and concern. I smiled, praying it looked like I was having fun and was in no danger at all.

I reached the fountain and was thumped onto the stone next to Ipstan with a shove. Ipstan steadied me before I toppled over the edge and into the fountain itself.

The cheers started again, probably loud enough to be heard all the way at the League. It worried me for a moment, but after losing the attack yesterday and then hearing us cheer today, the cheers might actually make the *blue-boys* worry.

"What do we do, Nya?" a man cried.

"When do we take them on?"

"We're with you, Shifter!"

Ipstan looked at me in almost the same worry-or-joy way Tali had. He scanned the crowd, larger than I'd realized now that I was higher and could see. There had to be well over a thousand people, and all looking to me to do something.

Well, I'd done what Ipstan had hoped. I'd gotten them looking. It was up to him now to tell them what to do. "So? What do we do next?" I asked.

"Collect your gear," he shouted, another uncertain glance my way. "Your squad assignments will be decided within the hour."

"Is Nya leading the attack?"

His smile twitched. "She'll work with me and my officers on strategy. Don't worry, she'll be instrumental in our attack and our victory!" He grabbed my hand and raised it in the air. "Together we will stop those blue-boys and make Geveg safe again!"

The crowd went wild, stamping their feet, waving their arms, cheering. Ipstan kept hold of my hand and pulled me off the fountain and toward the blacksmith's. Men and women in chain-mail armor lined the walk to the door. His officers? Surely they weren't his guards.

"I'm glad you decided to help us," Ipstan said once we were inside.

"My friends and sister were behind me. I can't—"

"They'll be brought in, don't worry." He gestured at one of the folks in chain mail. "People really respond to you."

"They were there when I woke up. I had nothing to do with it."

"You inspired them." He pushed open another door and we headed upstairs. "I tried, but I couldn't bring them together like you have. We stand a chance now, a good one."

"What's the plan?"

"Take back the League. We can do it if we act tonight." Ipstan stood at the head of the table.

His officers took places around him, eyes shining, excited. "There's a big storm coming in, and we can use it as cover. Get right up against the League before they even know we're there."

"What about the bridge guards?" his commander asked. I hadn't caught his name, but I was pretty sure he'd worked on one of Ipstan's fishing boats. "They have both Upper and Lower Grand Isles protected, and we can't reach the League without taking one or both of those."

"Nya can deal with them."

"They'll be expecting that," I said, trying not to imagine the new scars or the pain. Did I really need to go in first? Where was Danello? He understood military strategy better than I did, and this plan didn't sound all that safe. "They won't let me get that close again."

Ipstan shook his head. "No one survived yesterday's attack. They don't know what you did. If we're *really* lucky, with all the rain and confusion, they won't even see you."

That seemed like a lot of luck to rely on. But hadn't I relied on less?

"What did we find out about their pynvium weapons?" a woman with spiky blond hair asked.

"I don't think they have any left. Nya's the only

one who's flashed any pain in weeks."

I frowned. "What about those orbs the blue-boys had?"

"They're out by now."

I wasn't so sure, but Ipstan's officers didn't seem to care.

"Numbers?"

"Minimal on the bridge, under a dozen. A few hundred on the isle itself, the rest in and around the League. Best estimates on the remaining garrison say five hundred total."

"That's all?" I said. "The Gov-Gen's garrison had been ten times that before. What happened to the rest of his—"

Danello and the others walked into the room. Ipstan rubbed his hands together. "Wonderful, everyone's here. Now, this is what we're going to do. . . ."

Rain splattered against the windows, tap-tap-tapping like tiny feet scurrying across the glass. I adjusted my armor—leather like most folks in the resistance wore. Ipstan had offered me one of the few sets of chain mail, but it was hard to walk in it. I couldn't fight if I couldn't stand. I asked him to give it to Danello instead.

Ipstan had organized his squad leaders and

grouped everyone up hours ago. He'd handed out weapons and armor at sunset, created a chain of command. Not everyone knew every detail of his plan, but his officers and squad leaders knew where to be and when.

The storm hit just as he'd hoped, heavy wind and rain but no lightning to pick us out in its sudden brightness. Gray light reflected off gray rain, everything washed out in the twilight.

I turned to Soek, back in the pynvium armor. The second set didn't fit him nearly as well, but he'd added extra padding to fill in the gaps. "We're crazy for trying this, right?" I asked.

He nodded. "Nuttier than pecan pudding."

"That's what I thought."

Danello squeezed my hand, but he looked worried. The storm would hide us like Ipstan said, but the rain also made it hard for *us* to see. What if he was wrong about the numbers? What if the defense was tighter? What if what if what if . . . It rattled through my mind like the rain on the glass.

We waited in the staging area, a wide strip of warehouses behind a row of workshops. Ipstan had decided to attack Lower Grand Isle, claiming the upper isle would be more heavily guarded since that's where yesterday's attack on us had come from.

He'd posted extra guards and soldiers there to distract the blue-boys and make them think we were planning to defend that area. After all the noise this afternoon, they had to suspect something was up.

The door opened and Kione walked in. Water gusted in behind him.

"Slight change of plans," he said, expression grim. "We got a better look at the area beyond the barricades. It looks like there's a command tent a few blocks past the bridge, in the square that intersects the main roads. If you can reach that, you might be able to take out their command staff."

I knew the square he meant. Day vendors set up carts there in the summer, and street performers danced and sang for coins.

"The general wants to clear the way through for you and Soek."

"Ipstan's leading the attack?"

"He insisted." Kione glanced around and leaned close. "Said he wanted to fight alongside you. That it would be good for morale for the troops to see you two together."

And good for his reputation.

Danello raised an eyebrow. "Really?"

"Yeah. Everyone's excited about it."

We had hope and faith in buckets. Steel now,

too. Ipstan was confident, but I wasn't so sure. You didn't just hand someone a sword and expect them to know how to use it.

"Soon as you break through," Kione continued, "the rest of us will cross the bridge, secure the area, and wait for you to clear out the square before moving in. We'll work outward from there, secure the bridge to League Circle, and prepare for the final assault on the League."

"Okay."

"When you hear the quarter-bell chime, head out to the rally point." Kione wished us luck and headed back out.

"You can do this," Danello said softly. He and his da were in one of the rear squads. Danello had wanted to join Ipstan's squad, but I'd made Ipstan promise to keep Danello back. He had the right to fight same as the rest of us, I just didn't want him on the front lines doing it. Not unless I could be there to watch his back. And his front. Saints, all sides of him.

"I'm scared," I said. So much pain waited for us—for me.

"You have six hundred people standing right behind you. Including me."

All stuffed into buildings and hidden in alleys

between here and the Lower Grand Isle bridge. They wanted what we wanted and were willing to die to get it. If they could risk their lives, I could risk some scars.

The tower chimed and we headed toward the street perpendicular to the bridge. People stepped aside and let us pass, their faces frightened, hopeful, far too eager.

Ipstan stood in the rain with his command staff; all of them wore a white violet patch on their armor that hadn't been there earlier. He nodded a greeting.

"The weather is helping us out. Our people are prepared and ready," he said, then turned to me and Soek. "Now it's up to you two." He pulled out a silk cord.

Soek held out his hand and I took it, lacing my fingers through his. Ipstan tied the cord around our wrists, tight enough to keep us from yanking free, but not so tight it hurt.

"Three blocks," Ipstan said. His face was stone-still, but his eyes held fear despite his confident speeches. "Do whatever you have to do to make it to that command post. We'll be right behind you."

Three blocks. Through soldiers and barricades and an awful lot of pain.

Danello took my hand, ran his thumb across my

knuckles. "Don't die," he said, regret in his eyes.

"I won't if you won't."

"Deal."

Ipstan and the white violet squad moved out toward the bridge. Soek walked beside me, his pynvium armor gray in the downpour, like everything else. We moved across the bridge, the rain masking our footsteps and any clinks of our armor.

Though we couldn't see them yet, scouts had sketched out where the blue-boys were hunkered down behind barricades on the other side. Twelve of them.

Ipstan gave the order and his squad charged, a wall of steel and anger rolling across the bridge. Soek and I followed, waiting for a break in the fighting to slip through. We crested the bridge as Ipstan and the others hit the barricades.

Whoomp! Whoomp! Whoomp!

Flashes washed over me, prickling my skin one right after the other. Ipstan was wrong! The blue-boys *did* still have pynvium weapons! Soek staggered and fell against me, but caught himself and stayed upright. Ipstan and the others cried out and dropped, slamming against the stone bridge. I tugged Soek faster. We had to get in range before the soldiers reached our people lying helpless on the bridge. It wasn't the command tent, but maybe they had more pynvium and the flash would trigger all the way there anyway.

We reached Ipstan and the others. I turned and slapped my hand against Soek's chest plate. Pictured dandelions blowing in the wind.

WHOOMP! Whoomp! WHOOMP! Whoomp! WHOOMP!

The bridge soldiers screamed and dropped, but no echoing pynvium thumped in the distance.

I *drew* Soek's pain away and his eyes snapped open. He scrambled to his feet without a word. We knelt as one, and each grabbed one of the unconscious officers. We *drew* and they jerked awake.

A horn sounded and another answered it.

"Was that ours?" Soek asked.

"No." My stomach churned. "Heal faster."

Boot stomps shook the bridge behind us, our people moving forward, expecting us to have secured the bridge and cleared the square, unable to see in the rain that we hadn't. Shadows moved in front of us, becoming soldiers as they closed in.

So many soldiers.

Ipstan hollered orders and his squad attacked. "Nya, flash it!"

I had nothing left to flash. Nothing to use but my hands and whatever pain the blue-boys gave me. I pulled Soek into the approaching army, dread coursing through me. "Get ready to heal."

Two soldiers charged. I braced myself and stepped into them, catching their blades in my shoulder and side. Pain cut as skin cut. My hand tingled and it was gone.

I feigned a stumble and the soldiers came at me again. Stings from their swords, and Soek pulled it away. I spun, put a hand on the pynvium.

Whoomp!

No chain of flashes, but enough to make five or six soldiers scream and fall. Our people took advantage of the distraction.

More, I need more.

Bodies slammed against me, blades pierced my skin. Soek filled his chest piece with their pain and I flashed it, taking out as many as we could before they got to our people.

"Ipstan's in trouble!" Soek cried, pointing.

Ipstan fought twenty feet away, fending off men who seemed to be taunting him, pricking him with the tips of their rapiers like cats with claws. The thin blades slid between the links of his chain mail. I headed for them, weaving as if injured, luring in attacks.

I was almost to Ipstan. Soek's armor was full of fresh pain. Ipstan darted for a small opening in the circle. A soldier moved faster, stabbing him once—twice—three times before he even had a chance to fall.

Soek leaped forward into the circle, dragging me along with him. My hand hit his armor before my feet hit the street.

whoomp

A small sting, less than it should have been. Grit poured through my fingers as the pynvium chest piece crumbled to fine sand.

Saea, no, I flashed it too much.

"Nya?" Soek gaped at me, terrified.

"Run!"

The soldiers closed on us, thrusting their rapiers. I tried to take what I could but there were too many. Soek dodged and screamed. He stumbled sideways, blood speckling his lips.

"Soek!"

The soldier yanked the rapier out of Soek's chest and he collapsed, dragging me down with him. I struggled, flat on my stomach, my arm pinned beneath his body. I pressed my fingers against his head and felt my way in. *Please, Saint Saea, let him still be alive.*

Nothing. He was gone.

His heart. It pierced his heart.

Tears blinded me. I blinked hard, wiped my eyes with my free hand. *Cry later, but now you'd better move!* I rolled right, sliding my arm out from under him. I rose and was jerked back to my knees. Our hands were still tied together. My knife, I needed my knife.

A shadow fell over me. The soldier who'd killed Soek sneered, his friends circling in behind him. I scanned his body for bare skin, but he wore armor on everything but his face.

Something moved beside me, lunging past me. Armor clinked, steel met steel, and the soldier staggered back.

Danello!

More of our people appeared, leaping over me and skirting around those who had fallen. They crashed against the wave of blue-boys, swords flying, people dying.

Danello grabbed my shoulders. "Nya, come on," he cried over the shouts and screams of the fight.

"Soek!"

"Is he alive?"

I shook my head, trying to saw through the silken cord, but it wouldn't cut.

Danello took the knife and sliced the cord in one quick jerk. He hauled me to my feet, pulled me away from Soek, so still and pale on the bridge. Dragged me toward the safety of our people on the other side.

I stumbled, thumping off bodies as we passed, Danello's arm tight around my waist. I clung to him, shaking, hurting, my heart sputtering like a bird in my chest. Cold hands, hot face.

Another friend dead. Too many sacrifices.

My head spun, the street closing in around me. I couldn't get enough air. I tipped sideways against Danello, gasping.

"Breathe," he said, hand on my back. "Take a breath, that's it—no, slow down, breathe deep."

Soek was dead. Quenji was dead. Mama, Papa, Grannyma—all of them—dead.

More horns blew—two short blasts. Our order to retreat.

The rain continued to fall, turning dirt to mud and streets to rivers. I sat on the floor of a boardinghouse room not far from Aylin's old building. Danello and Aylin sat with me, though no one else had joined us. One lamp sat in the corner, the flame turned low. Danello held me while I cried.

"You need to get out of that armor," Aylin said gently when I was too spent to cry anymore.

I shook my head. I didn't want to see what was underneath it.

"Nya?"

I kept staring at nothing. When I closed my eyes, I saw Soek; when I looked at the others, I saw the fear. I couldn't bear to look at either.

"Danello, help me with this, would you?" Aylin tugged and lifted and together they pulled the armor over my head and set it on the floor.

Aylin gasped and pressed her fingers against her lips. "Oh, Nya."

I didn't look down. No point.

"Are those hives?" She reached toward my arm, then stopped. "You have bumps all over."

"Scars," I said. "They're scars." Every sword tip, every cut, healed so fast there hadn't been time to avoid them. They'd all left their mark. And it had been for nothing.

Kione entered the room. He shut the door and stood there, dripping.

"Ipstan's dead."

I closed my eyes. Saw Soek's face. Opened them again.

"Most of his officers, too. We've pulled back, but it's a mess out there. Can't see in all this rain, which is lucky for us. They won't attack tonight. Tomorrow? Who knows?" He sighed. "Nya, what happened? Why didn't you—"

"It's not her fault," Danello said.

"I'm not saying it is, but she was supposed to flash the armor at the soldiers."

"They were waiting for us," I said, throat tight. "They knew we were coming—that *I* was coming—and they were ready." Nothing else explained the lightly guarded bridge, the pynvium weapons, the sudden ambush of soldiers. It was a trap. And we'd fallen into it.

"How many did we lose?" Aylin asked quietly.

"A third, maybe a little more. Would have been twice that if the bridge hadn't gotten clogged with bodies. Folks couldn't get across to join the fight."

I twitched. All those lives, gone.

"People are talking about running. No one knows what to do. I was hoping Nya had an idea."

They all looked at me. I shook my head. Running sounded good to me.

"She might later," Danello said. "She needs rest right now."

"Yeah, sure, I understand." Kione paused in the doorway, and a fresh gust of hot, wet air blew across my face. "Get some rest."

How could I rest when I couldn't even close my eyes?

EIGHTEEN

Pale light cut through the window, draining the color out of the already worn carpet. At some point I'd fallen asleep, but nightmares had woken me long before dawn. I'd been standing at the window for hours.

Bedraggled men and women walked past, shoulders tense, jaws set. I'd seen those same faces years ago when Tali and I hid under bushes, crying. People who'd been thrown out of their homes, same as we were. Scowls that swore silent revenge against the man who'd killed their loved ones and turned them into beggars.

I hadn't sworn revenge. I was too young to know what it was back then. But I'd sworn a promise later with Aylin and Danello while we stood on a farm and said we would fight for our home.

"Okay, I'm in. The Duke can send only so many sol-diers at once, right?"

"It's a small island," said Aylin. Danello chuckled.

"Yeah, but it's our island."

"No, it's our home."

Look at our home now. Everything was grim and gray, our hope draining into the canals with the mud. But bits of blue sky poked out around the remaining storm clouds smudged across the dawn. It wouldn't be long before the sun followed.

And when it set, we'd meet Onderaan and . . .

What? Run?

Maybe we should. Eggs should never fight with stones. Hope and faith were nothing compared to steel. Soek was dead because of me, because I thought we could win—believed all those hopeful faces and thought that I could *do* something and *be* more than what I was.

A Shifter.

Shifted pain, shifted blame. I couldn't help any-one. The soldiers would come just as they'd come five years ago, yank us from our homes and throw us into the streets like trash.

Ipstan would never have charged the bridge if I hadn't been here. Soek wouldn't have put on the

Undying's armor and run right into pain and death. All those people wouldn't have stepped forward to fight because of their faith in me.

I killed them all.

Worse than that. Geveg wouldn't even *be* in trouble if not for me. *I'd* killed the Luminary. *I'd* exposed the experiments that had caused the first riots. It was *my* fault the Duke demanded more and more pynvium, trying to replace the ore I'd destroyed in Baseer. *My* fault the Baseeri in Geveg rebelled and killed the Gov-Gen over it.

If I hadn't gone after Tali, none of this would have happened.

"You're up early," Danello said softly.

"Couldn't sleep."

He nodded, gazing out the window. "The rain stopped."

"A while ago."

We watched people walk by, some with packs and travel baskets stuffed full. People were leaving, running.

"We never should have come back," I said. "Why did I think I could change anything?"

"Because you have before."

I shook my head. "I just made things worse. Got people killed."

"You didn't kill Soek," Danello said.

"I *got* him killed." Quenji, too.

"He volunteered to fight."

Quenji hadn't. "I flashed the armor too much. I didn't keep track of how many times."

"It was a battle. Even trained soldiers forget things in a battle."

"I panicked." I whispered, closing my eyes. Seeing Soek again, his fear, his pain. His death.

"That's understandable."

"No. When his armor disintegrated, I should have protected him, taken the attacks meant for him and shifted them, but I *panicked*. I wanted to get out of there and that got him killed."

"Nya, you can't blame yourself for that."

"Then who can I blame?"

He didn't answer. Not at first. Then he took a deep breath and turned back to me. "Blame the Duke."

"I tried, but it doesn't work anymore." They were my choices, my mistakes. That made them my responsibility.

"So what do we do now?"

Staying was foolish. We could do nothing but die, and still Geveg would burn. Leaving meant that Quenji and Soek died for nothing.

Like Mama and Papa? Grannyma?

Would they have run if offered the chance?

"Wait until sunset," I said. "Then we'll decide."

The noon sun shone bright, drying the puddles and the mud, steaming the air. More people were on the streets.

"Do you think the blue-boys are going to attack again?" Aylin asked. She hadn't said much since she'd woken up, just stared out the window with the rest of us.

Danello shrugged. "Maybe. Depends if they know Ipstan's dead."

"Would that make them more or less likely to attack?"

"Maybe less. No leader, no resistance."

And no reason to fight.

By midafternoon more people were passing our window, some in a hurry, and all going the same way. Hopefully an evacuation, boarding every boat on the isle and getting as far away as possible.

"Kione's coming." Aylin got up and went to the door.

He and three others stomped up the front steps of the boardinghouse. Aylin opened the door before he got there, and they walked in and looked around.

His gaze stopped on me.

"We need you at the plaza. Everyone is gathering there, asking what we're going to do." He gestured at the three people behind him—one man and two women. "We were all aides to the officers, but we can't lead the resistance."

I gaped at him. "You think *I* can?"

"No," the man said, "but people will listen to you, and that could hold everyone together until we *can* find someone to lead."

"I'm not sure they'll listen to me anymore."

"Yeah, that's what I said," muttered one of the women.

I frowned. "Then why ask?"

"Because we don't know what else to do, okay?" she snapped. "General Ipstan thought you could save us. That you were this unstoppable force, but he was wrong and it got him killed."

"His arrogance got him killed," Danello said. "His plan was flawed, but he went ahead with it anyway. He never accounted for an ambush, never planned for pynvium weapons to be used, never even thought for a moment that someone saw or survived the tradesmen's corner attack and reported back."

"And he put too much faith in *her*." The woman pointed at me.

"Yes, he did," Danello said. "We *all* did, and that was wrong."

My throat tightened. All true, but to hear Danello admit it?

"Because she's just *one* person," he continued. "An army isn't about one person—it's about a lot of people working together. What happened in the corner was lucky, and it was stupid for Ipstan to plan an entire offensive around it. Nya doesn't even know how she did it, so how could she possibly do it again on command?"

"Then she shouldn't have volunteered."

Aylin scoffed. "She *didn't*. You people forced her into it, with your flowers and songs and acting like she was Geveg's patron saint. How was she supposed to say no to all that?"

No one answered.

Aylin folded her arms. "Right. Don't put this all on her shoulders. You drag someone into the lake, don't blame them when you get wet."

"Will you come?" Kione asked. It felt odd, him asking me for help when I'd practically had to beg him to help me save Tali all those months ago.

"I don't see what I can—"

"She'll be there," Aylin said. What was she up to? No one was going to listen to me, not after I got

281

so many killed. "Soon as she gets cleaned up."

"Thanks." Kione and his friends left, joining the growing crowd headed toward, I guess, the plaza.

"You *want* me to speak?"

"I think you have to or the resistance is doomed."

"It's already doomed. I failed."

She huffed. "So what? That doesn't mean you give up. And you *never* give up."

I gaped at her. "Aylin, you don't even want to fight."

"Not even a little, but I'm behind you all the same."

"Why?"

She took a deep breath and pointed at Tali. "Because of her. I've spent a lot of time with her the last few days, and she's been singing. I thought it was just lullabies and nursery songs, but they're stories about you."

"Me?"

"Some of it is recent, but a lot of it is old, from when you two were little. 'Nya stole me breakfast, Nya stole us beds. Nya tricked the soldiers and now we won't get dead.' Things you did to protect her."

"I failed there too."

"No, don't you see? You've been fighting your *whole* life. Tali's songs made me realize just how much, and you're not the only one who's had to struggle. Everyone in Geveg has. If you leave, everyone gives up and everyone dies. You have to fight, because if *you* can fail and keep fighting, so can *they*."

". . . don't know anything more than that," Kione was saying as we worked our way through the crowd in the plaza. His friends stood behind him. Not a one inspired any confidence. No cheers today, nobody passing back information. Fewer people stood around the fountain, but they were more closely packed together, as if clinging to each other for comfort.

"Nya's here," someone said after I elbowed past them. "Do you know what we should do?"

I didn't even know what *I* should do.

People pushed closer. I didn't like the looks on some of their faces. The angry ones were easier to face than the hopeful.

"Give her some room," Danello said, pushing back. He stayed close, keeping Tali between me and him. I'd wanted her to wait in the boardinghouse with Aylin, but Aylin refused to stay behind.

"Nya's going to say a few words," Kione said, looking relieved.

I stepped onto the edge of the fountain. Folks talked among themselves and waited for me to speak, though I had no idea what I was supposed to say. I stared out at the people looking back at me. They wanted to blame someone, too.

And still no words came.

People fidgeted. Anticipation turned to annoyance. Wonder to worry.

"You didn't stop them!" a man shouted.

"What happened?"

"You're supposed to protect us!"

I laughed. I couldn't help it. There was no humor in it, just the same bitterness and anger they felt.

"I'm supposed to protect *you*? Where were all of you five years ago when *I* needed protection?" I didn't know where the words came from, but they were there, just like the memories that had been floating in my mind since last night. "The Duke invaded three days before my tenth birthday. How many of you fought him *then* when you could have stopped him?"

Shocked looks, some ashamed. I knew people in this crowd, had worked for them, shared food with them, been chased off property by them.

"I was *ten* and the Duke took my family. He sent men to the governor's estate and killed my grandfather. Papa fought with our army and died at the Healers' League. Mama left after that, forced to take the last battlefield brick to the front lines to heal those she could. We never knew where or how she'd died. The Duke sent her body to Grannyma in a box."

I held my hands a foot apart and took a shaky breath.

"A box *this* big."

Cries of dismay and sympathetic mumblings ran through the crowd.

I wiped my eyes. "You can't hide from the Duke or expect someone else to save you. If you want protection, you stand with your friends and your family, and you protect each other.

"My grannyma used to say you can do more with a friend and a stick than you can with just a stick. If you need me to remind you of that, then I will. And I'll even stand with you when you fight. But I won't swing that stick by myself. I can't, and those who think I can stop an entire army on my own are just fools."

"But you caused the Great Flash!"

"So what?" I was tired of hearing that. Tired of being blamed, or worse, credited for it. "What good is a flash when there's no one standing in its way?

You think the Duke's soldiers are going to line up and wait for me to hurt them?"

"How do we stop the Duke then?"

"What do we do?"

"What's going to happen?"

I sighed. They weren't listening to me. "I can't tell you what's going to happen when the Duke gets here. I don't have some great battle plan to save the day. Even if I did, I *still* couldn't tell you how many will die, or if we can win."

"Then what *do* you know?" The angry words were cast across the plaza.

"That giving up means death, sure as spit. That we need to stand together and keep fighting to survive. We need to defend Geveg and the people in it. We need to prepare for fire and smoke. We need a leader who can make all those things happen. But what we really need is—" A man stepped forward, his gray-blue eyes filled with sadness. "Jeatar?"

He stood in the crowd, Onderaan and Ellis on either side of him. I spotted a few more familiar faces around him, members of Jeatar's guard. What was he doing here? What were *they* doing here? It wasn't sunset yet, and this wasn't Analov Park.

"Who's Jeatar?"

"Is he taking over for Ipstan?"

The crowd kept talking, kept speculating. I kept staring.

Kione nudged me. "Say something."

"We need a leader, or our city will fall." I spoke to Jeatar. To the one person I knew could help me fix the mess I'd made. Who could show me how to defend Geveg and everyone in it. "We need someone who knows the Duke's tactics, knows how he thinks and fights, knows what he's capable of and can prepare for his tricks."

A few people cheered, then looked embarrassed when no one else did.

"We need your help," I said, putting all my hope, my faith, my steel, into it, "because I can't do this on my own."

Everyone was looking now, whispering and wondering who this person was I had singled out. Jeatar looked at me, unreadable as ever.

Then he smiled, and the band crushing my chest slipped.

"What's going on?" Kione whispered.

"I've found us a new leader."

"Him? I don't even know him."

"I do."

Jeatar moved through the crowd and up to the

fountain. "You've been busy," he said, climbing up next to me.

"How did you know where I was?"

"Nya, everyone's talking about you. Soon as we got to Geveg, we knew where you were." He glanced around, a small frown on his face. "Did you have to draw so much attention?"

"It was an accident."

He chuckled. "With you, it always is."

I ignored that and turned to the crowd. "This is Jeatar, and he's going to tell you what we need to do next."

He raised an eyebrow at me. Sure, it wasn't much of an introduction, but we didn't have a lot of time.

"Who here has military command experience?" he called out.

No hands went up.

"Who has captained a crew of ten or more?"

A few hands rose.

"How many worked as foreman of any trade or industry?"

A lot more hands.

"If you raised your hand, line up over there." He pointed left. "You're my squad leaders. The rest of you—we'll find out what your skills are, what you can do to help, and put you where you'll be the most effective."

"What if we don't want to fight?"

"Then leave right now. Because Nya is right. The only way we can win is if we all work together."

"What about the Baseeri?"

"Yeah, or them looters?"

Jeatar turned to me, questioning.

"Looters control the middle isles. Baseeri have the Aristocrats' Isles. The Duke's men have the League and Upper and Lower Grand Isles."

He turned back to the crowd. "By the time we attack, we'll have their support. Commander Ellis and the sergeants will meet with you shortly. I'll have squad assignments by sunup."

Jeatar looked at me, then glanced at Kione and the others. "You four have command experience?"

Kione hesitated and the others seemed uncertain. "We were officers' aides. Sir."

"Not anymore. Talk to every person in the plaza and build me an army."

Kione blinked. "Sir?"

"Put together squads with like skill sets. Swordsmen, fishermen, rope makers, whatever they can do and do well. And separate those ready to pick up a weapon. They'll start training in the morning."

"Yes, sir."

"Where's my command post?"

"Uh, I'll show you, sir."

Jeatar waved a hand. "Just tell me—Nya can take me there. I need you to get out and interview everyone."

"Above the blacksmith's."

"Thank you." He jumped off the fountain and headed for the blacksmith's. I shot a *follow me* look at Danello and Aylin and hurried after him.

"So," he began when we were out of earshot of the others, "tell me everything so we can plan our defense."

The resistance had a real leader now. Maybe we also had a real chance.

NINETEEN

W hy, if it isn't the girl everyone is talking about," Optel said, leaning against the side of the bridge that connected the warehouse district with North Isle. The sun was barely up and I was surprised Optel was even awake to meet us. But with so little time before the Duke arrived, Jeatar thought it best if we contacted the looters and the Baseeri as soon as possible. If they weren't going to help us, we needed to know right away. "Rumor has it you brought someone back from the dead."

"The rumors are wrong."

"Oh, I'd say inaccurate. You must have done *something* to get tongues waggling." He waved a hand at Danello, Jeatar, and three of the farmhouse guards standing behind me and looking pretty darn intimidating. "And you've brought friends."

"Not in the mood for a kidnapping today."

He chuckled. "What can I do for you then, Nya of the Great Flash?"

I twitched, trying hard to hide my surprise. Even the *looters* knew about that? "Where did you hear that?"

"The blue-boys of course. We maintain an ale-house they frequent." He grinned, just as irritating as he was the last time we'd met. "No one else is offering any recreation, and I've found myself with a surplus supply of ale and other things. I'll sell to anyone—for a premium."

Traitor. Bad enough he stole from Gevegians, kidnapped them for profit, but to do business with the very soldiers attacking us? He was worse than I'd thought.

Jeatar came forward, nudging me a step back. "You're in contact with the garrison holding the League?"

"We do business from time to time."

"I'd be very interested in hearing about that—for a premium, of course."

Optel's greedy eyes sparkled and he glanced around. "I'm sure we can work something out. Join me inside?"

292

"Certainly."

I didn't much like the idea of going anywhere with Optel, but Jeatar had told us to expect this. No self-respecting thug would do business out in the open. It might work in our favor, but I still didn't like it.

Danello stuck close to me, his hand near his rapier. I could feel the glyphed pynvium strip tucked away in my pocket just in case Jeatar's plan didn't go quite *as* planned.

The barricades were still at the base of the bridge, palm fronds stuck into the top as if to make them look more like trees. They weren't fooling anybody. Optel's guards watched us warily. Had any of them been on duty the night Quenji died? Maybe the big one there with the scar had been the one to grab my arms. Did they even know it had been us that night?

Of course they had. I'd shifted into at least one of them. They weren't here, though. No one looked like he was carrying shifted pain. Maybe he was dead by now.

Good.

I took a deep breath. We needed these people, horrible as they were. And if they had information about the League, we needed them even more.

So what if working with them even a little made my skin creep.

Optel led us to a town house well shaded by grapefruit trees. A few yellow fruits tugged down branches at the tops of the trees, but the rest of the branches were bare.

"Welcome." Optel opened his arms and gestured inside. "Make yourselves comfortable, though your friends will have to wait outside."

Jeatar gestured at the guards and they took position along the front walk. "After you," he said.

They might have looted other homes, but this town house hadn't been touched. Thick carpets covered the floors, artwork graced the walls, and someone had even polished the carved furniture to a glossy shine. It wasn't his, but at least he took care of it.

"Now then," began Optel, sitting on the softest-looking chair in the room, "I believe you were interested in guests at my alehouse?"

"Why are you helping them?" I said. "They're the enemy!"

"She gets right to the point, doesn't she?" Optel said to Jeatar.

"She does." He shot me a look. "It's not time for that, though."

I shoved my hands into my pockets and flopped

back into the chair.

"What *are* the soldiers saying about her?" Jeatar asked.

"That she's a weapon even deadlier than the Undying. They're scared to bits of her, or were until that mess yesterday. Ipstan made a huge blunder there, didn't he?"

I put my hands in my lap and gripped the pynvium strip tight. *Just stay quiet and let him talk.*

Jeatar shrugged. "I wasn't around for that."

"The blue-boys have been celebrating all day. They fooled the Shifter—aren't they clever? Been good for business, so anytime you want to lose a battle, I'm behind you."

"So much better than joining us," I said.

"Why join the losing side?"

"What if it wasn't?" Jeatar asked, still calm as morning water.

"You're the new Ipstan?"

"I've stepped in to help."

Optel leaned back, thinking. Or pretended to think. I liked him less and less. "I'm not sure you have the numbers or the training to beat them."

Jeatar straightened the cuffs of his shirt. He wore silk again, green like the first day I'd seen him. "I didn't come alone. I have good people with even better training. And I'm willing to share if you'll join us."

"I don't know. There's eight or nine hundred blue-boys around the League. I don't remember seeing any ships dock in the last few days that were big enough to bring in an army."

"I can be stealthy."

Optel laughed. "I like you. You should join *me*. We could do lots of business together."

Jeatar pulled out one of the gems we'd found and held it up to the light. The emerald twinkled. "Start by telling me what else you know about those blue-boys. We'll see what happens after that."

Optel licked his lips. I couldn't see him passing up a chance to make money *and* show off how much he knew that we didn't. He seemed to enjoy hearing himself talk.

"Solvaat's in charge now, but the men don't like him. The women like him even less. Something about his breath. He has the bridges well guarded, with duty houses close by for quick reinforcements should they be required. You won't be able to get past them, not even with the lovely Nya's special talents."

Jeatar grinned. "I'm pretty good at getting around guard posts."

"No doubt, but those guards can call for a hundred more with a single toot of the horn." He looked at me. "She can attest to that."

"You do realize the Duke is on his way here, don't you?" I said. "He's not going to care who you sold drinks to. He's just going to try to kill you, same as he will us."

"No, he won't." Optel sighed happily. "Because we'll be leaving with the garrison."

I gaped. "You'd side with the Duke?"

"Oh please, staying here is suicide, but the resistance and those 'Crats have all the boats. What else could we do?"

"Did you ever try *not* betraying your fellow Gevegians?" Danello asked.

"Not really, no."

"What makes you think the Duke will honor his side of the bargain?" I said. "He could leave you here. He probably will."

Optel grinned again. "Not if I have you to offer in trade for passage." He rapped on the wall behind him, and six men with swords came through the door.

I looked at Jeatar. "Told you."

"You were right." Jeatar pulled a coin out of his pocket and tossed it to me. "He is greedy enough to be that stupid."

Optel's grin vanished. "You were dumb enough

to bring the Shifter right to me. Do you have any idea how much Solvaat will pay for her?"

"Not nearly as much as she's worth," Danello said. My cheeks warmed just a little.

"Kill them all."

"Not so fast." I held up the pynvium strip. The guards froze. "You know what I can do with this."

"Flash it if you'd like," Optel said, but he clearly hoped I wouldn't, "but you're not walking out of here."

Jeatar rose, easy as if he were getting up for a drink. "By now my people have this town house surrounded, the bridges secured, and are rounding up *your* people."

"You're bluffing," said Optel, but he didn't seem sure of that.

"We came in last night. Right past your guard posts." Jeatar smiled at me. "Nya can also attest to how little you watch the canals."

I'd love to have seen Kione leading the squads through the canals, or Ellis bringing in more squads along the lakeside coast. Crossing the thin boarding ramps she'd devised to get folks from the boats to the shore where there were no docks wouldn't have been any fun in the dark, but fishermen were pretty surefooted on the water.

Optel jumped to his feet and gestured at one of his men. "You, check outside."

The thug nodded and hurried to the door. He ran back almost immediately. "They got troops out there!"

Optel paled and ran a hand over his mouth. "Listen, we can work something out."

"I tried that. Now we do it my way." Jeatar looked at Danello, who nodded and left.

"Unwise." Optel's gaze darted about the room. "You were outnumbered before, but you're down to two against seven."

Jeatar chuckled. It even gave *me* shiverfeet. "It's Nya against you. She wins."

Optel's men dropped their swords.

"Jeatar, you were right about those overwhelming numbers," Kione said. "The bridge guards didn't put up much of a fight, and some didn't put up any."

"Thugs survive on intimidation." Jeatar paused while another set of looters was hauled past. Ellis was rounding them up and loading them onto a ferry. Jeatar still hadn't decided whether he wanted to dump them in Dorsta Prison or just dump them on the mainland shore. I was leaning toward dump them in the lake. "They prefer the advantage and run when they don't have it."

"What about Optel?" Danello asked.

"I'm going to hold on to him. He might be useful later."

Kione nodded. "You impressed folks with this, General Jeatar."

"I'm no general. And this?" He waved a hand around at the hundred or so looters we'd captured. "This is nothing. This was opportunistic men taking advantage of an abandoned neighborhood. Had the Baseeri and their guards still been here, they never would have gotten a foothold, much less control. It won't be this easy when we go after the League."

"But you have a strategy?"

"I have a few ideas." Jeatar turned to me and smiled. "How about you?"

I glanced at Optel. "Oh, I have a plan. But we'll need the Baseeri to make it work."

It was midafternoon by the time we secured North Isle. We still had South Isle to worry about, but Optel admitted to not having control there like he'd been boasting. Nice to hear we wouldn't have more looters to deal with, but that also meant we had no idea what we were walking into.

"So what's the best bridge to take to the Aristocrats' Isles?" Jeatar asked, shocked.

"There's just the one that connects to South Isle."

Ellis scoffed. "No wonder they chose that side to defend."

"We can go by boat," I said. "The lakeside won't have as many hyacinths clogging it."

"Just the blockade."

Ellis had told us about that. The east side of the city was surrounded by boats, like our side. She hadn't seen any smoke that suggested they had fire rocks though. We either had to get past the boats or take our chances with unknown troops on South Isle.

Jeatar tapped one finger against his lips. "Let's go by boat. Baseeri skiff, Baseeri flag, Baseeri crew— we shouldn't have any trouble getting through. Convincing them to help will be the challenge."

"I'll get the skiff ready," Ellis said.

Jeatar shook his head. "I need you back at tradesmen's corner. Kione was a little too pleased with the 'victory' here, and I don't want him or the others thinking they can just sneak past the bridges and go after the League."

"Yes, sir."

"Oh, and get someone over to talk to the farmers."

"The farmers?" I asked. Ellis just looked confused.

"There are several large farming isles right below the League and Lower Grand Isle," he said. "Don't you think someone should talk to them and find out which side they're on? If we get troops down there, we can attack from all sides."

"And risk the *food*?" I asked.

For a heartbeat he looked like he might laugh but thought better of it. "You won't need that food if there're no Gevegians to feed."

"I'll put a team on it right away," Ellis said. "Anything else?"

"If we can work things out with the Baseeri, we'll have to act fast, so make sure everyone is ready to move when I need them."

"You'll have them."

"Now let's go find us a boat."

Finding one wasn't much trouble, since the skiff they'd used to get here was still docked where Ellis had left it when she'd brought in the wave of fishermen. Jeatar hung a Baseeri flag, raised the sails, and we headed for Upper Aristocrats' Isle.

We spotted the blockade just after we rounded the tip of Geveg. Danello started counting.

"Twenty-seven boats that I can see, and there's

got to be more behind those."

"Pick the closest."

"That one."

I adjusted the rudder and headed toward a skiff a little smaller than ours. Unlike the ones patrolling the lake, this one was anchored.

"They've seen us," I said. Bodies moved on deck, sunlight reflecting off their swords. "And it looks like one of the patrol boats is heading this way, too."

"Good." Jeatar patted my shoulder. "Easy, Nya, we want them to come to us. They'll take us to someone in charge."

If they didn't attack us first.

Waiting for a patrol felt wrong, running right at one felt ridiculous, but these weren't typical Baseeri. They had defied the Duke, triggered Geveg's rebellion. They wanted their freedom as much as we did.

As long as they remembered it was *our* freedom, too, not just theirs.

"Wait here." The Baseeri who'd escorted us in pointed to stone benches at the edge of a dock I hadn't known was here. Boats filled eight of the ten berths.

"I didn't even know they *had* a dock like this over here," Danello whispered.

303

"Me either." It wasn't nearly as big as Geveg's main docks, but it was all the harbor the Aristocrats' Isles needed. It's not like they had people coming and going all day.

Jeatar stayed standing, and his guards took positions around us. The Baseeri dock guards seemed a bit nervous about that. Oddly, neither of them wore blue. Just basic leather armor with red patches on the shoulders.

"I don't suppose you know who might be in charge?" Jeatar asked me.

"Of the Baseeri? No."

I stuck my hands in my pockets. The pynvium strip was still there. Not as comforting without the army backing us up, but if trouble showed, it would be enough. I'd escaped with less.

The man finally came back, along with two others. One wore a uniform—red, just like the guard patches. The other looked like a typical Baseeri aristocrat. Well dressed, well fed, and well accustomed to staring down his nose at folks. Which couldn't have been easy considering the size of his nose.

"You have five minutes," he said.

The bluntness surprised me, but Jeatar didn't even hesitate. "I represent the Gevegian half of the resistance. If you're as organized as I've heard, you'll know the Duke's army has mobilized and is headed here. Our best chance to defend Geveg is if we work together and coordinate attacks."

"Work together?"

"Combine our resources, our forces. Create a solid base on which to defend the city."

"Protect your bunch of freeloaders, you mean?"

I rose. "Excuse me?"

Nose Man folded his arms. "You think parading a bunch of orphans around is going to make us more sympathetic?"

"Considering you people turned us *into* orphans, I doubt it," I said. "We came here to help save *you*."

He laughed. "We don't need saving. We have everything under control."

Jeatar grabbed my shirt, right at the small of my back, and tugged me to a stop. "There are two legitimate and separate forces and one formidable enemy. No matter what you think, you *don't* have him under control."

Big Nose scowled. "You have no resources, you have no soldiers, you have nothing worth forging an alliance with."

"They have *me*," I said. Jeatar tightened his grip on my shirt, scratching my skin with his nails.

His expression hadn't changed, but it was clear I shouldn't have said that.

"And that matters why?"

"Because, Neuss," a woman said, coming down the docks behind him, her glossy black hair in a perfect bun at the nape of her neck. "If anyone can defeat the Duke, it's her."

Danello gasped. "Saints, Nya, is that—"

"Vyand," I whispered. "That's Vyand."

TWENTY

"What are *you* doing here?" Last time I'd seen her, we were all trying to get out of Baseer. She'd already been paid for bringing me to the Duke and hadn't cared that I'd escaped him. She claimed that unless someone paid her to capture me again, she had no interest in me. She'd even helped us get past the gates and the panic to reach the wharf.

Had she been hired to find me again?

Or kill me?

No, Vyand was a tracker, not an assassin. If she was here, it was because someone paid her to be. Money was all she cared about.

"I was about to ask you the same question," she said.

"How did you find me?"

"I wasn't looking for you, didn't even know you were in Geveg. I had business here and was just leaving."

"You work for the Duke," I said.

"I did a few jobs for him, yes. But I don't work for anyone but myself."

"Then why come to Geveg?"

She smiled her cat's grin. "That's my business. I am curious why *you're* here, however."

"Maybe that's *my* business."

She chuckled. "Wouldn't it be interesting if we had the *same* business?"

We wanted an ally against the Duke. Vyand didn't care what happened to anyone but herself, and she sure wouldn't risk her life for a bunch of people she didn't even know. She was here for another reason. Knowing Vyand, it couldn't be good.

"You have that look again," she said. "You're up to something. I do love your little plans."

"You know this child?" Neuss asked.

"I'm surprised you don't. What is she asking you to do?"

"Protect the whole—"

"I don't want your protection, I want an alliance," I said.

"A unified army against the Duke," Danello added. Jeatar stayed silent, though his eyes narrowed as he stared at Vyand.

She smiled, ignoring Danello and scanning Jeatar head to toe. "My, my, aren't you intriguing. The strong silent type?"

Jeatar turned back to Neuss. "It's in your best interests to relay my message up the chain of command. I'd hate to see the Aristocrats' Isles fall because you were too shortsighted to inform your superiors."

Neuss snorted and spun on his heel, muttering something about worthless 'Vegs as he left. His guard followed. Vyand stayed.

"You could have handled that better," she said.

"He had no intention of helping us."

"And no power to. You need to speak with Balju. He's the man in charge."

Jeatar paused, studying her again. "Could you make the introductions?"

"What? No!" I stepped between them, a hand out to either side. Danello moved with me, keeping his gaze on Vyand and his hand on his rapier. "We can't trust her," I said. "She'll probably turn us over to, I don't know, one of the Duke's spies."

"No, I won't."

"Then why are you here?"

She smoothed her hair and looked at Danello. "What have you been whispering into her ear? Does she really think everything is about her?"

"It usually is."

She laughed. "Not this time, Nya. I'm here to conduct business, nothing more. I had weapons, Balju needed weapons. I have more weapons, if you or your handsome man here wants to purchase any."

Jeatar actually looked like he was considering it. "What do you—"

"No. It's *Vyand*."

"Excuse us." He dragged me off to the side. "You need to calm down."

"And you need to remember that woman kidnapped me, sold Tali to the Undying, and handed Danello and Aylin to some Baseeri jailer to be executed. I'm *not* going to work with her."

"I'm not asking you to. But if she can get us into the same room with Balju, we'd be fools to refuse her help."

"She'll trick us somehow."

"I doubt it. There's nothing in it for her."

Trust Vyand. No, just believe her. Take her at her heartless word. I glanced over. She waited, as perfectly pressed as ever. Saints knew how she managed to stay so neat. Maybe not even dirt wanted to be near her.

"I guess Danello can stab her if he has to."

Danello nodded. "I'm willing to do it even if I don't have to."

Jeatar shot us both stern looks. "You want to wait on the skiff?"

"No."

"Then stay quiet, don't tell anyone who you are, and let me do the talking."

I folded my arms. "If I can't say anything, why am I even here?"

"You wouldn't let me leave you behind."

True.

"You also know the area, and I don't," he continued. "If something went wrong, I figured you could get us out of here."

"I'm your protection?"

He grinned. "More of a guarantee."

"Anytime now," Vyand called. "I haven't got all day."

I raise my hands in surrender. "Fine, I'll shut up and be dangerous."

"Thank you." We walked back to Vyand. "We accept your offer."

"Which one?"

"The introduction to Balju," I said. Jeatar glared at me.

"I don't believe I made an actual offer on that,

but why not? Getting you two together should be fun."

"Where does he live?" I ignored Jeatar's glare.

"The terraces."

My stomach fluttered. I hadn't been back there since the Baseeri soldiers threw us out.

We followed Vyand to the street. Servants hurried past, most carrying baskets and crates. The canals may have been clogged, but the streets were swept clean, the hedges trimmed, the trees neatly shaped. Wrought-iron fences surrounded the villas, and flowering vines of various types provided some privacy.

"Wow," said Danello under his breath. "This place is as nice as where the Underground's villa was."

We passed the turnoff for the gardens and headed for the bridge. Soldiers stood guard on either side, their red uniforms glowing in the setting sun. Even their swords sparkled.

"This way," Vyand said, turning onto one of the long avenues that cut the isle in half. "Down near the end."

No fences on these villas. High stone walls in shades of white, pink, and gold surrounded them instead, with gates of sturdy wrought iron with family crests carved into them. I recognized some, though the families had been gone for five years. Did the Baseeri know what the crests meant? Maybe they thought they were decorations.

I don't know what would have made me angrier—if they didn't know or didn't care.

Yellow petals drifted on the wind, falling from the flowering trees along the sidewalk. They gathered on the grass like pale, sweet-smelling carpets. Children laughed and water splashed. So different from the sounds on the other side of Geveg. At least today.

"Girls!" Mama ran across the grass toward the fountain. "Come inside."

Tali giggled and kicked more water at me. I didn't splash back, my gaze drawn past Mama to the soldiers running toward the bridge.

"Tali, Nya, out of that fountain right this instant."

Someone screamed. Then another person. Harsh clangs rang out and Mama gasped. She grabbed our hands and hauled us out of the water.

"Nya, hurry!"

That was the first attack. Not the invasion that came a few days later but the one that surprised us all. A small force sent to kill the Governor, destroy our ability to organize and fight back. Not that different from what they were doing now with the Undying.

"It's beautiful here," Danello said. "I've never even seen that kind of stone before. And enamel on the gates? That must cost a fortune."

My steps slowed, my heart raced. The street ended up ahead in a graceful cul-de-sac lined with curved hedges. A two-story villa of cream-colored stone sat at the end. Dark rosewood shutters shaped like butterfly wings hung on the second-story front windows. Tali's room.

I shivered, cold from head to toe. Home. I was home.

"Nya?" Danello stared at me, worried. "What's wrong?"

Were the stained-glass butterflies still hanging from the ceiling? Did they still catch the morning light and send rainbows across the bed?

"Sniffles," I said softly.

"What?"

"Tali's cat. Her name was Sniffles. She'd chase the light all over the room, trying to catch the sparkles from the mobiles. She'd knock over everything, and Tali would laugh so hard she'd fall off her bed."

Danello put a hand on my shoulder. "That's where you used to live? *Here?*"

I nodded. "There were flowers under the front window. A whole garden full of lake violets. Mama's favorites. Soldiers trampled them."

Heavy banging on the front door. Tali and I huddled together at the foot of the stairs with our housemaid, Lenna. Her husband, Wen, answered the door. We were the only ones left.

Soldiers. Always soldiers.

"On the order of Duke Verraad of Baseer, you're to vacate the premises immediately."

Wen stood tall. "This is my master's villa, and you'll not step foot inside. I hold no allegiance to your Duke."

A soldier moved—one swift sword thrust. Wen doubled over with a grunt and a gasp. The soldier yanked the sword out and Wen dropped to the floor.

Lenna screamed and ran forward, dropping to her knees beside him. Another solider grabbed her by the hair and dragged her outside. She kept screaming; then metal shringed and she was silent.

"Lenna!" I ran after her. A soldier caught me and threw me back inside. "Anyone else in the villa?" he asked.

"Get out!" I screamed at him.

"Anyone else in the villa?"

Tali darted forward and wrapped her arms around my waist. "Nya, I'm scared."

"Where are your parents?"

"Dead. Your friends killed them, and I hope one of Papa's friends kills you."

The soldier called to the others, and they grabbed us like sacks of coffee, carrying us outside. Lenna was lying in the violets, her blond hair covering the purple blossoms soft as spiderwebs. Her eyes stared at nothing.

The soldiers threw us into the street and slammed the gate shut behind us.

The anger, the fear—it felt as real as it had then. "After the soldiers threw us out, Tali and I cried and banged on the gate, begging to come back inside, but they ignored us. I stopped before she did. It was getting dark, it wasn't safe out after dark. I went to a neighbor's villa, but their gate was locked. Everyone's gate was."

"That's awful. I'm so sorry, Nya."

"We slept in the gardens, under some bushes. I didn't know where else to go. I was only ten. How could they do that to us?"

Danello hugged me and I clung to him, barely able to breathe.

"We'll get your home back, I promise," he said.

Would we? Even if we beat the Duke, the Baseeri had claimed these isles, these villas. Maybe Neuss's opinion wasn't the same as all of theirs, but my

316

guts said more than a few felt that this was *their* home now.

Jeatar turned around and walked back to where I'd stopped. "Is everything okay?"

No, but I wasn't about to let Vyand know that.

"Rock in my sandal," I said, shaking my foot. I don't think Jeatar believed me, but he glanced at Danello and nodded.

"Vyand says Balju's in this one."

"Okay."

The gate opened smoothly. A stone walkway led to the front door. No flowers, no benches, no decorations of any kind. Bushes and grass were trimmed in neat lines. A soldier's yard. I guess she did take us to the right place. I forced my feet to keep moving.

The yard was open and lush, the trees well spaced, planted for the best view—from inside and outside the villa—but not the most convenient spots for cover. A low row of gardenia bushes ran along the side of the building, but there were far too many windows overlooking that part of the property for anyone to hide in them effectively. Anyone inside could see us walking up.

"Where are the guards?" I asked.

"Along the perimeter. No need to post them on the interior of the isles."

Vyand knocked on the door, and a man in a red uniform answered. Maybe they didn't have guards outside, but he was guarding the inside.

"Did you forget something?" He eyed the rest of us with less caution than I'd have expected.

"No, but I need to see Commander Balju if he's available."

"I'll see if he has a minute." He let us in and told us to wait in the foyer. Danello gaped at the tapestries hanging on the wall. Baseeri design, which surprised me. I hadn't thought anything here belonged to them.

"Was your home this nice?" Danello whispered.

"I don't really remember," I lied. I couldn't see much of the villa from here, but what I could glimpse looked just like the outside—ready for war, not entertaining. No crystal, no blown glass, no artwork on the walls. Our villa had been filled with light and color and laughter.

The guard returned and waved us inside. Vyand walked ahead, smiling at a large man in a pose I'd seen a lot lately. Standing at a table covered in maps, with other men gathered around him.

"Thank you for seeing me, Commander."

"Always a pleasure."

I glanced at Danello. Seriously?

"I'd like to introduce you to someone." She stepped aside and Jeatar came forward.

"Saints' mercy, you're alive!" a man on Balju's right cried. He ran both hands through his dark hair, then hurried to Jeatar, grabbing him in a hug. "We feared the worst when we lost track of you in Baseer."

"Riendin, it's good to see you too."

Vyand raised an eyebrow. "I guess introductions aren't necessary after all."

Jeatar looked happy, but worried too.

Riendin let go of Jeatar and held him at arm's length. "You've no idea how glad I am to see you, especially now."

"Perhaps you should let us all in on why this is such a good thing?" Balju said. A solid man, handsome, yet hard and sharp, like broken marble.

"This is the man I was telling you about. He's Bespaar's son!"

Jeatar's shoulders tensed. The rest of the men in the room gaped. Vyand got a strange look on her face. "My, my, my," she mumbled.

Danello leaned close. "Who's Bespaar?"

"The Duke's brother."

Danello coughed. "*The* Duke?"

"Yeah. Jeatar's kinda the rightful heir to the throne."

"Of *Baseer*?"

I nodded.

"Why didn't you *tell* me?"

"And why didn't you tell *me* you knew that?" Jeatar said, more interested in me than in the men all talking over each other behind him. "How did you find out?"

"I figured it out."

He stared at me, shock and a bit of pride on his face.

Balju banged his fist against the table and the room fell silent. "Bespaar's son, here." He shook his head as if unable to believe it. "We've been looking for you a long time."

"So has the Duke. I thought it best to disappear for a while until we were ready."

"Riendin said the Underground wasn't dead. That even if you were, there was still hope."

"There's not much left of the Underground, but Geveg's resistance is strong. That's why I'm here, to forge an alliance between both sides."

Balju seemed confused. "You're working with the Gevegians?"

"I am."

"Why?"

I opened my mouth and Danello slapped a hand over it. "Shut up and be dangerous, remember?" he whispered into my ear. I nodded, swallowing my words.

"Because this is their home," Jeatar said for me, "and they deserve to have it back."

The men around Balju didn't care for that. Frowns and suspicious glances passed among them.

"You're saying we should just walk away and hand the city over to *them*?"

I didn't like the way he said *them*.

"I think we should save it first, then decide how to fix the mess the Duke's created afterward."

Balju paused, rapping his knuckles softly against the table. "I supported your father," he said. "Fought against Verraad when he tried to steal the throne and drank my vengeance to him after he did. *You* should be on that throne, not him."

"So let's change that."

Balju pursed his lips. "Who's the girl? Too old to be yours."

"She's an Analov."

Balju's eyes widened. "*Is* she?"

Every gaze in the room focused on me. I reached for Danello's hand, squeezed it tight. He looked at me, puzzled. Was I allowed to speak now? Jeatar didn't say anything, or look my way, so probably not.

"Regeer's great-granddaughter."

More whispers in the room and strange looks on the faces of the older people.

"Onderaan with you?"

They knew him too? I looked at Danello, who seemed just as surprised as I was. How did these people know my family? Who *were* they?

"He is. He fights for Geveg and so do I. So does she." Jeatar stood tall and crossed his arms. "We've waited a long time for this opportunity. You join us, we can fix a lot of old wrongs. You don't, I'll take back Geveg with the Analovs and watch while the Duke lobs his fire rocks at you."

Riendin sucked in a breath. Balju leaned forward, eyes narrowed, but there was respect in there too. "The Analovs and the Bespaars, united again."

Jeatar offered his hand. "Do we also have an alliance?"

Balju paused, then took Jeatar's hand. "We do. Grab a seat—we were just about to discuss tactics." He looked over at Danello and me. "Vyand, would you be so kind as to escort Miss Analov and her guard into the other room?"

"Certainly, Commander."

"But—"

Jeatar shook his head. "Not this time, Nya. I'm sorry."

Sorry? He was throwing me out and he was *sorry*? I had questions, so many questions.

Vyand ushered us out and closed the door behind her. The same guard waited in the foyer, talking with a girl in a housemaid's uniform.

"How could he kick me out?"

"He had to," she said. "Balju isn't going to discuss battle strategy with a child in the room, no matter what family she belongs to."

"I'm hardly a child. And I'm a *de*'Analov. They keep getting that wrong."

Vyand flicked a hand at me. "Don't be naïve. If your man there was in trouble, you'd take on the whole group and win, but that's not the point. Balju doesn't know you."

"He sure seemed to know her name, though," Danello said.

"He should. Her family founded Geveg."

Danello paused. "You were serious about that the other night? When you said they helped build it, I thought you meant they were masons."

Vyand laughed and Danello blushed. I wanted to strangle them both.

"There's a park named after her, you know," she said.

"My great-grandfather, not me."

Danello sank onto a couch. "Wow. I knew you were an aristocrat before, but that . . . wow, the whole city?"

Vyand chuckled again. "I must ask. Where did you meet that man of yours? Bespaar's son? You do associate with very interesting—and powerful—people."

"We ran into each other at the League."

"Must have been some meeting." She stared at me, who-knew-what spinning in those blue eyes, like she wanted to ask more but didn't want to appear ignorant of anything. "Well," she finally said, "this has been delightful, but I must go."

"Of course," I said, frustrated and confused and not knowing who to yell at first. Or even if I should. "Because you can't *possibly* stay and fight for something worth defending."

"Do you truly think me so callous?"

I snorted. "I think if I offered you the two bean-sized sapphires I have in my pocket, I could hire you as my personal guard."

She grinned and held out her hand, palm up. "Deal."

"What?"

"I accept your offer. You have my full team at your disposal."

She couldn't be serious. This was a joke, an

insult, a way to rob me of two gems. "I was being sarcastic."

"I mean it. I guard you, I guard your man."

"Will you please stop calling him that."

"Fine." She stepped closer and the playful maliciousness vanished. Her eyes were clear, strong, and Saints forgive me—*sincere*. "Bespaar's heir has aligned himself with you. *That* is a man worth protecting, and the only way he'll let me is if he thinks I'm guarding you."

"Why in Saea's name would *you* want to protect *him*?"

She stepped away and the glint in her eyes returned. "You're not the only one who wants to see the Duke pay for his crimes."

TWENTY-ONE

What do you *mean* you hired Vyand to be your bodyguard?" Aylin stared at me as if I'd lost my mind, which maybe I had.

"I didn't do it on purpose."

Danello nodded. "Vyand dived at the chance. She's got to be up to something."

Something that involved Jeatar and the Duke— and I didn't want Vyand even *thinking* about them in the same sentence.

"I've never seen anyone go from bounty to boss before. Are you sure it's a good idea?"

I sighed. "It's *Vyand*, so it can't be. Maybe she won't actually show up." Vyand had some more "business" to deal with and had said she'd meet us later. She didn't say where and I didn't tell her where we'd be.

"Does Jeatar know?"

"I'll tell him if she gets here."

"He does plan on coming back, right?"

"He said he would." Jeatar had come out of his meeting with Balju after a half hour and told his guards to take us back. Part of me wondered if he just wanted to get us out of the way before our frustration made us do something foolish. "He wanted to get everything in place with the Baseeri before speaking to our people."

Someone knocked on the door.

"That's Onderaan with an update on Tali," I said, rising. He'd spent all day with her while we were out. Aylin said she'd kept staring at him like she couldn't quite figure out where she knew him from.

I opened the door and Onderaan came inside. Tali looked up and started staring again. "Evening," he said, taking a seat. "I hear you had some excitement today."

"My life is nothing *but* excitement these days. Did you find anything in Zertanik's book to help her?" I had so many other questions for him, but Tali came first. I could ask why the Baseeri resistance leader knew who he was—and who *we* were—later.

"Perhaps. He made extensive notes on the kragstun, but nothing about reversing the effects of it."

"That doesn't sound helpful," Danello said.

"Oh, it was. I did find out the metal affects the nervous system and the brain. I don't know how yet, but if something was done to the body, there must be a way to heal it. You did say she improved after healing Danello."

I nodded. "She stopped trying to hurt people."

"She may have inadvertently healed some of the damage."

"Can she heal the rest?"

He shook his head. "I doubt it. I believe she'll need someone trained in brain or nerve injuries to repair the rest of the damage."

"One more reason to take back the League." As if we needed another. I had no idea if Heal Master Ginkev was still there, but if anyone would know how to heal a brain, it would be him.

"Papa?" Tali said. She walked over, hand out-stretched.

My breath caught. "No, Tali, that's Onderaan, Papa's brother."

She ran her fingers across his forehead. He

waited, still as stone, while she felt her way around his face. "Where's Papa?"

"He died."

"Soldiers come, soldiers stay, can't you make them go away?" she sang quietly.

"That's what we're trying to do."

She nodded and wandered off, her fingers trailing from Onderaan's cheek. She found the window and curled up in front of it, resting her chin on the sill.

Danello slipped his arms around me from behind. "We'll find a way to help her."

I nodded, my throat too tight to speak.

Onderaan rose, sadness in his eyes. "I'll keep researching."

"Wait, before you go," I said. "Balju, the Baseeri leader, asked about you. He knew who we were. Our family. Everyone there seemed to know."

"We were close allies with Jeatar's family. Father and Bespaar were good friends."

"They plotted to overthrow the Duke together?" I assumed as much, but the bits of information I'd been told didn't satisfy.

Onderaan nodded. "After Verraad took over, yes. Your grandfather helped Jeatar escape Sorille when it was burned. He smuggled him out in a grain cart, sacrificed his own life to do it. Peleven helped hide him in Geveg for a while; then we managed to get him to the farm. It was his great-aunt's and needed a lot of repair, but it was forgotten by the family."

"Is that why the Duke came after Geveg?" I asked, dreading the answer. But I'd heard the accusations in Baseer, in the Underground's villa. That my family had brought the Duke down on Sorille. "Because Papa hid him here?"

Onderaan stepped closer, cupped my shoulders in his palms. "Nya, no. The Duke was already planning to invade Geveg and Verlatta. He had no idea Jeatar was here, or he'd have destroyed it too, not invaded it. He thought Jeatar was dead."

"But not anymore," Danello said. "He probably knows now, doesn't he? He went after the farm."

"He might not remember the farm. We don't have any contacts close to him anymore, so we can't know for sure."

My guts said he knew, though maybe not for very long. Jeatar had stepped forward, admitted to a roomful of Baseeri who he was. Maybe it hadn't been his choice, but if his friend had known he was alive, then others probably did, and saying that the legitimate heir was alive and willing to fight was a good way to gain support for your side.

"What if he does know?" asked Aylin.

"Then he'll attack with everything he has."

Jeatar finally returned and called a late meeting. Lamps brightened the map room above the blacksmith's, the shadows of several dozen people flickering on the walls. Ellis stood on Jeatar's right, his friend Riendin on the left as the Baseeri representative. Kione and the other newly appointed sergeants were also there, along with a few faces I didn't know. Their scowls suggested they were part of Balju's group. Our people scowled back.

"We have an alliance with the Baseeri resistance," Jeatar began, though no one cheered. "We've contacted the farmers and ranchers, and they're willing to fight with us as well. We took control of North Isle this morning and placed our people at the bridge guard posts. Ellis was able to convince Optel to help us, and we were able to infiltrate the alehouse. We've been gathering information on their troop size and movements, and we have a plan of attack."

He picked two red stones up off the map. "The Baseeri are moving in through North and South Isles. South Isle is mostly abandoned, large portions of it in ruins." He set the stones down at the bridges to League Circle. "They'll be ready to move when we need them."

He grabbed two more stones, violet ones, and placed them on the bridges to Upper Grand Isle. "The Gevegians will take Upper Grand. Kione will come in from here"—he pointed—"and Ellis from there."

Ellis had the lower bridge, the same one we'd failed to take with Ipstan. According to the scouts, it was the harder of the bridges to cross and claim, with more troops in reserve to support attacks than on either Upper or Lower Grand Isle.

"The farmers and select troops from both sides will come in here and here." He dropped yellow stones on the bridges to Lower Grand Isle.

"Timetable?" Ellis asked.

"We hit the Grand Isles at dawn. The Baseeri hit the bridges from North Isle to the League. Once we've secured the Grand Isles, then we make a full attack on League Circle. By then we'll have control of every isle and bridge surrounding it."

Danello tentatively raised a hand. Jeatar grinned. "Yes?"

"If we attack that many bridges at once, won't they figure out something is up?"

"That's a risk, but I have people at the alehouse

telling the soldiers they heard another attack was imminent. Ellis will make sure some of her troops are seen massing at that bridge. I hope between those rumors and the Baseeri attacks on the bridges, it'll draw out and split the blue-boys' forces so we can ambush them from behind. If we get lucky, they'll commit the bulk of their forces before they realize all the bridges are under attack."

"The bait might not be big enough," Riendin said. "They're feeling cocky right now. They'd need a good reason to overcommit."

Dread tied my guts in a knot. "Like me."

He nodded. "Or someone posing as her. Put anyone her size in the pynvium armor and it can fool them long enough."

"Won't they also have the whole army trying to kill them?" Kione said, horrified.

"We could ask for a volunteer."

One of the sergeants scoffed. "You expect us to charge in there and die as a distraction?"

"Gevegians not brave enough to make the sacrifice?" a Baseeri said.

The yelling started. Jeatar slammed both palms on the table. "The fight is out there, not in here."

"It has to be me," I said, wishing it could be anyone else.

Aylin grabbed my hand. "Nya, no."

"You'd need a Healer to survive long enough to do any good, and we need every Healer *out* of battle, healing. Besides, I'll be able to flash and thin the ranks, giving our side an even bigger advantage."

Jeatar frowned, but he had to know I was right. "They'll be waiting for you."

"I know."

"You'll need protection."

I smiled. I guess Vyand got to earn her pay after all. "I have that covered."

Jeatar frowned. "You'll need more than Danello."

"I'll have a whole team at my disposal." One that I didn't mind risking one bit.

The pynvium armor still didn't fit. The chest plate hung on my shoulders, heavy and awkward, thumping my ribs when I moved. Even padding it with extra shirts didn't help much, though it did keep it from digging into my flesh. The bracers sat against the tops of my hands at the wrists, but at least they stayed on. The greaves were okay.

"Here." Jeatar lifted a helmet that looked suspiciously like a reforged pot and shoved it over my head. He pulled a visor down across the top half of my face, covering my eyes. A thin slit let me see, but not well.

"I'll trip over my own feet in this thing."

"It'll protect your eyes."

A lucky shot could end this fight fast. I had to draw it out, scare the blue-boys badly enough that they called in everyone they had to stop me.

We had to succeed. Capture the League and we stood a chance of beating the Duke. Of healing Tali. Fail here and he'd burn us all to ash.

Dozens of people surrounded me, hundreds more behind me. Our army numbered in the thousands now, but nowhere near the numbers the Duke commanded. All these people around me and I still felt alone. Danello was with his father, part of the farmers' attack. He hadn't been too happy about that, and my guts said he suspected I was keeping him out of danger again.

"Nya, are you sure about this?" Jeatar said. I wasn't sure where he'd be fighting, but Riendin had been pretty vocal about him staying off the front lines. Some of the resistance frowned on that, but others reminded them about what had happened to Ipstan. They needed to keep the people who knew what they were doing back where they could do it. "We can still use a decoy."

"I'm sure. I don't want to risk anyone else."

"Except me and my team," Vyand said. She'd arrived with the giant and silent Stewwig and a dozen men and women who looked like they could take on the blue-boys all on their own. Jeatar wasn't pleased when he found out about her, but he agreed that there was a certain justice in her trying to keep me alive. I'd rather he hadn't used *trying* though.

"You're well armored and well trained. You'll be fine," Jeatar said, barely looking her way. She and the others all wore chain mail, their faces already sweaty though the sun hadn't risen yet.

"This wasn't what I had in mind when I accepted your offer."

"You can always change your mind."

She sneaked a glanced at Jeatar. "No, I'm up for the challenge."

Ellis motioned me over. They were ready to go.

"Good luck," Jeatar said.

"You too." I turned to Vyand and her team. "Try not to get too close, unless you want to get caught in the flash."

"Hard to protect you that way."

"Harder to do it if you're unconscious."

"Very true."

I started across the bridge, walking, not running. I'd lose my balance if I ran. Vyand came in behind me. The blue-boys watched us come, their swords glinting in the sun that had finally peeked over the horizon. One girl against an army.

They'd go after my arms if they were smart. Hold me down, keep me from touching the pynvium chest plate. They wouldn't be fast enough, but they could reach me before I reached them, forcing me to flash before the bulk of the soldiers were in range.

A squad tried. They left the protection of the bridge barricade and stalked toward me, swords out, eyes hard. One small flash would take them out, but I couldn't do one small flash. It would trigger the rest, waste the pain in the armor on four when I needed to take out four hundred.

Steps away, coming closer. Chain on their bodies, smirks on their faces.

Almost in range.

Shadows flickered across the stone, like birds flying overhead. Several of our spears whizzed past and sank into the blue-boys' chests. More whizzed past, hitting two others and sending the last few running for the far side of the bridge.

Shouts from the blue-boys, some in pain as the poison flowed through their bodies, others in fear when they realized what had happened.

I wasn't the only thing to fear today.

The blue-boys fidgeted, as if eager to race out

and tackle me, but the threat of the poisoned spears kept them back. Unsteady feet or not, it was time to hurry. Close the distance and flash them all. Scare them, force them to call for reinforcements and make the other bridges easier to capture.

I hugged myself, holding down the chest plate and keeping my hands against the pynvium.

"Now!"

I charged into the battle, shoulders braced, head tucked. Swords clanged off my armor but didn't get through. Bodies slammed against me, knocking me off-balance, but hands steadied me. A body jumped between me and the blue-boys like a wall.

Stewwig.

He moved forward, sword swinging, silent as ever. But he cut through the soldiers like he was harvesting grain, clearing a path deeper into the blue-boys' defense. I stayed in his wake, my hands twitching to flash the armor and get it over with.

Something heavy smacked against my helmet and my head spun. I grabbed Stewwig's back and stopped my swaying, looked for the threat, but it was impossible to see much through the visor's small slit. Soldiers in blue battled soldiers in brown leather. Blue-boys twitched on the ground, victims of the poison. Vyand's team fought all around me, holding back the tide of pain.

They were good. They were *very* good.

I was deep enough. "Get back!"

"Do it now," Vyand yelled.

"You're too close."

"Do it anyway!"

I pictured dandelions.

WHOOMP whoomp WHOOMP whoomp whoomp

Pain flashed against my skin. Soldiers screamed, Vyand and Stewwig fell. For several breaths the street quieted, a lull in the storm. Then horns blared and men shouted, but farther away. Calling for reinforcements.

It was what we wanted, but I trembled anyway.

I knelt and grabbed Vyand's cheek, one of the few spots of exposed skin. *Drew.*

"It worked," I said after she snorted awake. "They called for help."

"Good. Nya, move!"

She shoved me, but something hit me and dragged me down. Not a body—a net! I slammed into the street, crushing my fingers between stone and pynvium. Vyand grabbed the net, but a man in blue tackled her, knocking her away.

I tried to get up, but the net tangled in the armor, caught on the straps and buckles. The armor's weight made it hard to move and the net even harder.

Another horn blew and the ground shook.

I curled into a ball, bracing myself for the stabs and strikes that couldn't be far away. The reinforcements were coming. No one saw me lying on the street, or no one cared, and soldiers trampled me. The straps of the armor broke and the protection skittered away, kicked by running feet. My bones cracked. Broke. Pain flared, and the soldiers kept coming.

Just like we'd planned.

Protect me, Saint Saea, please.

There was nothing else I could do.

TWENTY-TWO

The river of feet eventually subsided. I'd have sighed in relief, but my ribs hurt too much to take more than a shallow breath. I still wore the helmet and chest piece, but the bracers and greaves were gone. The net bunched around my visor, and all I could see were bodies and blood on the warm brick street.

"Nya!"

Danello, but he sounded far away. And scared.

"Here," I rasped, but it couldn't have been loud enough to reach him. I rolled and fresh pain shot through me. I cried out, louder than my call for help.

"It's her!"

Not someone scared—or friendly. My mind

screamed at me to move, but my body couldn't listen. Feet stomped closer, then metal against metal.

I squeezed my eyes shut, braced for more pain. None came. Fighting above me, near me, the quick swish of rapiers cutting through the air.

Someone tugged on my hands, my legs. I whimpered, suddenly alert. Had I blacked out? I couldn't focus, couldn't stay awake.

"Hold on, Nya," Danello said. "Help's coming."

"Nya needs a Healer over here," Ellis shouted. "Don't move her. Don't do anything until the Healer gets here."

The world swam past me, shadows moving, people talking. The helmet slid off my head. An older man stopped and knelt beside me and put his hands on my forehead. The pain in my chest eased, though my limbs still hurt.

"That'll hold her until you get her back to base."

"Thank you," Danello said.

"I gotta get moving. They've broken through the League's front lines. Shouldn't be long now."

"Good luck!"

Scraps of information came to me as Danello and someone I couldn't see carried me through the streets to the resistance's small infirmary. The soldiers had fallen for the ruse. The battle was still going on, but not here. They'd taken both Upper and Lower Grand Isles and were closing on the League.

Jeatar did it.

The sunshine on my face vanished, and a door thunked closed. My stretcher was lowered to the floor. I gritted my teeth while Danello and the other person lifted me onto a cot.

"Saints, what happened to her?" Lanelle sounded worried.

"She was trampled. Help me get the chest piece off her."

"No, leave it until I get those bones healed. It'll hurt her too much."

Lanelle pulled over a stool and sat beside me. I tried not to think about the last time she'd stood over me while I was in pain. Telling me to sleep, doing nothing to ease my suffering, same as she had to the others.

She's here to help this time; give her a chance.

Tingling fire surged through my bones, part from the healing, part from the pain as Lanelle set my broken legs and arms. I screamed my throat raw and she healed that too. The heat and pain faded and I sank onto the cot, weak as a duckling.

⌐‿⌐

I opened my eyes.

Danello and Aylin stood by the bed, dirty and worn, but alive. Framed paintings hung on the wall behind them. Wherever I was, it wasn't the infirmary. A nice room, even without windows. Light glowed in elegant glass lamps. Soft mattress. Thick pillows. Familiar, even.

"Did we win?"

"We won," Danello said softly. Yellow bruises covered half his face. "You're in the League and safe. The distraction worked even better than we'd hoped. We got past the bridges and took the League itself with minimal resistance. There's still patches of fighting, but the League is secure."

"Thank the Saints." I took a tentative breath, but the pain was gone. Lanelle really did know what she was doing. "You look awful."

He chuckled. "You look beautiful."

"Liar."

"You're alive. That's enough for me."

"Where's Tali?"

Aylin stepped aside. Tali sat on a chair, playing with the braided silver cords that marked a League apprentice. The last of the tightness in my chest loosened.

"Ellis found Ginkev and a bunch of other Healers

upstairs," Danello said, taking my hand. "They were hiding in one of the classrooms. Barricaded the door and everything."

"Took her twenty minutes to convince him to let her in." Aylin chuckled. "She was about to knock the door down."

I swung my legs over the end of the bed. "Where is he? Does he know about Tali? Has anyone spoken to him yet?"

"He's in the ward, and you need to stay here." Danello put both hands on my shoulders and pushed me back. "Want me to go see if he's free?"

"Would you? But only if no one else needs healing."

"Of course." He leaned down and kissed my forehead before leaving. People were hurrying past the door, most of them still in armor.

"You know," Aylin began, "he was running all over the place looking for you. There were reports you'd gotten hurt, but with all the bodies out there, they couldn't find you. He fought off four soldiers to protect you."

"He did?"

She rolled her eyes. "Well, yeah."

"But he could have gotten hurt—or killed."

"Let him be the hero once in a while, huh? You're not an easy girl to live up to."

I grinned. He wasn't going to let me keep him in the back after this. But maybe he'd stay close to the League. Surely we'd need lots of soldiers to protect it.

A soft knock at the door, and Aylin rose and answered it. She stepped aside and Jeatar walked in, still wearing his armor. Dirt and blood smeared his face, and I spotted several gashes he really should have had healed.

"I hear we won."

"We did, but it cost us."

I was afraid to ask how much. "Is Ellis okay? And Kione?"

"They're fine. You didn't lose any more friends. Not even Vyand, though it was close there. She might cancel her arrangement with you."

"You can have her then." She'd be happier protecting him anyway.

"I have enough people watching my back." Jeatar ran a hand through his hair, scratching at the back. "We received some bad news. One of the scouts I left upriver sent me a message that the Duke is two days out."

The tightness in my chest came back. "Two days? Do we have enough time to prepare?"

"We'll do what we can. Onderaan's already got

the forge stoked. We'll need healing bricks for sure, pynvium weapons."

"Did he find anything valuable in the forge?" Doubtful, but something could have been left behind.

"Nothing but barrels of blue sand. We were lucky they didn't think to break apart the forge."

"Can we still win?" Aylin asked.

"I don't know yet. We lost a lot getting this far, but morale is good. I've called a strategy meeting in an hour, and you're welcome to attend. I understand if you need to rest."

"No, I'll be there. Where is it?"

"Danello knows." He paused, his gaze traveling over the scars on my arms. For a moment, I thought he might say more, but the contemplative look vanished and he nodded. "See you in an hour."

Ginkev arrived not long after Jeatar left. He'd been Tali's Heal Master, in charge of teaching the apprentices at the League. He was just as short and bald as he was the day he'd taught me how to spot bleeds. Back then he'd had no idea I wasn't a real apprentice, or that I was at the League to sneak upstairs and rescue Tali. He'd been tough but nice. Even tried to keep me out of the spire room and away from Vinnot's experiments.

"Can you help her?" I asked after telling him everything that had been done to Tali. I'd tried to explain what Onderaan had said about the damage to the brain, but I wasn't sure I'd gotten it right.

"Won't know until I look." He walked over to Tali, a smile on his face. She tensed, but there was recognition in her eyes. My heart soared.

Ginkev reached out a hand. She flinched away.

"It's okay, Tali," I said, going to her. I took his hand and placed it on my forehead. "See? It won't hurt."

He reached out again and she held still. "Saea's mercy, who did this to her?"

"The Duke. Vinnot. Zertanik. Maybe all of them together."

He tsked and shook his head.

"Can you fix her?"

"I don't know. I've never seen such brutality before, not to a brain. Bones, muscles—seen those shredded many a time. But this?" He shook his head again. "Just criminal."

"I wonder if she's the only one," Aylin said softly. "There have to be more, right? Not everyone wanted to join the Undying."

I hadn't thought of that, but there probably *were*

more. Trapped in the armor and in their own minds. Forced to become something so awful, they closed out the rest of the world.

"I know she's still in there, Master Ginkev," I said. "Please find her and bring her back."

Ginkev sighed and put his hand on her forehead again. "I'll do everything I can."

An hour later, I left Tali with Ginkev and headed to Jeatar's meeting. Danello led us to one of the classrooms on the second floor. The same officer group as before sat around a table with maps again, but this time Balju was there.

"The Duke will be here in two days," Jeatar said after we took our seats. People gasped. I guess he hadn't told anyone else about his message. "He's been marching his troops along the river, but he'll have to load them all onto the transport ships once he arrives at the delta. The fireboats will most likely reach us first, and we can expect the transport ships to start ferrying troops over not long after."

"How many are there?"

Jeatar looked grim. "Fifteen thousand men. Five transport ships, plus smaller skiffs, scouts, and of course fireboats. Where are we with the fire crews?"

"Ready to go where needed," said a woman I

didn't know. "We found seven water pumps, and we'll have them placed around the city by midday. We'll start soaking buildings so the wood's good and wet. Won't protect them if they get a direct hit, but it should help keep the flames contained until the fire crews can get there to douse them again."

Seven water pumps wouldn't be able to cover all the isles. But hopefully our boats would be able to stop the fireboats before they could launch too many attacks.

"We need to keep the fireboats out of range," Ellis said.

"Anything we can get in range to hit them will also be in range of their boats."

"What about bigger catapults?" Kione said.

"No materials, and no time to get any."

"Ipstan blocked the canals by sinking boats," Danello said. "Can we block Geveg by sinking bigger boats?"

"We'd never find boats that big," Ellis said.

"The Duke's bringing them, though, right?" Aylin asked. "We sink those first and they block the rest."

Jeatar rubbed the back of his neck. "That's actually not a bad idea."

"Except we have no way to sink a ship that

size," Ellis said. "What's Nya going to do? Shift into it?"

"What about pynvium?" a sergeant said. "Something that will flash and make them scared to come closer?"

"A little pain won't stop a whole ship," I said. Except . . . I looked at the walls around me. Stones just like those that had crumbled from a *lot* of pain. If pain dissolved stone, it could also dissolve wood.

"I need to talk to Onderaan." I jumped out of my chair and headed for the door. Danello and Aylin both came after me.

"Nya?" Jeatar said. "What are you planning?"

"I'll tell you once I know it's possible."

And if we had enough time to do it.

Onderaan was in the League's foundry. It wasn't very different from the one I'd robbed—and destroyed—in Baseer. Double doors opened toward the lake, allowing the breeze to carry the heat of the smelters away, but the metallic tang of the pynvium stayed behind. Two forges blazed, one on either side of the room, the enchanter's glyphs carved into the bricks glowing bright blue. The fires inside burned a shade darker, the blue flames rising and falling with the breath of the bellows.

A half dozen barrels like the ones I'd found in the Duke's foundry lined the front wall. More pynvium sand. The only pynvium left behind.

Onderaan worked at one forge, heavy leathers covering his head, hands, and torso. He was pouring blue-hot liquid pynvium into a mold about a foot square. Another man worked the second forge. He spotted us, then went to Onderaan and tapped him on the shoulder. Onderaan turned and walked over, pulling the long cap off his head.

"You're looking better."

"Feeling better, too. Do we have enough pynvium to make large spheres? Something that can hold a *lot* of pain?"

"For healing?"

"Weapons."

"Such as?"

"If you flash enough pain, it disintegrates things, like wood." Flesh too, but I didn't want to think about that. "If you trigger it to flash when bumped hard, we can put pynvium balls around the isles. We can use buoys from the fishing boats to keep them just below the surface. If we do it right, we might even be able to weight them enough that they drag the buoys underwater too."

Danello whistled. "They'd never even suspect something like that."

"No, they wouldn't," Onderaan said. "We can make them, but filling them will be the problem. We don't have enough pain."

Aylin huffed. "We have Healers and soldiers and knives. We can *make* pain."

Onderaan gasped and stared at her as if he wasn't sure if that was ghastly or genius. Seemed like both to me.

"Can you make them?" I asked.

"I can." Onderaan went to a heavy metal box on a worktable and opened the lid. He pulled out the silvery-blue cylinder I'd found at Zertanik's. My stomach quivered, flipping around like a beached fish. He ran his fingers along a row of glyphs. "In fact, I'm almost certain these glyphs here enhance a flash. I'm still studying what these other glyphs are, though." He tapped along the bottom. "They're very similar to a traditional trigger, but I haven't figured out yet what *type* of trigger."

"Which means what?" Aylin said, frowning.

"Oh, I'm sorry." He grinned. "Zertanik was a dangerous man, but his work is astonishing. With his glyphs, I can enchant Nya's spheres to flash twice the amount of pain, if not more."

"Enough to dissolve a hole in the hull of a ship?"

"I believe so, yes."

Danello looked uncertain. "Is it wrong to be happy about that?"

"I don't know, but I bet Jeatar is going to be thrilled."

If this worked, we could even the odds. Saints, we might even gain an advantage. It would be nice if just once, we didn't have to do the impossible to survive.

TWENTY-THREE

The darkness hovered on the silver edge between night and day. No gray streaks of dawn lit the sky yet, but the orange glow from fires boxes on the blockade boats mimicked the rising sun. By full dawn, the Duke's men would be here.

"I can't take this waiting anymore," Aylin said, standing with the rest of us on the balcony of the tallest spire at the League. Jeatar had everyone on alert, the pynvium ready, the dorms and classrooms full of Gevegians who needed our protection. Children, old men and women, those who weren't able to fight. They'd been coming in for two days, carrying what was left of their possessions in baskets.

"They'll be here soon enough." Danello wore a League guard's uniform. He'd been assigned to protect the League, along with his father.

I tugged at the collar of my own uniform. Me, in Healers' League green. If that didn't say desperate, I don't know what did.

"Do you see that?" Aylin said, pointing out across the water. "I thought I saw something."

"It's still too dark," I said. "We'll see them before they land, don't worry."

She shivered. "All I've been doing *is* worrying."

I gazed into blackness. Pale light hovered on the horizon. It wouldn't be long now.

"How many ships do you think he'll have?" Lanelle asked, back in League green as well.

"Not more than we can stop," Danello answered. It sounded better than the truth. Jeatar had kept the Duke's numbers quiet, though they were bound to come out once he arrived. Hard to hide the truth when it was sailing right toward you.

Jeatar had troops spread around the isle at strategic points throughout the city. He didn't expect the Duke to risk a full invasion unless the fireboats failed, but he wanted to be ready. Vyand had gone with him this time, insisting it had been my idea. That I'd be fine tucked away in the League. After seeing her and her team fight, I agreed that she was a good person to have watching Jeatar's back.

He'd frowned, but he hadn't argued.

With so much ground to cover, our people were spread pretty thin. Every boat was on the lake, fire rocks ready to launch and spears ready to throw. The pynvium spheres, or sinkers, as Ellis had named them, floated below the surface of the water just beyond catapult range. The bulk of our foot soldiers were in the Aristocrats' Isles—where Jeatar felt the Duke would most likely launch his ground assault. The League had a decent-sized guard, but we needed our people more on the outer isles to work the water pumps and keep the fires from spreading. We placed extra sinkers in Half Moon Bay to compensate. The Duke's ships couldn't reach League Isle without coming through there.

We were as ready as we could be with the little time we'd had to prepare.

The sky brightened, black turning to gray. Shadows fled, but a moving darkness remained.

"There they are," said Aylin. No trace of hesitation in her voice this time.

Black on the lake. Ships of all sizes, sails unfurled. The transport ships led the armada, huge and unforgiving. Smaller ships trailed in their wake.

"Look at them all," Lanelle said. "Oh Saints, they're really here. It's starting."

"We're going to have burns first," I said, thinking about everything Mama had ever said about treating them. "We need to soak the cloths."

"We know what to do, Nya. We've been trained for this—you haven't."

I gritted my teeth. "It won't be the same." Words in a classroom couldn't prepare you for what was coming. Of course, neither could stories, no matter how horrible they might have been. Or the memories.

"There must be forty ships surrounding the isles," Papa told the group of men and women around our table. *"Dozens of fireboats."*

Gasps from those who'd been strong until now.

"He means to burn us out? Like Sorille?"

"He's threatening to."

"We'll fight him. We have our own boats. We can throw fire and pitch just as well as he can. Burn those fireboats before they can burn us."

They hadn't done it, but maybe we had a chance.

"Healers, time to go," Ginkev said, and I jumped. I hadn't even known he was there. The worst of the injured would be brought to the League, but the rest would be healed on the battlefield. Half our Healers had gone with the army, taking several pynvium bricks each.

"I'll be on the perimeter if you need me," Danello said before hurrying off. He had his own post to get to. He was ten steps away before I realized I hadn't gotten a good-bye kiss. I wanted to chase after him, say good-bye properly in case one of us died today.

"Nya, move it!" Lanelle hollered.

I followed the others, wondering if Mama and Grannyma had felt like this the day the Duke attacked them.

And wondering if they had been just as scared.

The city bell tower struck double clangs—another fire warning. Volunteers rushed around the treatment ward, preparing beds, stacking cloths and bowls, filling water tanks.

Healers waited for the rush of injured. A few dozen to help where there had once been a hundred. But it should have been two more. Soek should be here. And Tali should be able to do what she was so good at, but who knew what she'd do in all the chaos. Ginkev was making progress with her, but she wasn't ready to heal under battlefield conditions.

More burn victims would be coming in soon, but right now the treatment ward was empty. I had time to see what was going on, how bad the fighting was. How close the Duke's ships were. I ran for the stairs and the sunroom on the third floor. The lower windows had been boarded up, but the windows on the upper floors were unprotected.

Several of the Duke's fireboats were by the dock, some already burning from our attacks. Smoke from the fireboxes rose into the air on both sides, the curved poles of the catapults arching over the decks. Balls of flame flew through the air toward the docks. More flew toward the approaching fireboats. Smoke misted above the buildings, but not as heavily as I'd feared. The fire crews were probably there, keeping the fires under control.

I scanned the rest of the city, the afternoon sun stealing any shadows that might hinder my view. A half dozen more fireboats floated off the production district. Heavier smoke rose above the buildings there—had the fire crews failed? I didn't see any of our boats.

Tall masts rose above Upper Aristocrats' Isle, transport ships that had made it past the sinkers. We'd gotten reports that troops were in the city, but we hadn't seen any battle injuries yet. That would change soon.

WHOOMP!

Water sprayed. Wood vanished. A sharp crack split the air as a sinker's flash split the hull of one of transport ships off North Isle. Huge cracks spiderwebbed from the gaping hole in the bottom. The ship rolled to one side, and armored soldiers tumbled toward the water. Screams followed not long after, then splashes.

WHOOMP!

Another flash, a fireboat this time. Screams came sooner, the flash close enough on the smaller boat to hit the crew. Steam hissed as water flooded the fireboxes.

Cheers rose above the screams and hisses and splashes.

My stomach churned.

I turned away. This was my doing. I'd thought up the sinkers, devised the way to kill those people. I tried not to imagine it, but the images kept flooding my mind. The falling. The sinking. The dying.

I left the balcony. People filled the halls: soldiers left behind to guard the League, folks with nowhere else to go. People running with one message or another. I reached the main treatment floor. Lanelle was shouting directions and Healers were dashing from bed to bed.

"Wounded incoming," she shouted, and bells began to chime. Smaller bells than those outside— calls for the Healers.

The next wave of injured for the day. But not the last.

"Nya," Lanelle called, waving me closer. "Stabilize the patients and move on. Let the others finish the heals. It took too long this morning."

I held my tongue and nodded. I went to the first bed. A woman with stab wounds, confirming the Duke did have soldiers in the city now. I put one hand on her forehead and the other on her heart and felt my way in. Pierced lung, badly healed on the field by someone who didn't know how to close such a wound. We'd probably see more of those today, too. I *drew* the pain away, sealing the puncture and easing her shock. So much more I could do, but she'd survive until one of the others got to her to heal her properly. That was their job, this was mine.

I went to the next bed, a man bleeding far too much to have been moved in the first place. I *drew* in his pain too, closing the artery. Bed to bed, patient to patient, skipping those who weren't on the verge of death. I finished the row, my stomach throbbing, my lungs stinging, my head swirling. I staggered to the rear of the ward and through the curtains.

The apprentice assigned to help me jumped to her feet. Twelve years old, with just enough training to take my pain and put it into the pynvium. "Are you full?" she asked.

I nodded.

She closed her eyes. I wanted to shift into her and get rid of the pain faster, but it was easier on her if she took it herself.

My hands tingled and the pain slid away, my fingers throbbing as it passed from me to her. She gritted her teeth, the knuckles of her hands white.

Then the pain was gone.

"Got it." She turned away and went to our meager Slab, a cube of pynvium the size of a footstool, and pushed the pain into it.

Tali had once offered to transfer pain for me. She foolishly thought I could join the League and heal, that she could draw my pain from me and push it into the pynvium. Impossible then—the Luminary would have thrown me into prison—or worse, as I'd found out—but I was doing it now.

Without her.

Bells inside the League rang again. More wounded on the way.

I took a deep breath and ran back to the ward.

~⌐⌐~

By the end of the day, bodies and wood floated around the city, creating an effective barricade against the Duke's ships. Two transport ships broke the surface just off the Aristocrats' Isles, leaning so heavily to one side, their masts dented a villa along the edge of the isle. The Duke had tried hard to reach us but we'd held him back.

Another ship lay on its side in the water at the edge of Half Moon Bay, blocking the path to the League better than anything we could have built. The smaller boats we'd sunk had vanished, though they made the water equally treacherous. Two fireboats had tried to maneuver past them and had run aground on the wrecks, ripping out their hulls and sinking.

The Duke had diverted more soldiers to North Isle. Rivers of blue and silver were still pouring into our streets from the transport ships we hadn't been able to sink. We had them contained to the North and Aristocrats' Isles for now, but we were still outnumbered.

"I thought I'd find you here," Aylin said, walking wearily into the sunroom. Blood stained her shirt, and a smear of it crusted along her hairline. She'd been assisting patients and Healers all morning. "Best view in the city."

"Not today."

"Yeah, well." She sighed. "It'll get better."

"You really think so?" I said.

"Yes. And so should you. No one thought we'd last this long, and we're holding them back."

I tried to smile, but it wouldn't come. Could I at least hope? I gazed at the ships we'd sunk, the soldiers we'd stopped. The fires we'd put out.

We might not win, but maybe, just maybe, we'd survive.

TWENTY-FOUR

Two full days, and still we held our ground. The wounded kept coming into the League, and we kept sending them back out again. Fire crews staggered in, exhausted, and others staggered out to relieve them. We couldn't keep this up, couldn't keep pitting tired and worn soldiers against the Duke's fresh troops.

The docks were in flames, but the fires had been stopped before they'd spread to the tradesmen's corner. Most of the production district smoldered, some fires still burning, but the fire crews had put out most of them. One of the Aristocrats' Isles was nothing but cinders.

"No loss," said one of the soldiers recovering

from healing. "It was all Baseeri living there anyway. We'll rebuild it for Gevegians."

I held my tongue and kept healing. Gevegians had built those villas. Nothing Baseeri burned there—just all that was left of the families they'd already destroyed.

Another night fell. The sounds of metal clashing subsided, and campfires blazed in the east end of Geveg—the isles held solidly by the Duke. More fires burned in the west end, but no people sat around those. They were the last of the dock buildings finally succumbing.

"One more in bed six," Lanelle said as we passed each other. "I'm going to dump my pain and grab some food."

"I'll get them."

The soldier in bed six smiled. Ellis.

I smiled back and took her hands. "Good to see you, even if it is here."

"Better here than not at all."

"True." Someone had started a list of the dead in the main antechamber, but I hadn't looked to see who was on it. I had no time to grieve. I put a hand on Ellis's forehead and felt my way in, sensing the same cuts, the piercings, the bruises I'd been healing for days. I *drew* them all away.

Ellis sighed. "Thanks."

"How's it going out there?"

"Been hard, but we're not letting them through. Jeatar is amazing. He won't let us lose hope, keeps us focused and fighting, even laughing once in a while. Those sinkers made a big difference."

I winced.

She patted my hand. "We'd be dead now if you hadn't suggested those things. They cut the Duke's forces in half, gave us time to put out fires. They forced him to dock where we were the most prepared. Now that he's on the ground, he's being cautious instead of smashing through us. If we win, it'll be because of that."

If we win. She thought there was a chance, same as Aylin.

"Is Jeatar okay?"

Ellis nodded. "He's been hurt a few times, but nothing the battlefield Healer can't handle."

"Vyand taking good care of him?"

"Extremely. I don't even want to skewer her anymore."

I smiled. "I guess that's good. Tell him and the others I said good luck."

"I will."

I hugged her and left, carrying her pain back to

the Slab. I offered my hands to the apprentice and she sniffed back tears. I'd lost count of how many times she'd taken my pain.

"This'll probably be the last time tonight," I said, just as glad as she probably was about that.

"They won't attack tonight?"

"Not until dawn. They're probably tired." Though they had more soldiers, so they could be pretending to cease attacks, waiting for us to let down our tired guard. Then they'd send more troops, fresh from a day of rest.

"Okay," she said, taking my hand.

My hands and fingers tingled, aching in a way I'd never felt before. Had Tali ever felt this? Was this normal after healing all day? If so, she'd been tougher than I'd thought.

Is tougher—she's not gone. There's still hope for her.

"There's food in the dining hall," I said, voice cracking. I cleared my throat. "Get some food and some sleep."

She nodded and left without another word, feet shuffling across the floor.

Twelve was too young to go to war.

I followed her to the dining hall and filled a bowl with fishcakes. Aylin and Danello were sitting at one of the long tables. Tables Tali used to eat at. Laugh at. Live at. Just like Mama and Grannyma. I turned away. I couldn't eat in there, not tonight. Maybe not ever. I ran.

Footsteps echoed in the hall behind me.

"Nya, wait!" Danello called. I stopped. He and Aylin caught up. "You okay?"

"No," I said. "I just . . . I need someplace else."

They looked at each other, understanding in their eyes; then Danello looked back. "Sunroom. No one will be up there right now. Let me get our bowls."

I nodded, clutching my own bowl.

Moist air and darkness greeted us as we stepped into the sunroom. Someone had left the balcony doors open and a breeze blew in. The lamps were off and we left them dark.

We sat on soft couches and ate in silence. Kept sitting long after we finished our fish and set the bowls down.

Outside, Geveg was equally dark—save for the fires and lights of the Duke's army. It angered me, that boldness. Like he had no fear of us and could shout his location so clearly. We had to hide in darkness, mask our presence.

"I want him dead."

Aylin looked up. "The Duke?"

"Yes. I just wanted him gone before, but now I want him dead."

Danello nodded. "Me too."

Aylin paused, then sighed. "So do I."

Wood cracked, then something banged—wood against stone. Sounds we'd heard for two days, but this was closer. Much closer.

WHOOMP!

Water splashed, a man screamed. Just one.

"That didn't sound right," Danello said. He rose and went out on the balcony, peering into the darkness covering Half Moon Bay.

WHOOMP!

Again, just a single frightened voice screamed.

"How many sinkers are in the bay?" Danello asked.

"Six," I said. "Three at the front and three close to the League."

WHOOMP!

"That was the third front one then." Danello frowned. "He's not sending in fireboats or we'd see the flames."

My guts twisted. "One boat—one captain. He's looking for sinkers and triggering them."

The moon slid out from behind the clouds. Blacker-than-black shapes hovered at the edge of

Half Moon Bay. A transport ship. Smaller boats sailed ahead of them. Six were already sinking.

"Saints, he's clearing a path," Danello said, gripping the balcony rail.

"No, he's *cleared* it." I pointed to the ships closest to the League. "We heard the *last* three sinkers flash, not the first three."

He sacrificed all those lives just to get to us.

"I'll alert the perimeter captain," said Danello. "We'll need reinforcements."

"How many soldiers does a transport carry?" Aylin asked.

"Maybe five or six hundred?"

"We can't let them get to the League," she said. "The guard is what? Half that?"

"Yeah."

We had to slow them down, keep them back. Give our reinforcements time to get here. The Duke couldn't be sure he'd triggered all the sinkers, so he'd be cautious. That gave us some time, but not much.

"Maybe Onderaan had some pynvium weapons that haven't gone out yet," Aylin said.

We ran to the forge. The fires still burned, but I didn't see any pynvium in the ore bins.

"Onderaan!" I shouted over the roar of the flames.

"What's wrong?"

"We're under attack. The Duke's cleared a path through the bay sinkers and is about to land a transport ship on the League docks. Do we have any sinkers left? Or anything we can use against them?"

He shook his head. "Just you."

I groaned and scanned the foundry. "There has to be something. Scraps I can throw or—"

The barrels of pynvium sand. Six of them along the wall.

"Is there pain in there?"

"I don't know. We never checked. The sand is just a by-product of the smelting process."

I turned to Aylin. "Get me a Healer, fast."

"Got it." Aylin raced off.

Each grain might be small, but together that was a *lot* of pynvium. Would it be enough? I had the details worked out by the time Aylin returned with Lanelle.

"The sand in those barrels." I pointed. "Tell me if there's pain in there."

She went over and stuck her hand into each barrel. "What I can feel has pain, but there's no way to tell if every single grain has it."

Good enough.

"I need sacks. And people to carry them. And a

way to get these barrels to the rear courtyard."

Onderaan gaped at me, then understanding lit his eyes.

"That's—"

"I know, but it's all we have."

"You'll need a trigger," Onderaan said. "Something large enough to start the chain flashing."

"But there's no pynvium left," Lanelle said.

"Wait!" Onderaan cried. "The cylinder." He hurried to the metal box and pulled it out. The quivering started again in my stomach. "Would this work? It's made of pynvium."

"*And* kragstun," I added. "We have no idea if it'll even hold pain. Or what it'll do if we try to fill it, let alone flash it."

"Do we have a choice?" Aylin asked. "There's nothing else we can use to trigger the flash."

Nor time to find an alternative.

Onderaan handed the cylinder to Lanelle. "What do you sense?"

She shook her head. "Nothing. It's empty. And there's no one in the ward at the moment, so there's no pain."

Aylin huffed and lifted her shirt, exposing her stomach. "Nya, stab me."

"No!"

"Don't be stupid. We need pain. We have enough

between us to fill the cylinder. Lanelle can heal us right away."

No one moved. Lanelle smiled. She'd probably imagine stabbing Aylin at least once before.

"Don't make me do it myself," Aylin said. "You know I have terrible aim."

I shook my head. "There has to be another way."

"*Stab* me," Aylin said, slapping her stomach.

"Let me be the one." Onderaan pulled off his leather smelting jacket. "There's nothing left to forge, so it won't matter if I'm a little weak for a few hours. You'll need Aylin and you'll need your full strength."

"Onderaan, I can't—"

"Yes, Nya, you can." He smiled. "Analov blood has already been spilled to protect this city. What's a little more?"

Was this really any different from the folks fighting out there now? We were already fighting the Duke with our own blood, our own pain.

"Are you sure?" I asked.

He nodded. "It's the only way."

I drew my knife. If we were going to use my family's blood, then family should be the one to spill it.

The League guard was gathering in the courtyard when we rolled the first of the barrels out. Two dozen of those who'd evacuated to the League volunteered to help, with more offering to fight if they had to. Grandmothers and grandfathers, iron in their hearts and wills, even if their bodies were weak.

Children ran back and forth, filling bags of sand and taking them to those spreading it out in the courtyard.

"What can I do?" Danello asked, breathless. He'd sent messengers to both Jeatar and Balju, but who knew if they'd reach them in time. Or if they had any troops to spare to help us. If the Duke was sneaking up on the League, he might also send troops to distract our main forces.

After all, it's what we'd done to them.

"Make sure no one in the guard has any pain-filled pynvium on them. We can't risk them getting caught in the flashes."

The guards were well back from the lakewall, our secondary defense in case the sand didn't work. I tensed, even though the ship hadn't reached us yet. It was getting closer, the black shape creaking, gentle splashes of oars through water. They maneuvered without sails, quiet as a sigh.

We were just as quiet. Clouds blocked the half-moon, and the courtyard was dark, far enough back from the docks, with hibiscus hedges along the lakeside. There was a good chance those on the ship couldn't see us moving or spreading the sand.

We stood shoulder to shoulder across the court-yard, throwing out handfuls of sand, the ground gritty under our feet. When the sand ran out, we paused and stared into the darkness.

"Will it be enough?" Lanelle asked.

"I hope so."

Aylin turned to me. "Where do you want us?"

I pulled out a small horn. "I need one person at the far end of the courtyard to signal when all the soldiers are in the sand."

"I'll do it," Aylin grabbed the horn as Danello reached for it. "They'll need you if we have to fight," she said.

"You'll be caught in the flash," I said.

She nodded. "I know. Just come and get me when it's over."

I hugged her. "I will. Be careful and stay hidden."

"That's my plan." She dashed off, disappearing into the darkness.

"I guess that's it," I said, my stomach in knots.

"Yeah."

I looked at Danello, his features just shadows. "You should get back with the guards."

"I'm not leaving you." Shadows moved, and warm

lips brushed mine. I tugged him closer, not wanting to let go. He pulled away. "We fight together."

"Together."

We hid behind a hastily erected barricade fifteen feet from the edge of the sand. I'd have preferred stone. Wooden desks and chairs wouldn't protect Danello if the flash blew back toward us. The hundreds of League guards behind us also crouched low, some on their bellies, avoiding notice until the last possible second.

The transport ship reached the lakewall. I couldn't make out details, but its sheer size blacked out everything behind it. Metal rattled, faster and faster until a splash. The anchor? Wood banged against stone, then another just like it, then a third. Then footsteps. Lots of footsteps thunking on wood.

"Gangplank," Danello whispered. "They're unloading now."

I gripped the cylinder tighter, my stomach quivering, my skin itching.

Steps, movement, breathing. The gritty shuffling of soldiers walking through pynvium sand. They had to be close. I peered through holes in the barrier. Dark shapes focused, neat lines of soldiers so tight you couldn't tell where one ended and the next began. Hundreds of them filled the courtyard and dock area behind the League.

A horn blew. Aylin.

Startled cries rippled through the soldiers. I pictured dandelions scattering in the wind, pushing them as far and as fast as I could, and heaved the cylinder over the barrier.

Trigger every last grain of sand, you stupid flash.

WHOOMP!

Pain washed over me, sharp, prickling. *Too close!* Danello grunted and collapsed.

Whoomp, whoomp-whoomp! Whoomp . . .

Sparks flashed like blue fireflies dancing in the night. They floated on the wind, shimmering and casting a blue hue on the water. Light reflected off armor and windows, off broken glass scattered on the ground. Pynvium sand glittered as it fell, bursting with blue.

So beautiful.

Soldiers collapsed one by one, entire rows falling in unison. Soft gasps grew into cries and then screams farther down as soldiers started running.

Whoomp, whoomp-whoomp! Whoomp . . .

They couldn't run fast enough. The pynvium fireflies chased them down, exploded around them. They bit with our teeth, stung with our blood.

A chorus of childlike screams rose above the others.

WHOOMP!

Blue-white light lit the sky. A darker glow pulsed blue, then faded, pulsed again a little brighter, then dimmed and pulsed once more, over and over, brighter and brighter.

Blue glyphs.

Panic hit me a breath before the life-draining pulse did.

The Duke's weapon. It was here!

TWENTY-FIVE

S aea save us.

Cries of shock and fear behind me—the League guards.

I heard the noise again in my mind. The grinding of rock on rock, the sound that had twisted inside the huge disk of glyphed pynvium and silvery kragstun—and in me. The Duke must have gotten the weapon working again. Must have found someone besides me who could trigger it without dying.

I shivered, picturing the boats sent in to trigger the sinkers.

Maybe he didn't care if they died.

I had to stop it. The pulse would expand every time, stealing life from everything it touched. Brick

and wood would withstand it for a while and protect those inside, but soon even stone would start to
crack and crumble, same as the Duke's palace.

I grabbed Danello's hand and *drew*. He opened
his eyes, groaning. "What happened? I feel weird."

"The Duke's weapon is here."

"Oh Saints, no!"

"My flash triggered it, like in Baseer."

He winced. "Can you stop it?"

"I don't know."

He rose, and another pulse hit us, draining the
life from us. The League guards ran. How soon
until the pulse reached the League's walls? How
soon until it covered all of Geveg? Maybe that had
been the Duke's plan all along. Control the League
and trigger the weapon to drain the city.

"What if we shoved it into the bay?' Danello said.
"Would the water stop it?"

"I don't know. It's too big for us to move on our
own, though."

"Aylin's still down there, maybe she can help."

Last time I couldn't stop it—I'd only made it
worse. Flashed enough pain to shatter the Duke's
palace and several blocks around it. I wasn't sure
there was anything I *could* do.

Except find Aylin. Get her away from it. Get as

many people to the edges of the city as possible.

Danello's hand tightened on mine. "We'll find her together."

We started running. I tripped at the edge of the pynvium sand, right before the bodies. Danello lurched for my arm, but I crashed onto the street, grinding pynvium sand into my palms.

"Nya? Are you okay?"

"I'm fine."

Something heavy rolled past me. Glints of silvery blue sparkled in the faint moonlight as it spun.

The cylinder.

"Wait."

Silvery blue. Just like the metal on the weapon.

I pictured it, sitting there in the Duke's palace, a misshapen disk of pynvium and kragstun, that same silvery blue metal. It had a spire in the center of the disk, with a hole right in the middle of the spire.

I looked at the cylinder. A hole *that* size and shape.

Vinnot's voice drifted into my mind. . . .

We had someone working on a control device, but then I heard about the Shifter's flashing ability and her amazing immunity.

Zertanik. He *had* to have been the one working on a control device. Was this it?

Onderaan had said the glyphs were odd, forcing a flash, not just enhancing one. The size and shape couldn't be a coincidence. The cylinder had to control it, and if it could control it, maybe it could stop it.

I grabbed the cylinder, my hand itching where it touched me. My stomach flipped as fast as my racing heart.

"Find Aylin and get her out of here."

"Nya, what are you going to do?"

"See if this fits the weapon."

We ran toward the light. Danello broke away and headed for where Aylin had gone. I continued toward the weapon. My steps faltered when I got closer and the pulses got stronger, draining more and more. Running slowed to walking, then staggering. Then crawling. I dragged the cylinder along with the rest of me.

Almost there.

I kept crawling. Over the unconscious bodies of the Duke's soldiers.

The weapon loomed ahead, a glowing blue beacon with unconscious Takers chained to it. Carved glyphs shone bright in the dark, the blue and silver metal shimmering around it. It seemed smaller in the open. The pedestal rested on a cart this time, the driver lying on the bench. Even the horse was unconscious, trapping a soldier under its bulk, its harness snapped and dangling.

The weapon pulsed again—brightened—and drained. I screamed and dropped the cylinder, but swallowed the pain and snatched it again. Kept moving.

I braced myself for the next pulse and clawed my way across the fallen horse, the unconscious soldiers.

A girl lay where the Duke had once chained me, in the trigger position. I covered her hand with one of mine. Felt my way in. Faint pain cycled through her, her heart barely beating. I had to get her out of there. Had to get all them all out of there.

"Hold on. Fight it."

The weapon pulsed again and I shrieked, curling into a ball against the pain. So different from the blades or the kicks. Deeper, stronger. *Move—you can't quit now.* I gathered the draining pain between my heart and my guts, forced it back, trapped it. Hand over hand I climbed onto the disk, my stomach quivering so badly, it was hard to walk. My skin itched where the disk touched me, but I grabbed the spire, pulled myself up, and shoved the cylinder into the hole at the center.

Please work.

Light burst from the weapon. I dropped back to the disk and squeezed my eyes shut. The light stabbed through my lids, bright as day. Wind sucked at me, pulling me toward the device. My skin stretched, cracked—

Silence.

The wind eased. The pulsing stopped. Blue light dimmed to black. I trembled, every muscle sore, my skin stinging as if I'd flashed all the pynvium in the Three Territories. Was it over? Had it stopped?

No pulse. No more light.

I opened my eyes. White aftershimmers hovered before me for a heartbeat, then faded. The Takers weren't moving. Were they even still alive?

Weak and shaking, I crawled to the edge of the disk and rolled off, dropping to the street. I landed on my back on a soldier, but it was better than being on that pynvium. My stomach still quivered, but I didn't have the energy to move farther away.

"Nya!" Danello called.

I stared at the stars. They were twinkling blue. My eyelids drooped closed.

Leather scraped against stone. Swears, grunts. Staggering steps, coming closer, getting louder. "Nya!" Danello gathered me in his arms. "Can you hear me?"

"Help them," I said, shivering, but not cold.

"Are you hurt? Can I take any of your pain?"

I hurt, but not the same as when I carried pain. More weak than sore. I touched his arm, hot under my trembling fingers. *Pushed*.

"Nothing to shift." Every word took effort. So much effort.

Hands on my cheeks. Warm hands. "Nya, hold on," Danello said. "Aylin's here, but she's unconscious. Wake her up, and she'll get help." He put my hand on her arm.

I *drew*, just a little. Shuddered.

Aylin woke. Gasped. "What happened to her?"

"Get Lanelle. Now!"

More running feet. Danello stayed with me, stroking my hair. I tried to lift my head, but my neck felt made of lake weed.

So many sounds floated in the air: shouts, running feet, clanking armor. War. There was a war going on. And Danello, yelling. Yelling at Lanelle to move faster.

Tali. I had to say good-bye.

"I need Tali."

Soft hands pressed against my skin, tingling. "There's no injury—she feels . . ."

"Feels what?" Danello said. "Lanelle, is she *okay*?"

"I don't know! Last time I sensed something like this, the person was dying. I don't know what to do to help her."

Nobody spoke. I tried to feel my way into my own body. Was I dying? Felt more like falling asleep.

"Danello," I whispered, "get Tali."

"I'm not leaving you," he said. He sounded angry.

"Maybe you should find her," Lanelle whispered. "Nya may not"—she paused—"she doesn't have long."

"This wasn't part of the plan," Aylin yelled, grabbing my shirt. "You're supposed to beat him. You're supposed to win."

"I believe that's *my* plan," a man said. I knew that voice.

"No," Aylin whispered.

Whoomp!

Thuds, like bodies falling, as pain stung my skin. I forced my eyes open a crack, my heart pounding. A man stepped out of the shadows, then another, and another, with even more behind. Soldiers.

"Hold her."

Two soldiers pinned my arms to the street. The third man knelt over me, trapping my legs.

The Duke of Baseer.

TWENTY-SIX

"W here in Moed's name did you get the control rod?" the Duke asked, pulling a knife from a sheath on his belt. "Zertanik swore he couldn't make it work, the lying rat."

I struggled, helpless as a bird in a croc's jaw. My fingers flexed, straining for skin, but I had no real pain to shift even if I touched someone.

"I'm going to make you scream."

"Now, now, Verraad," another man spoke. I knew that voice too. He'd been with the Duke when they'd put me into the weapon. Erben, Eker—no, Erken. "No time to play."

"There's a little time."

"No, she's too dangerous to keep alive, even to torture."

"You . . . won't win," I gasped. So hard to breathe with them holding me down.

The knife came closer. "Yes, I will."

I clawed at the ground, unable to move more than my fingers. I brushed against Danello's pants leg. Found a rip at the knee.

"The best way to kill a Healer is straight through the heart," Erken said.

The Duke raised the knife. "Let's see if that works for Shifters too."

I stretched my finger and touched Danello's skin. *Drew* with everything I had left. He snorted awake. His pain surged through me, mingling with Aylin's.

The knife plunged down.

Danello leaped at the soldier on my right, knocking him over. My arm came free and I rolled right. The Duke's knife sank hilt deep into my chest, barely missing my heart. I gasped, unable to breathe in enough air to scream. Danello crashed against the second soldier, and he jerked back. My other arm pulled free.

The Duke. Get the Duke.

I swung uselessly at him. Missed. My hand dropped and landed on the hand of the second soldier. My fingers wrapped around his, and I *pushed* the knife wound into him. He shrieked and fell away.

Stop him. Stop the Duke, then *you can die.*

"Get her!" Erken yelled. The Duke charged forward. He grabbed my throat in both hands and squeezed.

My vision blurred. I grabbed his cheeks and *pushed*.

He sucked in a breath but didn't let go. "Shift all you want, but I'm stronger than you."

Soldiers surrounded us, swords out, looking confused. If they stabbed me, I could shift it into the Duke. But maybe they knew that.

"Don't touch her!" The Duke squeezed harder, far too much pleasure on his face.

I *pushed* harder. The shifted pain crashed against a wall, like he was keeping me out. Something strong.

Light sparkled at the edge of my vision. My lungs felt ready to burst. I needed air. Needed . . . strength . . .

I *drew,* clawing at that wall, trying to tear it down, get past it and make him let go of me. My vision cleared. I dug deeper, *drew* harder, reached beyond blood and bone and muscle. He grunted but still held on. My fingers ached, but I didn't let go. I had to get through that wall or I was dead.

The Duke's hands tightened more and my head spun. I kept *drawing.* Fire raced into me, sizzling up my arms and filling my lungs. The wall cracked and his grip loosened. Mine stayed firm. I *drew* harder. My heart beat with his heart. My blood sang with his blood. The strength of that wall poured into me. He tried to pull away but I held tight, *drawing* more and more, bringing it down.

"Look at her," Erken gasped. They'd pull me away now, make me stop. Kill me.

"She *is* Saint touched!" a soldier cried.

I held on. One last *draw*, one last heartbeat.

And then it was gone.

No, *he* was gone.

I shoved the Duke away. His body fell in a heap and lay still, his hands curled and pressed against his chest. His skin was flaky, his cheeks sunken like a frail old man's. His black hair was lighter, even in the dark.

What had I done?

My heart pounded strong. My pain was gone. I felt . . . *powerful.*

"Saints, what did you do to him? What *are* you?"

I looked up. Erken and the soldiers stood around me, swords drawn. They gaped, fear and confusion on their hard faces. Erken's held fascination as well.

"I'll do the same to you if you don't leave my city," I said.

The soldiers turned and ran. Soldiers, running from *me*.

Saints forgive me, but I kinda liked it that way.

Erken stood his ground, watching me. "He went about this the wrong way," he said. "Force was wrong. He should have asked you to help him."

"I would have said no."

"I imagine you would have. Perhaps *we* could strike a deal?"

I lunged toward him, hands outstretched. He shrieked and backed away, then fled into the night toward the transport ship still docked in the bay.

Grunts caught my attention. Danello wrestled on the ground with the two soldiers, kicking one while he swung at the other.

"Leave him alone," I said, moving toward them.

Neither soldier listened. I kicked the first in the chest. He fell back with a gasp.

"Now!"

They rolled away and staggered to their feet. Danello rose a second later, bleeding, but alive and ready to fight. The soldiers turned as if about to come for me, then cried out, horrified. They raced off after the others.

"Nya?" Danello said softly, staring at me. "Are you . . . what did you . . . ?"

"Please. I . . . I need a minute."

"Okay."

Nothing made sense. I stared down at the Duke. Hardly more than bones wrapped in skin. What had I done? What was that wall I'd tried so hard to tear down? His life? I'd drained him, drawn his life into me. The Duke had put me into his weapon all those months ago.

Had he *turned* me into it as well?

"Nya?"

"I didn't mean to do it, but I'm not sorry I did. He'd have killed us all if I'd let him live."

It was war. You killed in war—you had to. They *knew* that. They couldn't hate me for doing what had to be done. I spun back around. "You believe me, don't you?"

Danello took a step back and my heart nearly broke. "Of course I do."

"Then why are you acting scared of me?"

"Your eyes." He walked toward me, one hand out. He brushed the skin around my eyes. "They're, I don't know, blue."

"They changed color?"

"No," Danello said. "They're *glowing* blue."

I pressed my fingers against my face. I didn't feel anything. At least on the outside. Inside I felt strong. I felt *new*. I felt terrified.

"What happened to me?"

"I have no idea."

Soldiers were still unconscious all around us. Lanelle and Aylin too. I knelt and woke them both up, drawing away their pain.

They jerked away from me, then crept closer, the same horrible mix of fear and wonder on their faces.

"I know—they're glowing and I don't know why."

Lanelle gasped again and pointed to the Duke's body. "Is that the Duke?"

"Yes."

She kicked him. Twice. Then spit. "He deserved even worse than whatever you did."

I wasn't sure anyone deserved what I'd done.

"We need to get those Takers out of the weapon," I said. "And find where the League guards ran off to. The Duke might be dead, but his men are still alive. We have to deal with them."

"What about the weapon itself?" Danello asked. "You can't just leave it here."

I didn't want to touch it. It was hard enough looking at it. "Maybe we can get it inside the League."

"Maybe we can use it and flash the rest of those blue-boys back to Baseer," Lanelle said, heading for the Takers. "Do you have any idea how powerful that thing is?"

"I'm not using it on anyone. I don't even know if I can."

Aylin crossed her arms. "And let's not forget it uses *Takers* to work."

"Not anymore," Lanelle said. "They're dead. All of them."

"What?" No, they couldn't be. It wasn't fair. I turned the weapon off—it should have saved them. *It didn't save you. You had to drain the Duke to survive.*

He'd killed them, just like the boat captains, just like so many others. Why did he bring this weapon here? Why did he have to make me trigger it, make me kill so many just to stop him?

"Listen, the Duke needed to use Takers," Lanelle said after a bit. "Maybe she doesn't. She made it work in Baseer without them."

"Does it even matter?" They were dead because of me.

Lanelle huffed. "Of course it matters! Don't let him win. You made it work before, didn't you?"

"Yes." It *had* pulsed before when no one was attached to it. I didn't know why, but it didn't need to be full of pain to drain life.

"Then make it work now. Make those blue-boys

pay for what they've done."

"Um, I'll go get the guards," Danello said. "I'll make sure to warn them about your eyes."

"Okay." I stared at the weapon, the dead Takers. "We need to get them out of there."

We gently uncuffed them, pulling them out of the weapon, and then carried them to the soft grass. They deserved heroes' funerals, all of them. I took a deep breath and walked back to the weapon. Glared at it.

"Tell me you're not really thinking about touching that thing," Aylin said.

"Every inch of me itches just being this close to it."

"Then why do you still have that *look*?"

I sighed. "If I can figure out how to make it work, maybe we *can* end the war."

"By doing to others what you did to the Duke?"

I shivered. "No. But even elite soldiers are running from me right now, and if I have the weapon with me, maybe I can scare *all* of them and make them leave us alone for good." And then no one else had to die.

I stepped up and put my hands on the disk. It hummed under my palms. My stomach felt like something was eating away at me.

"Well?" she asked.

I closed my eyes, sensed my way in, shoving past

the quivering and the twisting and the humming.

Anything in here?

I hadn't expected an answer, but a soft *click* filled my mind. I followed it. Felt it. Like a huge room lurking there under the pynvium and the silvery blue metal. I felt around in that empty room, looking for the door or the key or anything that would make it turn on.

Blue fire flickered at the edge of my vision if I didn't look at it directly. I blew on the fire, gently, a soft breeze.

The glyphs in the weapon glowed.

"Nya, please get off that thing," Aylin said, her voice shaking.

"Wait, I think I got it."

I pictured a lamp with the blue flame inside and closed the flaps, shutting out the light.

The light in the glyphs dimmed.

I pictured opening the flaps.

The glyphs flared bright; the hum grew louder.

I had control. I could do this. I could *use* this.

You could kill with this.

But I could also save lives with it. Gevegian *and* Baseeri.

"Soon as Danello gets back, we're getting this thing to the front lines."

Geveg's army filled the streets. We'd been fighting all night, holding on to one block at a time, losing some, gaining others. The Duke's forces were still trying to seize a foothold in North Isle, but they had a solid hold on the Gov-Gen's isle. The fighting in the Aristocrats' Isles was fierce, and losses were high.

That was where Jeatar was.

So that was where we were going.

Fifty League guards surrounded me. We'd managed to wake the horse, and she pulled the cart with me and the weapon on it. I kept my hands pressed against the weapon and the glyphs glowed blue, same as my eyes. The light reflected off the armor of the dead, the shattered windows, the broken souls.

Aylin swore I would scare the Saints themselves.

"What—how—is that?" Jeatar gaped at me, blood caking his hairline just above his ear.

"It's the Duke's weapon. He's dead. I'll explain later."

"She's needs to get through to the blue-boys," Aylin added. "While it's still dark."

Jeatar gaped for another heartbeat, but Vyand shook him, staring at me the same way. He stepped aside. It took him another minute to issue orders.

Our soldiers parted, letting me and my escort though.

Battle sounds grew louder as we grew closer. Grunts and shouts, the *shring* of metal, the clang of swords. Then gasps of shock.

"What *is* that?"

"It's the Shifter!"

"It's the Saints!"

I blew on the blue fire in my mind, and the weapon glowed brighter. More than just the Duke's soldiers cried out and backed away.

"The Saints are protecting Geveg!" a woman yelled. I wasn't sure who, but it sounded suspiciously like Ellis.

The cries turned to shouts, the shouts to screams. The Duke's soldiers dropped their weapons and ran—a wall of retreating backs. Horns blew, quick bursts signaling retreat. The wall became a tide, sliding away from our shores, back into the lake.

I followed them through the streets, across the bridges, and onto the terraces. Past the villa I grew up in. Jeatar and our forces came with me, their blades reflecting blue in the light. Making the Baseeri run even faster.

They fled ahead of us to the Gov-Gen's isle, racing for the ramps to the transport ship looming above the governor's estate. Soldiers shoved each other, knocking people off the gangplanks and into the canals.

They were still running on board when the transport ship raised its sails. Wind caught canvas with a snap, and the ship pulled away, dragging the gangplanks along the lakewall.

We'd won. We'd actually won.

Cheers and chants floated above the screams and the running feet of those trying to make it onto the moving ship before it pulled free of Geveg. Our soldiers surged past me, after the last of the blue-boys, the Baseeri, the invaders.

"Nya, you hear that?" Aylin asked, jumping up and down beside me.

I listened and smiled. "They're chanting to Saint Saea."

Aylin laughed and slapped my leg. "No, they're chanting *Nya*."

They couldn't be! The wind gusted, bringing the words right to my ears.

"*Ny-a!*"

"*Ny-a!*"

"*Ny-a!*"

TWENTY-SEVEN

Eight days they'd been gone. For eight whole days we'd been free.

The first two days, the fires had burned. The last of the Duke's soldiers had fled Geveg in terror, dropping lamps and torches, kicking over camp stoves, igniting homes and fences throughout the North and Aristocrats' Isles. The fire crews put out what they could, and the Duke's soldiers never regrouped, never returned. They'd left Geveg burning, just as they'd intended, but they'd *left*.

The next six days *we* regrouped.

Families found each other, and friends mourned the dead. We grieved for those we'd lost and celebrated with those we'd saved.

Sunshine warmed my face while I stood in a room that used to be mine. It was charred now, blackened by the fires that had raged through the terraces and the rest of the aristocrat district.

"All gone," Tali said, crunching her way into my old room. She was better now, talking some, but not fully healed. Ginkev wasn't sure she ever would be, but I had hope.

"It was nice before. Soft colors, soft furniture. Always smelled like food."

"Mama smelled like flowers."

I nodded, eyes watering. "She did. She was beautiful too, and kind, and strong." I held on to her strength. I needed that today.

I walked to the wardrobe and knocked aside the charred door. Found wet clothes in sooty piles. I pulled one out. Pants big enough for me *and* Tali together. I dropped them.

"This is foolish. There's nothing here that's mine." I don't know why I expected to find anything of ours in our old villa. Just that . . . we'd won. Everything should have gone back to the way it was.

What's done is done, and I can't change it none.

Mama was still dead. Papa, Grannyma, Wen and Lenna. Soek and Quenji. Even Ipstan. Hundreds more whose names I didn't know, faces I'd never seen.

I'd never play in the fountain again. Never roll in the grass with Tali. Never curl up on the couch while Mama read to us.

My old life was nothing but ash, just like my old home.

"Come on," I said. "There's nothing here but a burned villa."

I led Tali down the wrought-iron spiral staircase in the back—the only stairs left—and exited through the hole that used to be the rear kitchen door. Crossed what was once the garden, where Mama had weeded her violets while Tali chased butterflies. Lake gulls and buzzards circled above, looking for bits of charred things to fill their bellies.

Two guards waited by the front door, standing on the blackened stone path where Wen had died. They fell into step as I passed, one man in front and one behind. Just a precaution, Jeatar had said, until the curiosity about me died down.

I'd thought that would have ceased when my eyes stopped glowing, but they'd been normal three days now and there was no sign of it fading. I didn't mind the praise so much—we'd worked hard for that—but the adoration? I could do without that.

It *was* getting better, though. People were clingy at first, wanting to touch me, to meet me; but once they did, they realized I wasn't a saint. I was just a girl.

A *strange* girl, to be sure, but not that different from them.

We left the villa's grounds and walked into the street. The cleanup crews stopped working and cheered, chanting my name like the soldiers had the last night of the war.

I prayed that would stop soon too. Aylin said being a hero would last longer than being a saint.

A carriage waited at the end of the walk, with more guards around it, but not mine. They all wore League green and gold, though folks were working on a different style for Geveg's new uniforms.

"Wait, that's not my carriage." It was nicer and bigger.

"The Duke wanted to speak to you," one of the guards said, opening the carriage door.

My first instinct was to run, but I couldn't be afraid of that title anymore.

I climbed in. Jeatar sat on the far side, arms crossed, giving me his "you're in trouble again" stare.

Okay, maybe I should be a little afraid of it.

"What are you doing here?" I blurted. He should have left for Baseer by now.

"I was about to ask *you* that."

"I wanted to see my . . . the villa."

His stare softened. "You should have told me. I'd have come with you."

I took my seat, and Tali slid in next to me. "Mean and Nasty came with us." I waved a hand at my guards. Tali had nicknamed them, which they'd found funny and they had kept the names. That's when I started liking them.

"But not inside the villa," he said gently.

"No."

I didn't say anything else, and he didn't ask. He told Mean to take us back to the League, and the carriage lurched forward.

People were already lining the streets, waving and cheering as we passed.

"Any chance they're cheering for you?" I said.

"No." Jeatar chuckled. "I didn't save the city."

"Yes, you did. You held back the Duke's soldiers and planned the defenses and even led the attack on the Duke's troops. Geveg wouldn't be free without you."

"You'd have found a way."

"They think I'm a saint."

He smiled. "They think you're a hero."

"Nya saved the city, Nya saved us all. They thought that they would beat us, but Nya made them fall," Tali sang softly, watching the city pass outside.

"See? Even she knows it."

I sighed and leaned against the seat. I didn't want all this attention. Sure, it was nice to be appreciated, but so many people knowing my face and my name couldn't be good. It was always safer when no one noticed you.

"When are you leaving for Baseer?" Once he'd officially come out of hiding, all his contacts and supporters had started talking about him, spreading rumors that he was back and fighting for Geveg. The Baseeri practically demanded he take the throne.

"In a few days. I have some things I want to finish up here first."

"Like what?"

"Like making sure the Baseeri and Gevegians don't start fighting over who gets to run the city."

"Rumors say Balju wants the job." Balju was also doing just as much talking as everyone else about Jeatar taking the throne. I suspected he wanted Jeatar out of Geveg before folks started thinking he'd make a better governor than duke.

"What do you think?"

"He doesn't much like Gevegians." Sure, he'd fought alongside us, but I could still hear him asking why Jeatar would try to help us. The sneer in his voice. "I don't think we'd approve of his appointment."

Jeatar chuckled. "Neither do I."

"Is that going to be a problem?" We really didn't need another war.

"More of a headache." He paused, staring at me a moment. "I was thinking about suggesting Onderaan."

"Really? Does he even *want* to be governor?"

He shrugged. "He's never said, but he's Baseeri, so Balju and his people will accept him. And he's an Analov, so Gevegians will accept him. Best still, he's your uncle, so if they don't like it, you can go out and *convince* them otherwise." He grinned mischievously.

"Onderaan's nice," Tali said.

Jeatar nodded. "Yes, he is."

Onderaan, in charge of Geveg. I smiled. "You're right. I think he'd make a good governor."

Besides, it kept things in the family, and that felt . . . *right*.

"Nya," Tali called, jumping up and down in the doorway of my room in our town house. "Hurry, hurry."

"She's right," said Aylin. "We're going to miss the skiff."

"It's not going to leave without us." I shoved the rest of my things into my pack. Aylin groaned and snatched them away from me.

"You don't treat expensive clothes that way." She folded the fine dresses and tailored pants into neat squares and opened the pack. Gifts had been arriving for the last month. I hadn't wanted to keep any of them, but Aylin swore refusing them would upset folks, and I didn't want to cause another war, did I?

An exaggeration to be sure, but she did have a point. Some of the gifts were small, flowers or sweetcakes, but from Gevegians I'd helped. Refusing them *would* be an insult.

"What do you have *in* here, rocks?" she asked. "Do you really want to be all wrinkled for Jeatar's coronation?"

"They'll hang out by then. We have a whole week." Even if it was a whole week of parties and events I didn't want to go to. Neither did Jeatar, but he couldn't exactly skip his own coronation festivities. He'd put it off for nearly a month now, and while he *was* ruling without challenge, the aristocrats wanted their official crowning with all the pomp. Just to be safe.

Soldiers all over the Three Territories had been recalled, and Jeatar had worked with Onderaan and

Verlatta's new self-appointed governor to create a joint guard to patrol the roads and borders. Travel was much safer now, though there were still problems. Probably always would be problems, but every step got you closer to the end of the path.

He'd put Balju in charge of it, which made it easier to make Onderaan governor. Both had been surprised, but happy, with the arrangement.

"Nya, what are these?" Aylin pulled two books from my pack.

"I wanted to get in some studying while we were away."

She tossed the books onto the bed. "Ginkev gave you the week off. You don't have any classes to study for."

"I have a lot of catching up to do."

I wasn't an official apprentice, but Ginkev had offered me a spot in class anyway. He said my knowledge was scattered worse than scared mice, and it would take him at least a year to fill in the gaps of my training before he could figure out what cord I might be. I was okay with that. I didn't know who or what I was either.

"Here." Aylin handed me the pack, my clothes neatly folded inside. "Your assignment this week is to have fun."

I grinned. "I'll do my best."

We left my room and hurried down the stairs. Our town house was a gift from Jeatar—or as he claimed, a gift from Geveg. Small, only two floors, but with more than enough room for just us. Aylin's room was next to mine, Tali's across the hall. I hoped one day she'd return to her apprenticeship, same as the other Takers in Geveg. Most of them anyway. Some had chosen to enter the new Protectors' League and learn how to fight *and* heal. I didn't see her choosing *that*.

"No time for lunch?" Kelsea asked, poking her head out of the kitchen. She'd come with the town house, a sweet blond girl who was always smiling no matter how sour the rest of us got. Jeatar claimed she was the daughter of a soldier who'd died in the war, one who really needed a job, but she was older than me and seemed quite capable of caring for herself. She also chopped vegetables like they'd personally offended her.

She was a bodyguard, sure as sugar.

I was pretty sure Kelsea knew I'd figured out her secret, but we both pretended she was only a housemistress. I liked her, and so did Tali and Aylin, so it wasn't hard.

Mean and Nasty waved to Tali as she raced

toward the carriage. Not mine, one of Onderaan's. He was pretty busy with the governor's job, but he still worked with Jeatar, using Zertanik's enchanter's book to develop weapons. We kept that secret.

"Ready to go back to Baseer?" Danello greeted me with a kiss. He and his family had the town house across the street, another of Jeatar's gifts.

"No, but it's not like I can get out of it." I climbed in and took a seat in the otherwise empty carriage. "Where is everyone?"

"Da left with the twins and Halima a few days ago. They wanted to get there early and visit Ouea." He grinned. "I think Da's sweet on her."

I smiled. Ouea had taken care of Jeatar's farmhouse and probably had her hands full now running the palace. "You'd certainly eat better if they got married."

"I don't think it's that serious yet."

"It's almost spring," Aylin said. "Love is supposed to be in the air, right?" She took my pack and put it with her bag in the trunk on the rear of the carriage.

Danello flushed pink. "Yeah, well, maybe."

"Let's go, let's go," Tali said, leaning over the side of the carriage. She liked to ride on the driver's bench with Nasty. Mean took his place in the rear.

Aylin hopped in, and we rumbled off, moving slowly through the streets. A few shop windows boasted new glass, though most were still boarded up. Many shops hadn't reopened, and rumors had it the Finance Master was worried about there being too many jobs and not enough people to fill them. Quite the change from last summer, when I'd waited twenty deep to get a job unloading fish.

Geveg was wounded, but we'd heal. Healing was what we did best.

"They've done so much this week." Danello gazed out the window, his fingers entwined in mine. "You should see all the lumber coming in from Verlatta. The docks are stacked with it."

"I can't believe how fast they rebuilt them," I said.

The docks had been the first project. Our farming and rancher isles provided some food, but we relied on supplies brought over from Dorpstaad. Once the wharf was functioning again, work crews began rebuilding homes and shops. They ignored the ruined aristocrat district. Those who could afford villas would return eventually, but for now we had to focus on getting our people housed and fed.

And protected, of course. We'd been caught unprepared before, and we weren't about to ignore security again. Soldiers patrolled the streets, dressed in purple and white, with a white violet patch on their uniforms. The soldiers greeted folks as they passed, watching over us this time, preventing looting instead of leading it.

Then there was the weapon. Hidden away in the League, but ready to defend Geveg against any attack, same as I was. The threat of that would keep us safe well after folks stopped calling me a hero.

As long as those who wanted to hurt us didn't stop fearing I might be a saint.

"Let me ask you something," Aylin said, smoothing the wrinkles in her skirt. "I was thinking about apprenticing myself."

"Really? Doing what?" I asked.

"I'm not sure yet. Either with one of the dressmakers or the glassblower."

Danello thought it over. "I think you'd be good at both."

"You do?" She grinned. "Nya, which do you like?"

"The glassblower. You'd get bored making dresses all day. The most excitement there would be someone stabbing their thumb with a needle."

We laughed.

"You might be right," Aylin said. "There's fire

at the glassblower's. Danger every day. Much more exciting."

I grinned. "You can always try both. Pick whichever you like better."

"I *can*, can't I?" She smiled as if amazed she even *had* a choice, let alone two.

"I was thinking about teaching at the Protectors' League," Danello said quietly. "Kione says they'd probably hire me as an assistant rapier instructor."

"Your mother would have liked that. You teaching like she did."

"Yeah, I thought so too."

We passed Analov Park, cleared of refugees and now blooming with new flowers and bushes. Great-grandfather's statue sat at the center, his blank eyes gazing out across the lake, his arms outstretched. Birds perched on them, leaving a mess underneath. There were rumors they were making a statue of *me*, but I hoped it was just gossip.

"I don't know what I'm going to do." I'd never really thought about it before. I'd always been too focused on surviving my todays to think about my tomorrows. "I can't be a real Healer, even after I finish my training. Someone would always have to transfer the pain into pynvium for me. Onderaan showed me some enchanting, but it bothered my stomach whenever I tried it. I can't do anything else."

"You're good at organizing people," Danello said. "And really good at telling them what to do." He grinned.

"Very bossy." Aylin laughed.

"You could be a dock foreman," said Danello.

"Or a ferry director."

"Work your way up to harbormaster."

"Once you graduate from the League, you could be Luminary."

"Why stop there?" Danello said. "You could always be governor." His laughter stopped. He looked at Aylin, and she nodded, eyes wide and bright. "Actually, you really *could* be governor one day."

Me?" I gaped. "Running all of Geveg?"

"Why not?"

"Because it's . . ."

Impossible? No more so than what I'd already done. Onderaan wasn't the first one in my family to be governor. If it was in Jeatar's blood to rule, maybe it was in mine too.

"There's one problem, though," said Danello, frowning. But his eyes twinkled.

"Which is?"

"Governor is a step down from saint."

I smacked him in the arm, laughing. But I couldn't get the idea out of my mind. Me, Governor.

"I bet there are some apprenticeships open," Danello said. "Maybe even an assistant to one of the Council members."

Aylin nodded. "Who wouldn't want the savior of Geveg working for them?"

Plenty of folks, probably, but all I needed was one to agree. And as the Governor's niece, surely *one* person would.

I smiled. "Governor it is, then."

I guess both Geveg *and* I had a future after all.

ACKNOWLEDGMENTS

For four years I've been living in Geveg and following Nya on her journey. I'd have to say I've had more fun than she has, but I've also had a lot more people to help me through the rough spots. I never would have made it this far without the love and support of my husband, Tom. Even though I was too scared to let him read any of my writing until I got my agent, he still stuck by me and encouraged me to follow my dream. Now that the series is done, I think I'll finally let him read the whole thing.

Family you choose plays a big role in the trilogy, and like Nya, I'm blessed to have some wonderful "family" in my life that doesn't share my blood. My writing family has been instrumental in helping me develop my stories and my skills, discussing scenes and plots, characters and ideas. Ann and Juliette have both spent hours on the phone with me, and their insights led to plot twists and character understandings I never would have thought of on my own. Ann has read every draft of the entire trilogy (even the really bad ones) and probably knows this story as well as I do. Juliette made sure I spent as much time thinking about the who and the why as I did the what and the how.

My crit buddies have always been there to offer words of wisdom and advice. Bonnie helped me see the more romantic side of the tale (which I've never been great at), and used her wonderful people sense to help me give the characters more depth. The Bloodies—Dario, Aliette, Traci, Keyan, Doug, and Genevieve—dug in and chopped the first draft into the pieces it deserved and helped me find the better story underneath.

My editor, Donna, was wonderful and patient as I wrote not only this book but the whole series, and I'm grateful for her sharp eye. Brainstorming with her was a blast, and she always said exactly the right thing to spark my creativity and send me where I needed to go. And she never minded when a sudden epiphany sent the story in a new direction. How one small comment from her could help me see so much is beyond me, but she's amazing at it.

I've had a lot of support outside the writing side as well. Booksellers Sharon, Ellen, Karen, Jackie, and Myra have been wonderful supporters of me and my series, and helped introduce Nya and her friends to their friends and customers. Media center specialists have opened their doors and let me chat with their students many a time. Lisa, Cindy, Janice, Patricia, Becky, Kelly, Jean, Ruth, Anna, Anne, Katie, and Karen—thanks for inviting me to stop by.

Big hugs also go to my agent, Kristin, who believed in the story from the start; Anita, who keeps me updated on sales and laughing with trivia; Ruta, who is always so much fun to talk to; Lindsey, Laura, and Marissa, who also worked hard to make sure the world knew about the books; and Emilie, who always had something fun for me to do that involved a recording device of some kind. One more big thank-you to the copyediting team, who never cease to impress me with their skill and sharp eyes.

More hugs and thanks to the many bloggers and reviewers who gave The Healing Wars (and me) a chance and said such nice things about both of us. And to those bloggers who let me visit them on my blog tours, who tweeted and talked and chatted about Nya. Way too many to name, but you know who you are.

And of course, thanks to the readers. Books are all about you, and without you, telling stories wouldn't be nearly as much fun. I can't say what your emails and kind words about the books have meant to me. They've brightened my days and made me work harder, because you deserve the best story you can get. I may not always succeed, but I'll always try to live up to your expectations.

Writing is a solitary endeavor, but publishing a book is not. So many wonderful and generous people rolled up their sleeves and dug in to help make this series a reality, and I am grateful and appreciative of all of them.

Thanks doesn't even begin to cover it.